M000194963

Gale   2106   25.95

Immune Response

Other Five Star titles
by Steve Perry:

Windowpane

Immune Response

Steve Perry

Five Star • Waterville, Maine

First Edition
First Printing: February 2006

Published in 2006 in conjunction with Tekno Books and Ed Gorman.

Set in 11 pt. Plantin by Minnie B. Raven.

Printed in the United States on permanent paper.

Library of Congress Cataloging-in-Publication Data

Perry, Steve.
    Immune response / by Steve Perry.—1st ed.
      p. cm.
    ISBN 1-59414-448-6 (hc : alk. paper)
    1. Washington (State)—Fiction.   2. Physicians' assistants—Fiction.   3. Makah Indians—Fiction.
    4. Indian reservation police—Fiction.
    5. Policewomen—Fiction.   I. Title.
    PS3566.E7168I46 2006
    813'.54—dc22   2005028624

This book is for Dianne;
and for the grandsons:
Zach, Brett, Cy, and Dex.

Acknowledgements/Disclaimers

This book would not have been written without the assistance of a number of people. My thanks to: Dennis McCullough, Patty Lyman and Dennison Kerlee, Physician Assistants in Washington state. To Shelly Johnson and John Heinz of the Indian Health Service clinic on the Makah Reservation. To Richard M. Hill, Louis Tonore, Dwight Brower, and especially, Rusty Harvey, excellent M.D.'s all.

Special thanks to Larry Segriff and John Helfers, fellow toilers in the word mines and excellent editors, as well.

Outside of public figures, none of the people represented in this book are real; they are all cut and stitched together from imaginary whole cloth. Those of you familiar with the locations herein will probably notice I have taken a few liberties—with geography, politics and other stuff—I did so for dramatic effect. It is, after all, a work of fiction.

—SP

"If you meet the Buddha on the road, kill him."

—Anonymous

PART ONE

Phylogeny

ONE

It was a miracle.

Pretty good one, too. Step right up folks and witness the *amaaazing* magic X-ray and the incredible disappearing crab!

The lightbox smelled like burning silicone, had since he'd stupidly used half a tube of the nasty stuff to seal the bottom where the metal frame had warped away from the glass. The rubbery translucent goop filled the gap through which the light spilled but after the bulbs warmed up a little, the stink got pretty intense. It had seemed like a good idea at the time—and wasn't that always how it was? He needed a new box.

Yeah. He also needed a real lab and a tech to run it, a better fax and an ECG machine younger than his grandma. A nurse and a new surgical table would be nice, and as long as he was wishing, a whole stack of medical CD-ROMs for his Mac.

Monsters ravish sluts, love corn silk, do grab intestines and cry wolf.

That was the mnemonic he'd learned while doing his PA rotation in Dallas, from an old GP who always used obscenity to remember and teach such things.

Looking at a chest film, that was how you made the examination, first letter of each word in the silly sentence: Midline structures, ribs, spine, lungs, costophrenic sulci, diaphragm, GI structures and chest wall.

Rick Scales, PA-C, shook his head, still not believing

11

what he saw. Maybe there were gods; western medicine sure couldn't explain this. The primary site cancer, in the form of a silver-dollar-sized coin lesion in the left upper lobe, was gone. The clinic's smelly lightbox was barely wide enough to hang the two chest films side-by-side but anybody with one eye and half a brain could see the difference. The patient was Tom Inch, a fifty-four-year-old well-developed, well-nourished, Native American male—was that still allowed or had PC voided it? Whatever. Inch was an Elwha Indian from just up the road in Clallam Bay, Washington. Ordinarily, he wouldn't be seeing this patient, since the Trettevick Clinic on the Makah Reservation was a lot better staffed and ordained by treaty to provide medical treatment for the natives. Included natives being the Jamestown S'Klallam, the Quileute, the Makah and the Elwha. Inch didn't want to use the clinic, though. It seemed that in 1861, a Makah raiding party had attacked the Elwha village and during the battle, had beheaded Inch's great-great grandfather. Inch didn't much like going out to the reservation, even though he admitted to having about as much Makah blood in him as he did Elwha, purebreds being in short supply around here. Where once had been hundreds of tribes, there were now only dozens and some of those were tiny, only a handful of members.

Still and all, Tom Inch didn't want to go to the reservation medical center because of something that happened a hundred and thirty-five years ago and he wasn't the only one.

Some grudges were real old.

Scales' original DX of lung CA had been verified a week later by biopsy at the medical center in Seattle. Already metastasized, too, dug into the liver and bowel. Inch wasn't interested in letting them cut, burn or poison the monsters if they couldn't guarantee they'd get them all, and of course they couldn't guarantee that, so the MDs in Seattle had sent him home. Scales' precepting doctor, the sometimes-sober-more-often-not Howard P. Reuben, Johns Hopkins, class of '55, with a good-sized clinic in Port Angeles, had concurred fast enough with the DX. There wasn't much they could do. Scales had given Inch an RX for Demerol by mouth until it got bad enough to go parentally and, if it got to where IM injections wouldn't stop the pain when Inch went to ground, Reuben would come out and hook up the IV morphine drip—a euphemistic way of saying euthanasia. They'd passed the assisted suicide law down in Oregon but it was still tangled up in the courts. They were working on it in Washington; until it passed, if and when, the drip everybody winked at and pretended was for pain would have to do. It was a good idea, assisted suicide. Most people who'd worked in medicine more than fifteen minutes knew that. Watching somebody die of metastatic disease wasn't pretty. Anybody who'd ever sat up all night with a screaming, incontinent, hallucinating brain cancer patient terrified of monsters that nobody else could see sure as hell knew it. The only reason not to help them check out was religious and Scales didn't put much stock in that.

Looking at the stinking light box, maybe he ought to reconsider.

Three months ago the first X-ray had been taken, and that was just about half as much time as the oncology crew figured the guy would have left.

You can pop firecrackers on the Fourth of July, Tommy boy, Dr. Reuben had told him, but better not figure on seeing Santa Claus again.

Inch owned a charter fishing boat in Sekiu, his three sons ran it these days, and they made a small living taking tourists out to catch salmon and the occasional ling cod. Like a lot of the locals, the Inch family supplemented their income by hunting in and out of season, fishing over the limit in and out of season, and doing small projects with timber mostly swiped from the big tree farms: cedar shakes, odd bits of trash wood like madrona. Scales didn't blame them—they'd been here first and he figured they had a right to a few fish and elk. Weren't the Indians who'd nearly wiped out the salmon runs and laid down concrete everywhere?

Cancer. Only now, the film on the left showed the fuzzy-edged filimented white ball, the one on the right did not. There was no mix up because Scales had shot the new image and developed it himself.

In that corner, wearing ugly malevolent trunks, a malignant killer eating Tom Inch alive, big and mean and probably the chemo or the hard radiation wouldn't even have slowed it down had the patient had gone for it. Might as well eat peach pits and apple seeds and pray to his favorite deity.

And in this corner, poof! it was gone, ugly trunks, evil mitosis and all.

Spontaneous remission, Scales thought, as he stared at the chest X-rays. Amazing.

Of course, there were the other sites, but somehow, he knew those had gone, too. Knew without any logical reason for that assumption. Knew because of his *Augenblick*. His one trick, something he couldn't even take credit for.

He'd been in practice since '78, first in Texas, then New Mexico, finally here on the north coast of Washington, and he'd never seen a spontaneous remission this dramatic, this fast. It certainly brightened up his day. He was really going to enjoy walking back into the exam room. This was better than the time he'd been sent to the Fort Worth nursing home to pronounce that MS patient dead and found her staring up at him when he walked into the room. Hell, just send ole Rick out to see 'em and they Lazarus themselves right back out of that grave, thank you very much.

Tom's youngest-of-four daughters, Mina, was with her father in the room. She looked at Rick when he came in carrying the two chest films. Mina was twenty-four, gorgeous, had hair that hung down to the middle of her blue-jeaned butt, hair so black it was almost blue and a smile hot enough to peel the chrome off a car bumper, though she wasn't using it now. He was looking forward to lighting her grin, too.

Shame on you, Scales, you're old enough to be her father.

As always, the exam room smelled faintly of mold, despite the daily applications of Lysol and air freshener and the brief summer sunshine pounding down on it. You noticed the odor when you stepped in and then you tuned it out. The clinic, a converted old house out past the old Crown-Zellerbach Vista compound fifteen miles short of the reservation, had seen oceans of rain and better decades.

"How we doin', Doc?"

He'd given up trying to correct his patients on that one years ago. He was a Physician's Assistant, duly certified by the NCCPA and the state of Washington, had his own DEA number and all, but he was not allowed to present himself as a doctor, no way, no how. The MDs took a dim view of that, they had given up a lot more of their territory than they wanted: PAs, NPs, techs, not even to mention alternative medicines, and they did not want anybody stealing any more of it. Thing was, this far out in the boonies the PA or the Nurse Practitioner was the only medic a lot of people ever saw, not counting shamans, and Scales wasn't going to spend half his time explaining the AMA's paranoid neuroses. Dr. Reuben—"Just like the sandwich, m'boy."—a rheumy, claimed-to-be sixty-nine, came out once a week and signed off on Rick's charts, usually without bothering to read them. "Got any problems?" he'd ask. If Rick said no, Reuben would smile and nod and drive back to Port Angeles. Some weeks he didn't make it out at all.

So much for his supervising physician.

So, "Doc" or "Rick," or "Scales," he'd answer to any of them. Just like when he'd been in the Navy, he had been a corpsman, but he'd look up at "Medic," "Doc" or "Hey, you!" At least until he got to the jungle with the Marines . . .

"Tom, you believe in miracles?"

"Sure, Doc, I been on miracle time since my brother's fishing boat went down in '69."

"Yeah, well, somebody just made another big deposit in your account."

Mina said, "What do you mean?"

"I mean, either my X-ray machine has gone blind or that tumor in your father's chest has flat out disappeared." Sometimes the Texas panhandle twang condensed when he got excited; any thicker now and you could spread it like sweet butter on hush puppies.

Mina stood. He handed her the films. She held them up to the light. He'd shown her the first one when Tom had first come in, complaining of a cough and tightness in his chest, some slight fever and night sweats, and bloody sputum. Inch's thirty-five year history of unfiltered Camels wagged a fat finger at Scales' differential diagnosis: Lung cancer or emphysema, maybe both. Scales' hadn't even needed that, he'd known the minute he'd seen the man.

16

Augenblick: In the blink of an eye. A gift—or a curse—some medics had, to be able to look at a patient and without asking for symptoms or looking for signs, to know with near absolute certainty what the problem was. It didn't always work, but when it did, he was almost never wrong. Right now it was telling him not only was the chest tumor history, so were the metastatic spin-offs. Telling him that here was one for the medical journals to ponder and the faith healers to be gleeful over.

Well. Large favors gratefully accepted and thank you, whoever is in charge.

Mina had gone off to the U of W in Seattle and come back with her Master's in biology, she knew what—and after she'd seen her father's first chest series—she knew where the mother cancer was.

Scales stood there and relished the puzzled look on her face. God, it sure felt great to deliver good news, he so seldom got to do it this much of it at one chunk. Made the drudgery days worthwhile to speak thus of miracles.

She looked at Scales. Blinked.

"It's gone. The tumor."

"Amen." To Tom Inch, he said, "I don't want to get your hopes up too high, there are the other sites to consider, but I want you to take a run into Seattle, and let the oncologists poke at you again. Maybe you might get to toast the New Year after all, assuming you don't drive into the Sound after the drunken Christmas Party."

"Well, son-of-a-bitch," Tom Inch said.

"Amen to that, too."

The rest of the day after that was pretty much anticlimactic.

Scales treated a sty on Joseph Lowhorn's left eye. Gave

him some drops, told him to put a warm washcloth on it a few times a day, to come back in a week if it wasn't gone.

He sutured a cut on the meaty part of Leslie Jenkins thumb, she'd done it scaling fish, so he'd spent a fair amount of time cleaning it out before putting in five mattress stitches, four-O ethalon. Gave her a tetanus shot, told her to keep the thumb clean and dry and to take the stitches out in five days, come back if it got infected.

Billy Gross sprained his left ankle, the X-ray didn't show any cracks. He wrapped it in an ace, told Billy to go home and RICE it—rest, ice, compression, elevation—and to come back when the swelling went down for a walking cast.

"Jesus, not a fucking cast!"

"Either that or you hobble around for a couple of months and it hurts like hell."

"You gonna gimme some pain medicine?"

"Tylenol 3."

"Sheeit. Codeine? Might as well eat aspirin."

"Okay by me."

Billy took the script anyhow—it wasn't a heavy narcotic but it was better than nothing—and promised to come back on Thursday.

After lunch, he saw Minerva Watson, aged fifty-nine, who had a viral URI. He gave her some Actifed samples and told her to rest and drink a lot of clear liquids, take aspirin if she had a fever.

"How about a shot? Doc Stevenson, he used to give me a penicillin shot that cleared me right up."

Scales gritted his teeth. "Sorry, we're all out of that medicine. Budget cuts."

Minerva left and Scales wished he could get his hands on Stevenson, the NP who had run the satellite before he'd taken over last year.

Penicillin. Right.

Antibiotics wouldn't touch what Minerva had, they were for bacteria and most patients didn't know there was a difference between a bacterium and a virus. The cocktail Stevenson used for viral infections like colds or the flu was a mixture of Decadron and the long-acting version of it, Decadron LA. It was a potent anti-inflammatory drug, a steroid, though not the kind that built muscles. The short-acting Decadron injection began to work almost immediately, and the long-acting version kicked in and kept it going for several days. It didn't cure anything, but it masked symptoms, reduced the swelling and discomfort, sure enough. A patient was just as sick, but he or she felt well and usually by the time the injection wore off, they were better than half way to being well. It made for good patient relations but it wasn't good medicine. That bolus of chemical damped a receiver's own production of hormones so if the patient ran into something nasty infection-wise in the weeks after she'd been injected, her body was apt to have more trouble dealing with it. Could be robbing Peter, not to pay Paul—but to pay Charon.

Scales had raised the issue with Reuben, who'd shrugged it off. "Most of what we do is treat symptoms, Rick. A patient comes in feeling like shit and goes out feeling great. Nine hundred and ninety times out of a thousand, there's no sequel and if you make him think he's well until he actually gets well, I see no problem with that."

Scales nodded but stopped the practice anyhow. It was like shooting squirrels with an elephant gun and he didn't want that responsibility. Feeling great when you had a bad case of the flu wasn't necessarily a good thing. Better you should lie low and take it easy so you didn't catch pneumonia. He'd seen over-medicated patients who felt terrific—until they keeled over stone dead.

If you can't swim, you probably ought not try to walk on water.

After lunch he checked on the chainsaw cut he'd sewn up on Millard Justice three days before, no erythema, no edema, told him to keep taking the antibiotic and check back in a couple more days. He could justify prescribing medicine for Millard, a chainsaw carried a lot of crud and infection was not just possible but likely.

The way the bugs were mutating, another few years and antibiotics they had were going to be pretty much useless. He wasn't going to help that along.

He sent Becky Richards, age twenty, to see Dr. Campbell at Reuben's clinic in Port Angeles when her pregnancy test came up positive. He could deliver a baby if he had to and he would treat simple vaginal infections, but since it wasn't in the scope of his practice, he referred OB-GYN patients to Port Angeles or the new guy in Forks. The biggest problem with Becky would be when her mother found out she was pregnant again. Becky already had two children and neither of those fathers had come forward to claim paternity. He'd given Becky prescriptions for birth control pills, a case of condoms and the standard lecture but it hadn't done any good. Maybe she liked being pregnant.

Before he shut the office down at seven, Scales saw two more bad colds, a plantar wart, a scratched cornea, a diabetic who told him she needed to up her insulin, a boxer's fracture of the left hand.

Jimmy Lewis, his AIDS patient, skipped his appointment. The man was thirty, had moved to Seattle ten years past and gotten into bad company and IV drugs. He had come home to die. That would be within another six months, if he were lucky. Scales called his house and his mother said Jimmy had gone out to the reservation to see his friends and had probably just forgotten the time. He seemed to be in good spirits to her, no particular aches or pains.

At seven, Scales knocked off. He loaded the autoclave with instruments and surgical packs to sterilize—nobody was going to spend any money giving him disposable anything if they could help it—then went to the kitchen to see if there was anything to eat. He found one of those Aussie pot pies in the freezer and threw it into the microwave. He opened a Henry's and poured the beer into a glass while he waited for the pot pie to get hot.

No workout tonight. He'd hit the weights yesterday.

He'd turned half the garage into a gym, had about four hundred pounds of plates, a few bars, most of which he'd picked up at garage sales. When the weather was good, he liked to walk along the beach or drive out to the gravel pit and plink cans with his .22 pistol, but when the weather was bad—and it was rainier here than Texas in the summer time—he'd just as soon stay inside. Kept his skin a nice fish-belly white most of the time. He was in pretty good shape for a man his age—same age as Sly Stallone—and he kept tight as a matter of course. No threat to the steroid boys, but he still wore the same size pants he'd worn in Steel Springs High when he'd played cornerback. Overweight, according to the insurance company tables, but at six feet even and one-ninety, he had only about five pounds on his best shape ever. After forty it was patch, patch, patch but he figured if he let the holes get too big, he might fall apart before he could fix them.

Just another day in paradise, healing the sick.

Well. And a spontaneous remission, don't forget. That made him smile. You lost the war against the Reaper in the long run but sometimes the battles went your way. He took his joy where he could find it.

He sipped his beer and wondered if he had anything left to read.

TWO

It was not yet seven in the morning and James Robert "Jim Bob" Harrison sat at the counter of the Dungeness Cafe in Sekiu, drinking his sixth beer, trying to pick a fight with Tank Louis. The Dungeness was done in a Swiss-chalet architectural style that would doubtless have had most Swiss architects and anybody from that country with any taste holding their sides laughing had they seen it. Ugly, brown wood, multicolor brick, dark strips crisscrossed over the windows. A big orange and black sign over the door said, "Cocktails, Breakfast, Ice," trying to cover as many bases as it could.

Jim Bob wasn't getting a rise out of Tank, and just as well, since Tank was sober, six-five and two-seventy to Jim Bob's plastered five-nine and one sixty. Tank was thirty, a French-Canadian gypo logger with his own truck. He was trying to get to his cereal. Jim Bob was fifty-six, a Makah fisherman but unemployed for six years, couldn't get on even a bad shift at the prison. And looking to get himself put in the hospital. The other patrons were hurrying hard to mind their own breakfasts and get out before the fight started rearranging the imitation Swiss-chalet furniture— dark brown wood stained ugly to match the outside of the building.

It wouldn't be a contest. If he wanted, Tank could pour the milk, break Jim Bob in half and get back to his corn flakes before they got soggy.

A drunken Indian. What a cliche.

Tribal Deputy Jasmine Hughes shook her head. She tugged her service belt up, a black leather basket weave rig from Safariland she'd bought while on the job at LAPD. Nylon would have been better in the north coast climate, but she thought the nylon belts and holsters looked tacky. The four-inch S&W .357 revolver was stainless, that helped, though with all the rain a .40 or .45 Glock or one of the Smith polymer composites would have made more sense. A lot more firepower, even though she figured that if you only had six instead of sixteen, you had to put them where they counted. She remembered a deal down in Seattle where a patrol officer put nineteen rounds from his Glock into the air at a perp from twenty feet and missed all but once—and that a glancing hit on the leg. It was a fluke he hadn't taken out half the neighborhood—the stray 9mm's had punched holes through the walls of two houses and an apartment building and it was a real miracle they hadn't hit anybody. The fed now said the new ones for civilians could only hold ten but still, if you couldn't get it done with six, you probably couldn't get it done. She'd had a trigger job and Spegel boot grips put on the Smith, but that was as much customizing as she wanted to fool with. The weather was hard on steel, even stainless, but—a Tupperware gun? No way.

She had cuffs, a six-cell flashlight and a can of pepper spray on the belt but she hoped she wouldn't need them with Jim Bob. He had two inches and ten pounds on her but she was fifteen years younger—and the Law. He was sometimes a mean drunk but not completely stupid.

Technically, she didn't have any authority off the reservation, except for her status in the State Patrol Reserve and that didn't mean much here. Not that anybody in Sekiu was likely to complain—like the cafe, it wasn't much town, mostly a thin and moldy crescent lining the bay, charter and fishing boats in the water, ramshackle motels, dive shops and bait shacks on the shore. Outside a rainy fog hung over the bay like a fat man's waistline, rolls of drooping gray-on-gray.

Ugly sky, ugly town, ugly cafe. And an ugly drunk.

Jim Bob was one of her people and he was going to cause trouble unless she did something. She took a deep breath, blew it out in a sigh, and moved toward the counter.

"—what I'm sayin' is, you white men came in here and fucked it all up. Crown-Zellerbach chopped all the old growth down and didn't get it replanted fast enough. There was a fucking ten-year-gap when there wasn't nothing big enough to cut. And you caught all the damned fish and killed most of the fucking elk."

Tank sipped at his coffee and pretended he didn't hear Jim Bob. He saw Jasmine moving in. "Hey, Jay. How's it going?"

"Can't complain, Tank. Jim Bob, are you looking to lose a few more teeth?"

"Hey, Jay! Lemme buy you a beer!"

"Another time," she said. "Why don't I give you a ride home?"

"I got my truck outside, besides, I ain't ready to go yet. Me and Tank, we got some things to get straight. Fucking blue-eyed white devil. I might just have to kick your ass."

Tank glanced at Jay, gave her a small smile and shook his head.

She nodded, thanking him for not turning Jim Bob into a bloody paste.

"I don't think so, Jim Bob. What I think is, you need to get home. Madeline will be wondering where you are."

Jim Bob turned away from his beer and stared at her. A

hard glint flashed in the rheumy eyes. For just a second, she thought he might try her again. The last time, she'd clobbered him with her Magnalite, bounced the heavy aluminum tube off his skull and knocked him to his knees. He hadn't lost consciousness and later, claimed he didn't remember it, which was too bad. She wanted him to remember it.

"What the hell," he said. "Okay."

As they started out, Tank said, "Thanks, Jay. I wouldn't have your job."

She smiled at him. Rounding up drunks before they did too much damage to themselves or anybody else was a whole lot easier than chasing heavily-armed gang kids down L.A. alleyways.

The rain had stopped and the sun was out. After she dropped Jim Bob off at his house on the reservation, Jay drove with the truck's windows down to clear out the stale beer-and-sweat stink the man had left behind. Being unemployed and poor left its mark, like dirt rings in a bathtub. A lot more of the tribe drank and fought these days than when she'd been a child. She'd grown up on the reservation with her mother, though she was only a quarter-blood. Her mother was half and half, her father had been half-white and half-black and fast on his feet and the mix left her a little darker than some but not as dark as others who were supposedly pure blood. More exotic-looking, though. A lot of men had told her that.

Too many men.

Her truck was a five-year-old GMC pickup with a beat-up aluminum shell over the bed and the best the tribe would do was give her a magnetic light and siren for when she had to get somewhere in a hurry. She had her own CB and two-meter band, everybody out here did, plus a cell phone that worked some of the time. Didn't do much good to have the light and siren anyhow; most of the roads were narrow and shoulderless and turnouts were few. You got behind somebody, they had to go faster rather than pull over and that was dangerous. Not that she had much occasion to hurry anyhow.

She turned south and headed along the old Crown Mainline toward the gravel pit. Crown was gone, eaten up and crapped away by some corporate raider a few years back and the new company was named after the raider's mother's hometown or something, Cavenham. The trees didn't care who owned them.

The gravel pit was across the Waatch River, south of the old Air Force Station and down a side logging road. She tried to get out there to practice once a week or so. Lately, she'd been making an effort to get there on the morning Doc Scales usually went shooting.

She grinned at herself. He was probably six or eight years older than she was, fifty-some-odd, but he kept in good shape. Had his garage all tricked out with weights. She'd pumped a little iron in the police gym when she'd been on the job in SoCal, not much since. These days, she did a lot of hiking and most of her heavy lifting was helping drunks to their feet or into the back of her truck.

She wasn't looking for a boyfriend, the last one had been a disaster, but Scales was all right, even though he was a doctor. Well, a half-assed doctor. As far as she was concerned that described most of them. She didn't have much use for medical people, not given all the shit she'd gone through. But Scales didn't push, was pretty smart, could shoot that target pistol of his real well. She wasn't sure what she wanted from him. She'd never had a man friend, not one that didn't want to jump her bones. It might be interesting.

She hit a pothole. The truck jounced, mud splashed up against the sides, rich brown spatters against the dark blue. The gravel pit was just ahead on the left. In theory, you weren't supposed to bring guns onto the reservation if you didn't live on it, but that was mostly for the tourists. Some of the local whites had been coming to the pit for forty years, were as much a part of the land as anybody. When times got tough, a man who knew you was a lot more likely to share some of his beef or salted salmon than one who didn't know you, and you didn't much care what color his hand was if it was holding out food. Sure, there were some in the tribes just like some whites who were racists. And grudges, sure, in all directions. The Northwest Indians had been fishermen, whalers, hunters, but they had also been war-makers and slave-takers long before the Spanish showed up in their ships. That crap about the noble savage who lived in total harmony with the land, that was some writer's invention. The local tribes hadn't seen the big picture any better than any of the other Indians in North America. In the long run the encroaching white tide rolled over them all. Took their lands, their dignity, and it was only now the casinos were starting to take some of it back. The S'Klallam were raking it in at their Seven Cedars casino just outside Sequim, and if the Makah could get ever the land swap worked out, they'd be doing the same in a few years. Couldn't build it here at the end of the world, the roads wouldn't take the traffic and it was a long way from the nearest town of any size. The bus from Forks or Port Townsend would only carry so many at a time.

Hughes felt a little stab of disappointment when she pulled over next to the pit and saw there was nobody else there. Maybe Scales decided to bag it today. Too bad.

She got out of the truck, walked around back and opened the gate and hatch, pulled her shooting bag onto the tailgate. She unzipped the heavy canvas bag and pulled out a couple of boxes of the reloaded .357s. She had a Dillon press, an old Square Deal progressive, and she mostly shot ammo she'd reloaded herself. It was easy enough. You filled the tube with primers and the hopper with powder, put a shell in the plate, cranked the handle. You had to put the bullets in one at a time, but it was simple. Once you got going, you could load a couple hundred rounds an hour, just pull the handle. The press was guaranteed for life, if anything broke, you called, they sent you the parts, free.

She cheated a little, in that she used wadcutters, flat-nosed lead target rounds and about three-quarters as much powder as her duty ammo. That way the Smith didn't beat her to death. She'd thought about having a compensator milled into the end of the barrel to cut felt recoil, but hadn't gotten around to it. Besides, those made for a lot of flash and noise. The reduced charges were close enough and she always put a few full-power loads through the gun so it wouldn't be a surprise if she ever had to pull it and pop a few in the line of duty. She hadn't had to do that here. Well, unless you counted putting down deer that had been hit by cars or shooing off a black bear now and then.

She pulled the headphones out and draped them around her neck, slipped on the shatterproof shooting glasses. She spent a couple of minutes filling four extra speedloaders. Counting the two on her belt, that made six altogether. She'd shoot the carry ammo in the gun first, then the two full-power loaders, then go to the pansy loads for the rest of the session.

With the gun stuff all set up, she crawled into the truck

and slid her target onto the tailgate. This was a squared-off human silhouette of quarter-inch steel plate with a mounting hole drilled through it. She slid off the truck, took a deep breath, and lifted the plate. It was heavy, forty-five, fifty pounds, and she grunted as she hurried across the uneven and muddy ground to a sawed-off tree stump where she propped the target. She went back to the truck, fetched the stand, a metal pole and a folding cross-base. She screwed the pole into the steel supports, spread them, and undid the wingnut from the bolt. Now was the tricky part. She had to lift the heavy target, line up the holes while holding it one-handed, and shove the bolt through without dropping the plate on her foot and crushing her toes.

It was really a two-person job, or one for a strong man. She took a certain amount of pride in being able to do it herself.

She held the bolt in her mouth as she lifted the plate. *Get it lined up, there . . . easy, grab the bolt, slide it in . . .*

Got it. She spun the wingnut on the threads, tightened it.

She went back to the truck, got the can of white spray paint from her bag, returned to the steel plate. It was pretty much the same size as an official IPSC cardboard target, but she preferred the metal. It rang when you hit it, it worked in the rain without getting soggy, and it would outlast a thousand targets made of cardboard. If you sprayed it with paint every so often, you could see where your shots hit, plus that kept it from rusting.

She finished dusting the target and moved back to a point about fifteen yards away from the flat-white plate. That was about twice as far as what was generally considered combat distance. Most shootings took place a lot closer and she figured if she could keep them all on the target at this range, she'd be okay for anything closer. Every now and then she'd back off to forty or fifty yards and practice slow fire and she could pretty much ring the target at that range, if she took her time.

She slid her hearing protectors up, easy since she didn't wear a hat except when it was raining or cold. She took a deep breath, let it out, took another and let about half of it escape.

Go.

She went for the Smith. Grabbed the smooth wood grips, flicked the thumb-break snap to the left and pulled. Brought the piece up, looking all the while at the target, indexed on it by the gun's profile as she slapped her weak hand around her strong hand's grip and squeezed double action—

Boom! Clang!

The .357's roar was loud even through the hearing protectors. The recoil of the full-power hot-loaded Cor-bon round shoved the barrel up and she pulled the weapon down to crank the second shot—

Boom! Clang!

She lowered the Smith, her right hand stinging a little from the recoil and looked at the target.

The first shot splashed pretty much dead center, a hair slightly to the right, the second shot was higher, just below what would have been a collarbone on a human target.

Hughes nodded and reholstered the gun. She didn't have a timer but it felt pretty fast. She'd taken the WSP refresher course and knew that on a good day, she could still cook off two from a snapped holster in a second and a quarter. She also qualified with a 95 percent, and had hit a clean 100 percent on several passes while training. Master Sergeant Leroy Perkins, her pistol instructor in the Army, had laid the bottom line in pretty hard: If you cannot hit it, you will not shoot it. And that had been with the old slab-side issue Colt .45 auto, a dependable piece but hardly famed for its pinpoint accuracy right out of the box.

The smell of burned powder was strong, the vibrations from the explosions still warm on her face. This ammo had a one-shot stop record of better than ninety percent. Two solids hits to the torso should give just about anybody not wearing body armor good reason to cease being a threat, if that's what they had in mind. And these two shots were the most important of the day. It didn't matter if you could pick flies off a wall at a hundred yards with the last few rounds in your practice session. If you missed the first couple on the street, anything else was likely to be academic.

She rolled her shoulders, getting ready to do another double tap.

"That's pretty good shootin', ma'am. For a cop. And a woman."

She grinned, turned and saw Scales standing next to his old Toyota. He wore a blue workshirt and jeans, black cowboy boots that put him up to maybe six-two or three, and his short hair looked almost blond in the sunshine.

"Well, well. Look who's here. Doctor Feel Good and his mouse gun."

He smiled back at her. "Like I said before, anytime you want to shoot it out, any range you want, you give me first shot and then you can blast back with all you got."

"That's not how it works, Scales. You don't get a free shot. Time you got that piece of yours out of its box, I'd have shot you full of holes, be home watching the late show."

He laughed, walked to the trunk of his car, opened it,

pulled his shooting gear out. He had a big box, looked like cherry wood, fitted with shiny brass hinges and clasps. He closed the trunk, set the box on it, opened the lid. Pulled his headphones out and slipped them on.

"Okay, you can touch off that cannon again," he yelled. "I'll be with you in a minute."

Hughes nodded and turned back to her target. She was not sure what she wanted from Scales, but she was glad he'd showed up.

She took a deep breath and went for her gun.

THREE

Scales sat at the kitchen table cleaning his disassembled target pistol. He knew a little about guns, having grown up on a ranch and been in the Navy, but he only owned two: a 12-gauge pump shotgun and this slicked-up .22, a gift from his brother. It came with a fat nine-inch barrel and an electronic dot-scope. When it was turned on, a tiny, glowing red spot appeared in the center of its field. You put the dot on what you wanted to shoot and, out to about a hundred yards, that's where the bullet went. On a good day, he could hit a matchbox as far away as he could see it. Made it real simple.

Scales smiled as he ran the cleaning brush soaked with solvent in and out of the barrel. Tom Junior had always been interested in guns. He was seven years older than Scales. He'd taught Scales how to shoot, from a BB gun to a rifle to a shotgun to a pistol. He'd taken him for his first beer, taught him how to drive, let him borrow his old Chevy to raise hell on Saturday nights with his friends. Been best man at Scales' wedding.

Tom Junior came back from his second tour in Vietnam in '72 missing his left arm. He'd gone to work on the family ranch, though he and his wife Linda lived in Steel Springs proper. Their kids were grown and gone. Little Tommy lived in Amarillo, was married with a two-year-old son, worked as a cop. Susie was a senior at Rice.

Every Christmas, Tom Junior sent Scales some kind of gun thing, and last year, it had been this pistol. What

Hughes called a mouse gun.

Scales took a tooth brush and solvent to the pistol's rails, enjoyed the chemical smell of the stuff as he scrubbed the burned powder and dirty dry lube off. He'd also enjoyed the visit to the gravel pit, now looked forward to seeing Jay Hughes there when he went. She was sharp, tough and drop-dead gorgeous. He hadn't made a pass at her, asked her to lunch or dinner or done anything other than small talk, that mostly about shooting. She could clear leather like an old-time gunslinger and ring that metal target she used, very impressive. He was attracted to her but he was also a little leery of pushing it and scaring her away. He liked her and if the choice was between having a friend or a fuck, he was leaning toward the friend side.

The fucks had gotten him into a lot of trouble.

Not that he was sure he'd have that choice anyhow.

Well, when in doubt, do nothing. Story of his life.

He ran a couple of patches through the bore until they came out clean, sprayed the parts with Break Free, used a dab of the military spec fluorocarbon gun grease on the rails. He reassembled the pistol, tightened the two take down screws, then wiped the outside with an oily rag. He stuck the gun back in its box, washed his hands and sighed.

Since today was Saturday, the office was officially closed, though he had his cell phone and his Motorola handset in case of emergencies.

He also had an appointment at Magic Fingers, in Forks.

The actual massage part was done, his naked body warm and oily under the sheet, his muscles relaxed.

Honey told him to roll over.

Scales did, already getting hard. She smiled. Leaned over and let her bare nipples touch him on the leg, moved them back and forth in little circles.

She rolled the condom onto him and said, "Hang on, baby, I'm gonna suck you dry." She grabbed his now-erect penis at the base and bent down. Her lips were warm, her tongue active as she slid her tight mouth down and up on him.

He bet they didn't teach her that in massage school.

She was good at it. He closed his eyes and gave himself up to it.

It didn't take long. A minute later he spasmed and came.

Honey squeezed him with her mouth and hand, lifted her head away. Slid the condom off carefully, knotted it, then wiped him with a towel.

"All better now?"

He smiled at her. "Oh, yeah."

She turned and headed for the bathroom to dispose of the condom. He watched her go, filled suddenly with post-coital depression. The room had that stale, damp, cum smell.

When was the last time he'd been with a woman he hadn't paid for sex?

Scales remembered: Peaches. Talk-dirty-to-me Peaches.

He'd gone to Portland for a weekend conference in February, the Northwest Physician Assistants annual meeting. It was a long drive, six hours down, six hours back, but he got a few hours of high-class CME credit, a couple days off, and his preceptor paid for it all. He'd missed the snow, the big storm had melted away, turned to dirty slush, the rain washing the last of it down the drains as he arrived. It rained Friday and all day Saturday, a slow, steady drizzle that made the sky and air a monochromatic gray the color of old lead.

He'd met Peaches—originally from Georgia, naturally—

during the cocktail hour on Saturday after a deadly dull lecture on emergency airway procedures. The Benson Hotel was old-money lush around them. They had a couple of drinks, he'd thickened his Texas accent in southern solidarity, and before long they were all but waving their negative HIV test results at each other. She was in her late twenties, maybe thirty, and because he kept in shape and the gray didn't show too much in his own dishwater blond, she didn't seem to notice he was old enough to be her father. She was a short-haired bottle-blonde, a tad on the plump side with a good smile and she seemed like just the thing—no complications, no responsibilities, just good clean piston-and-cylinder fun.

Peaches was doing some work up on Pill Hill in Portland, had an apartment in a bedroom community just west of town. Beaverton, she said and he thought that particularly appropriate considering what he had in mind.

He followed her home in his car.

It started out okay. They got there, went inside and practically tore each other's clothes off.

The first time had been too fast. One minute they were unbuttoning and shucking shirts and pants, the next minute he was in her and throbbing. What happened when you hadn't done anything in a few weeks.

He used his mouth on her, nibbled and teased her for a few minutes and brought her to a hard, shuddery orgasm. He didn't really think he was going to catch AIDS eating pussy and the idea of putting a dental dam or sheet of Saran Wrap over her to protect himself was just too silly to consider: Hold on, sweetie, lemme run to the kitchen, I'll be right back . . . If he did catch something, he'd probably be dead of old age anyhow before it got him. Which was, he knew, a hell of a stupid attitude for a PA who knew better.

Her natural hair color, he noted, was brown.

She liked his muscles. He liked the way she smelled and tasted. It looked like the rest of the weekend was going to be just fine.

Half an hour later—once it would have been two minutes, even a couple of years ago, fifteen minutes, max—he was ready to go again.

"Tell me what you want," she said.

"Just about anything you want to do is fine by me, honey."

"No, I mean tell me. Exactly. Tell me what you're gonna do to me." Her face was flushed and she looked excited by the idea.

Oh, Lord.

He tried. But he was more than fifty years old and in bed with a woman he'd met three hours earlier: "I'm going to shove my cock into your hot cunt," he said, and then he couldn't stop laughing.

In a moment, he didn't have anything to back up his threat, unless she happened to have a spare ramrod lying around.

Peaches, it seemed, didn't have much of a sense of humor.

The rest of the weekend went under, drowned by his giggles.

"I think you'd better leave," she said. Her voice was like liquid nitrogen on bare skin.

But before he went back to his car, he took a walk through the neighborhood. It was after midnight, the rain had blown away and it was quiet, cold and clear. As he ambled down the street, half-smiling, half-upset at himself for not being able to play lead in Peaches' personal porno movie, he saw the stars.

Well, he'd seen them thousands of times before, had been something of an astronomy buff as a teenager, but Texas was a long ways off and he hadn't seemed to have much time for that kind of thing lately.

The moon wasn't up. Sirius, the dog star, hung low, flashing white and blue, with a blink of red now and then, brightest thing in the sky, so bright he thought it was a plane at first. Orion the hunter was right there next to the dog, both of them stalking their prey now in the west, growing expansive as they neared the horizon.

He stopped walking, smiled and looked straight up. His breath made fog in the cold air. They were all there. Overhead, Castor and Pollux, Gemini. Near the twins, Leo. That red star, the one that wasn't blinking, that must be Mars.

He turned on the sidewalk to look to the north. There stood the Great Bear, the Big Dipper. He followed the cup pointers to Polaris, the North Star. Ran his gaze the other way along the handle: Arc to Arcturus, spike to Spica . . .

Amazing how much of it came back. Now, where was Cassiopeia . . . ?

A lot had changed in his life over the years, but the stars still looked the same. Maybe not so bright through the city glow as they had been when he'd been a boy in the country outside Steel Springs, but still there. That was comforting, somehow . . .

Back in the massage-present, Honey got back from her wash. "You want anything else?" She stroked the dyed-blond thatch of her pubis suggestively.

"No, I believe I'm done this time."

"Ah, you must be getting old, Rick."

He smiled. Yeah. He was getting old.

"Next week, same time?" she said.

He nodded. "Yeah. See you then."

She smiled, turned and padded away. She had a great ass.

He sat up, blew out a sigh. Peaches. That was the last consensual sex he'd had where money hadn't changed hands and it hadn't turned out too well. Maybe this way was better. No entanglements, no responsibilities.

Yeah. Right.

Christ, what a life. He was over the hill, his sex drive was winding down, he was alone, getting blowjobs in massage parlors. He'd expected at this age he'd be long-married, thought he'd have somebody to sit in the rocking chair next to his, to smile at the passel of grandchildren, yell at the dogs, hold hands as the sun went down on their lives.

The divorce had sure fucked that up, hadn't it?

Maybe if he'd gone back to medical school, got his M.D. like she'd wanted, maybe Janet would have stayed . . .

Maybe he could learn to fly by waving his arms.

If his daughters had any interest in having kids, he hadn't seen it. He had nieces and nephews who had given him grand-nieces and -nephews, but they weren't going to come to the great Northwest and throw blankets on him as his life heat slowly faded.

Well. That was how it went. You paid your money and you spun the wheel and you couldn't tell where the little ball was going to wind up. You could be a doctor in New Mexico with a wife and kids and grandkids, a pillar of the community, loved and respected. Or the wheel could flip the little ball one slot to the left and you might be at the end of the paved road in the Washington woods, taking care of cut-up loggers and sick Indians too pissed off at the government to take the free medical they at least deserved. You could be going to town once a week to get your ashes hauled by an undoubtedly bored masseuse at fifty bucks a whack.

He slid off the table and went to take a shower, to wash off the massage oil.

Honey was right: He was getting old and there was nothing he could do about it.

FOUR

Jimmy Reese, eleven, had fallen while in-line skating. No surprise, because most of the concrete and asphalt around here was full of potholes and cracks. Because Louisa, his mother, made him wear a helmet, he hadn't crushed his skull. But because she didn't make him wear pads, he had a road tattoo full of shredded blue jeans on his left knee. Scales had picked the denim bits from the scrape, foamed the wound with peroxide and put a Teflon bandage on it. Jimmy's tetanus was up-to-date. Scales didn't shoot an X-ray since nothing felt out of whack, but since it was a slow day, he went ahead and did a physical exam.

He put his stethoscope on the boy's left sternal border and heard the whisper of a faint cardiac murmur. He frowned.

The front door slammed and there came a wheezy yell: "Rick, you around?"

"In the exam room, Dr. Reuben."

Howard Reuben shoved the exam room door open. He carried a big cardboard box that hid his face. He squatted and put the box on the floor. "I have some samples and vitamins from the detail men," he said. Reuben was sixty-five, probably five-nine and a hundred and sixty, a fair portion of that in a potbelly. He had long gray hair combed straight back and held in place with Vitalis and a short, well-trimmed white beard. His eyes were a bloodshot brown. He wore a gray, three-piece pin-stripe suit that had to be thirty years old, with a gold watch chain draped across the vest. The shirt was white with a starched collar, his too-short tie a dark blue. He looked up, saw Louisa, smiled. "How do you do, Mrs. Reese?" Looked back at Scales and the boy. "What's our Mr. Reese here up to?"

"Jimmy decided it would be more fun to practice his racing dive than roller skate," Scales said. "No water around when he did it."

Jimmy grinned.

"He hurt his chest?"

Scales pulled the stethoscope's diaphragm off the boy's sternum and draped the scope around his neck. "Nope. But I'm picking up what sounds like a grade 2 systolic ejection murmur."

Reuben went over, took Scales' stethoscope, plugged it into his ears, warmed the diaphragm with his palm, then put it back against the boy's chest. Moved it a couple of times, listening.

Scales got a whiff of Old Spice and beer.

"What's wrong?" Louisa said.

Scales looked at Jimmy's chart. No history of rheumatic fever, pneumonia, asthma. He looked at Louisa. "Jimmy's never been really sick, has he? High fever?"

"Nothing more than colds or the flu."

"You didn't have measles while you were carrying him?"

"No. I was healthy as a horse with all three of them. What's wrong?"

Probably nothing, Scales thought. But before he could speak, Reuben pulled the stethoscope from his ears and turned to face the worried mother. "Nothing is wrong, Mrs. Reese. Jimmy's got a little music in his heart."

"Music in his heart?"

"Yes, ma'am. What they call a Still's murmur. Don't worry, about half the kids running around have a murmur at one time or another. This one is probably caused by his blood zipping past the mouth of a big vessel. Think of it like blowing across the top of a Coke bottle, how it makes a little hissy, hooty noise. It will stop when he hits puberty. Not going to hurt him at all. He can go right back out and fall down skating again."

Scales watched the relief wash across her face. Reuben was probably right, though Scales would have hedged a little. Still, with the history and the sound, it probably was an innocent murmur.

"You all done with Mr. Reese?"

Scales looked at Reuben. "All done."

"Okay, get dressed, son." Reuben handed Scales the stethoscope and walked over to the cardboard box. He took a brown plastic bottle from the box and moved over to Jimmy's mother. "Here, here are some new vitamins. Give Jimmy one of these a day, they'll fix him right up."

She smiled. She was a logger's wife and according to what Scales knew, barely finished high school, but she knew that if all it took was vitamins, then Jimmy's problem wasn't serious.

After they were gone, there weren't any other patients waiting. Reuben walked from the exam room down and across the hall to the kitchen/lab and opened the refrigerator. Pulled a beer out, twisted the cap off, and took a big swig. He leaned back against the stove. "Is there anything I need to look at? Any problems?"

"Nope. Pretty slow week. Oh, except for Inch, you already know about him."

Reuben grinned. "Hell of a remission, son. Good job."

Reuben had been born in Erie, Pennsylvania, during the Great Depression and the more he drank, the more a steel-mill-twang seeped into his voice. Scales wondered how many brews he'd pulled from the cooler on the long drive out here.

"Yeah, right. Heal the sick, raise the dead, walking on water my specialty."

"Charts?"

"Upstairs in the office."

Reuben took another big swallow from the beer, then shook his head. "The man who designed this clinic must have been a fool—or a lot younger than I. Why'd he put the office upstairs?"

It was Scales' turn to grin. Reuben had designed the clinic. And it actually made pretty good sense. On the ground floor were a waiting room, exam room, bathroom, a storage and emergency room—though they couldn't call it that legally, it was a "Trauma Stabilization Room"—plus the kitchen-slash-lab. Upstairs were a library, office, utility room, plus a bathroom and two bedrooms. It had been a pretty good-sized wood-framed house sixty or so years ago when it had been built, and it made a small but functional clinic. "My guess is the guy who designed it figured he'd only have to climb the stairs once a week to sign charts."

Reuben grinned again, finished the beer in four swallows. Scales had seen the man drain five beers without any change in his demeanor, save for the folksy ring in his voice. He would have bet a year's salary that the doctor was an alcoholic, though he seemed to control it most of the time.

"I suppose I should exert myself and see what damage you did to the local populace this week. You could bring the charts down and leave them here, you know." He tapped the empty bottle on the counter next to the stove.

"What—and miss hearing you bitch about having to climb one whole flight of stairs? Probably the most exercise you get all week."

"Actually, you're right, m'boy." He opened the fridge, pulled out another beer, toasted Scales with the unopened bottle. "Though I expect I'll live to walk on your grave—all that iron pumping you do, I have to tell you, it's bad for the constitution."

He shook his head and headed for the stairs.

Hughes sat in her pickup, looking at two men across the road. They were wandering around the museum grounds, looking at the cedar plank house built out front. She was parked across the street at the Coast Guard station eating a sandwich and drinking coffee from her thermos.

Since the tribe decided to build a casino, there had been a lot of strange visitors to the reservation. They got plenty of tourists in season anyway, but the guys looking to sell their services as builders and operators of the proposed gambling facility looked particularly out-of-place here at the end of the world. As reservations went, this one was better than some she'd seen, but there were a few rusted-out washing machines and car skeletons scattered about and other unburnable trash piled up in yards here and there. Here was a house that could sit in any upper-middle-class neighborhood in Seattle or San Francisco; next to it, a ratty three-room shack barely standing and only a cut above tarpaper. Not the kind of thing you'd see in the normal realm of men in suits with slicked-down hair, driving Jags or a drop-top Mercedes, carrying briefcases made out of emu that cost as much as a tribal deputy made in three months.

The brief sun-break shined through air washed clean by the most recent shower, so that things had a sharpness bathed in a kind of actinic Maxfield Parrish golden glow. She'd had a Parrish illustration from a picture book, The Arabian Nights, stuck it on her wall with thumbtacks when she'd lived in the Haight. Right next to her "Fuck Communism" poster. When the place had caught on fire and the firemen had kicked in her door, that poster had been the first thing they'd seen. "Strange attitude for a hippie," one of the firemen had said. Well, yes. She'd been a strange hippie . . .

She pulled her attention back to the present. It was threatening rain, the wind blowing damply through her windows. The golden glow would be gone in a few minutes. She catalogued the pair of slicks standing outside the museum right now, next to a shiny new blue Cadillac—the "Buy American" union types liked domestic iron. What they'd paid for the clothes and jewelry they wore would pay her salary for a year. Talking expensive shades, silk jackets and ties, linen slacks, Italian leather on the ground, exotic endangered briefcases on the hood and roof of the Caddy. They were young, maybe thirty, thirty-five, and if she'd seen them in L.A., she'd have figured them for movie producers or drug dealers—maybe both. They represented an east coast company that wanted to make the tribe a great deal on slot machines and while they could be upstanding businessmen, Hughes would not be the least bit surprised to find out they were connected to families whose names all ended in vowels.

She mentally shrugged. The tribe wanted to get into this bed, there was a lot of money to be made doing it, and they were going to sleep with somebody. If not these two, then others like them. Before it became legal in most places, gambling had been very big business among the bent-nose crowd, no matter what their ancestry, and they had a running start on how to set up a working casino. Since she was supposed to be head of the new casino's security, she expected she'd be dealing with men like these. The money would be very good, the work easy, plus the tribe would benefit greatly from the casino. But there were always drawbacks. Men like the two laughing next to the museum made the cop in her twitch. She knew bad guys when she saw them. The best she was going to be able to do was make sure these guys wore rubbers when they started fucking the tribe.

A fitful gust of wind brought with it a wave of fat drops, like a handful of pea gravel flung against the truck. The two slick boys grabbed their briefcases and scrambled into the Caddy as the next gust unloaded a heavier spray of rain. In five seconds more, it was coming down hard. She could see the slick boys laughing inside the safety of the Cad.

She rolled her windows partway up and started the truck. She pulled into the road and headed toward the west end of the reservation. The tribe really needed the money and the jobs but it would come at a price. She just hoped they could afford to pay it.

Reuben had been gone for more than an hour. Scales unloaded the freebie drug and vitamin samples and put most of them away. A lot of antihistamines, some antibiotics, a few asthma inhalers, a few packs of eye drops, some BP meds. The usual eclectic mix of whatever came through the Port Angeles clinic that nobody there wanted. Leftovers, but he was happy to get them. A lot of his patients were stone cold broke, especially some of the vets hiding in the woods.

He paused to look at the label on the vitamins. They were Medical Frontiers Corporation multiples. Five thousand of A, twenty-five hundred of beta carotene, four hundred of D, a hundred of C, thirty of E, the MDR and then some, the Bs and most of the minerals, iron, phosphorus, iodine, only partials on the calcium and copper. Not bad for prenatals or general one-a-days for most people. He flipped the bottle into the air, heard the capsules rattle around inside. He took a daily multiple, of course, but also added heavy doses of the antioxidants C and E, plus a couple caps of ginseng. Exercising regularly had a lot of benefits but it also created free-radicals and those didn't do you any good. Supposedly the antioxidants cleaned a lot of those up. Maybe they worked, maybe all they did was give you real expensive urine as some doctors thought, but Scales believed in vitamins. He felt better when he took them and if that was just placebo effect, what-the-hell. If he only thought he felt better, so what? Better than thinking he felt lousy. He'd give these a try.

The phone rang.

"Medical Clinic."

"Hey, Ricky."

"Hey, Momma." His Texas accent thickened instantly, like a time-lapse film of a bowl of cooling Jell-O.

"How you doin'?"

"Fine, Momma. How y'all?"

"We all fine here."

"Daddy okay?"

"Daddy's fine."

"Tom Junior and Eliza?"

"They're fine. Everybody at the house is fine."

He waited for a second. His mother never called him unless something—or somebody—wasn't fine, though she'd never admit it until she got good and ready.

"You hear from anybody?"

By anybody, his mother meant his immediate family. Since Tom Junior worked at the ranch and his oldest sister Eliza lived there, that meant: Had he heard from his other sisters—Sassy, who lived in Alabama, or Annie, a freelance book illustrator in New York City?

He said, "I got a letter from Sassy over the wire, e-mail a few days ago."

Sassy—Sarah, though nobody had ever called her that—was two years older than Scales, twice married and divorced. She now lived in Tuscaloosa with an assistant DA, where she worked editing a locally-unpopular left-wing weekly paper, *The Alabama Spectator*. They weren't married and neither of them had children from their previous marriages or this living in sin they were up to.

"She doin' okay?"

"Just fine, Momma. They're thinking about getting married."

"Well, I wish they would." A beat. "You ain't heard nothin' from your baby sister?"

He smiled. Annie was a year younger than he was. Still the baby, though.

"No, not for a month or so."

"Nothing from little Dana?"

Little Dana was Annie's daughter. She was twenty-six? twenty-seven? and a second-year Family Practice resident at Brothers of Providence Hospital in Cambridge. The bright light of the grandchildren, Dana had graduated from Harvard Medical School three years ago. Last Christmas when everybody had gone home to visit, he and his niece had swapped black humor medical stories until people started leaving the room in disgust. A very bright young woman.

"Reason I'm askin' is, I was wondering if you knew anything about her new boyfriend?"

No, he didn't, and now they were fixin' to get to the reason Momma called. He grinned. He even thought with a thick Texas accent when he talked to his family back home.

"I haven't heard about him, no."

"Well, she met this fellow at the hospital, he's a doctor, one of those Ontologists." This last was pronounced "Awn-tollow-jist."

"Oncologists?"

"That's what I said, didn't I?"

"Yes, Momma. Go ahead."

"Well, Annie says he's sharp as a tack and been offered a job somewhere out in California next year. And his folks are pretty near rich, too. Thing is, he wants Dana to move out there with him."

"So? What's the problem?"

"Well, Annie doesn't seem to think there's a problem but she sent me a picture of them together and, well, he's some kind of black man."

Scales blinked at the phone. "Some kind of black man? How many kinds you figure there are, Momma? He a purple black man? A red black man?"

"Don't go gettin' smart mouth with me, son."

"I'm sorry, Momma." Jesus, she still made him feel as if he were nine-years-old. "Where is he from?"

"Well, that's the thing. He's from Pakistan." This was: "Packy-stan."

My. Black *and* a foreigner. "Oh, well, then he's not black. He's a wog," Scales said. He tried to keep his voice deadpan.

"A wog?"

"A worthy Oriental gentleman."

"He looks pretty dark in the picture."

"But he's not a Negro if he's Pakistani, Momma. He's probably got a straight nose and thin lips, looks just like anybody else except for his skin is a little darker."

"Well, I don't know."

As much as he loved his parents, sometimes he got exasperated with them. So what if Dana's boyfriend was Pakistani? It wouldn't matter if he were Bantu or a Zulu, as far as Scales was concerned. That was her business, wasn't it? If the family didn't approve, they didn't have to invite them home for Christmas.

"She's a grown woman, Momma. If this guy is what she wants, she's old enough to make that choice on her own. What do you want me to do, call her and talk her out of it?"

"You're her favorite uncle."

"And I'm the uncle likely to tell her to go for it, too."

In Vietnam, he'd been a corpsman working in the bush with the Marines. There had been an ambush and a couple of the patrol took hits. He'd gone out to get a wounded corporal and they'd gotten pinned. It looked like they were history when Alfred the Chemically-Treated Night Fighter, and as black a man as he'd ever seen had come out, hosed Charlie dead in the bushes with his personal Thompson .45 submachine gun and helped Scales drag the shot-up corp back to cover. Crazy as a shithouse rat, Alfred was, but nobody ever doubted his bravery. Since Scales had never leaned toward heavy racial prejudice anyhow, after that, no way was he ever going to look at black folks as inferior. A man saves your life, he buys a lot of equality.

There was a short silence on the phone. "Daddy said you'd say that, that I was wastin' my time trying to get you to say anything to her."

"Much as I hate to admit it, Daddy was right."

"Well. I just thought I'd mention it. Maybe it's not all that serious."

They chatted for a couple more minutes but the main reason for her call being over, she was in a hurry to hang up. Momma hated to spend money on long distance charges.

When he had cradled his own phone, Scales shook his head. Thing was, if Dana and her boyfriend got serious, got married and had little coffee-colored babies, Momma would be the first one there to help out, and a standing offer of babysitting would be tendered. She loved babies, didn't matter what color they were. Sixty-odd years living in redneck country hadn't touched that in her. Momma would be happy running a daycare center and it wouldn't matter if the babies were green: mothering was what she did best.

He shook his head. Time to go hit the weights.

FIVE

One of the biggest problems with being out in the boonies was labwork—or rather the lack of it. Scales could cook petri cultures for strep or pseudomonas or gonorrhea, do throwaway pregnancy, TB, AIDS or even cholesterol tests, but to get a simple CBC, he had to ship the blood into Port Angeles and wait for the lab to call him. Reuben had been promising to pick up an old Coulter Counter for several months but so far he hadn't delivered.

Scales could do a diff, could drop-and-streak a slide and run a count under the microscope to get the proportion of white cells, and that's what he was doing. He'd stained, buffered, blotted and immersed the glass slide and was now scrolling the thing and punching the old mechanical counter. Back to the Stone Age, but it worked.

Nasty little men eat babies.

Another of the memory devices he'd learned. This phrase gave the white cells on the grid under the scope—neutrophiles, lymphocytes, monocytes, eosinophiles, basophiles—and in normal proportional order. Segmented neutrophiles—segs—usually ran 50-60 percent in a well patient. Lymphocytes came in at 20-33 percent, Monos 4-8 percent, Eos 1-3 percent, Basos 1 percent or less. Big deviations from the norms gave you major clues as to what might be wrong with a sick patient. Bacterial infections had a different shift than viral, allergies brought up one kind over another, even many parasites had a distinct signature.

He leaned back from the microscope and rubbed his

eyes. He'd have to wait until the complete blood count came back, but according to this slide, Timothy Joseph Canton, age seven, had a perfectly normal white cell differential. Which was highly unlikely, given that he also had an acute lymphocytic leukemia and ought to be so sick he couldn't get out of bed.

What Scales ought to see on this slide was a major elevation of leukocytes, which had been that way less than a week ago, a whole shitload of half-grown lymphoblasts, and a big drop in platelets due to a severe anemia. The kid should be pale as Casper the ghost, bruising if you looked at him crooked, with nose bleeds, weakness and general malaise. He'd been that way a week ago. Scales had wanted to send him to the hospital. He knew his limits. He wasn't an oncologist, and he'd called Reuben for back up. Let it ride a couple of days and see how he does, Reuben had said. We can always ship him if it gets worse.

But today, the boy looked great on the exam and seemed in good spirits and health. According to his mother he had sneaked out of the house and gone to play with his friends, had been running, jumping and generally having a fine old time when she'd tracked him down.

Leukemias sometimes had pretty good remissions and most patients this kid's age tended to have a favorable prognosis with current treatment, but even so, this was fairly sudden and dramatic. Timmy's risk factors had been mixed: He was young, but two weeks ago his total WBC count had been almost a million, he'd still had pseudodiploid karyotypes and cytoplasmic immunoglobulin blast cells swimming around like crazy and it hadn't looked good.

Scales shook his head. Must be something in the water.

Well. He wasn't going to look a gift horse in the mouth,

long as they kept coming. Getting well was better than the option. Though it was interesting as hell that he had two miracles this week. Had to be a statistical trick, but still . . .

He went back out to tell Timmy and his mother the good news.

Bobby Lost-a-Lot Mitchell had finally found a buyer for his charter fishing boat, some retired airline pilot who wanted to dabble in the business, so Bobby was celebrating by having a salmon cookout. His backyard was fairly large and he'd built a good-sized fire and surrounded it with fish, whole salmon flayed wide and propped up lengthwise on green sticks in the old way. The trick was to get the fish close enough to cook without burning it. He used a lot of butter and lemon juice to baste the fresh-caught fish. When it was done right, salmon didn't taste any better. Smelled pretty good cooking, too.

There was a big pot of mussels ready to steam open, a few Dungeness crabs somebody had brought by, even a sack of geoduck somebody had scored.

It was close to dark, and maybe thirty people were wandering around in Bobby's backyard, drinking Cokes and Oly beer from ice chests and eating potluck snack food, mostly potato chips and Fritos, with store-bought bean dip. Before the night was out, maybe a hundred more people would drop by.

The party noise was a nice background drone and the humming UV bug zapper dangling from the house's overhang was also working pretty good, frying insects attracted to it with pops and crackles and flashes of brighter blue.

Jay Hughes had shucked her police gear—it was locked in the toolbox in her truck—and stood nursing a beer of her own. She and Bobby went way back, they'd been kids together, and she was happy for him. With the money he made on the sale, he could pay off his bills and prop his feet up for a few months and do nothing while he decided if he was going to invest in the cedar shake business with his brother Russell. Which likely he would.

She felt a little edgy and her breasts were full and sore. Probably ovulating. Not that she had to worry about getting pregnant. First, you needed a willing man you could stand; second, you needed working tubes, and she didn't have either.

She knew everybody at the gathering. This was not a party for the tourists, though a few non-Makah were there. There were a couple of grad students come to see the Ozette Dig, attractive young women, which was why they'd been invited. Bobby had five brothers and while all five were married, all of them were always looking for women who didn't know about their wives. There were a couple of long-time local loggers, a few people from a couple of other tribes. And Doc Scales was there, sipping from a can of beer and listening to Millie Cippoli ramble on about her gallbladder surgery. Millie was east coast Italian, had married a man from the tribe who was killed a few years back in a logging accident. She had decided to stay around. She was a graying brunette, all of five feet tall and built like a rain barrel.

Hughes took pity on him and moved in.

"Hey, Millie, Rick."

Scales looked relieved to see her.

"Millie, mind if I borrow Doc for a minute? I've got something I need to show him."

"Sure thing," Millie said.

She took Scales' arm and urged him away from the obese woman toward her truck. She noted how firm his triceps were under her fingers.

When they were out of Millie's sight, Scales said, "Something to show me?"

"An empty spot where Millie was blocking the view," Hughes said.

"Thanks. I owe you one. I was getting the grand tour of Millie's gallstones."

"One of them was shaped like a heart," she said, deadpan. "Did you know that?"

"I know those stones better than the backs of my own hands. Poor Millie. The classic example of four-effery."

"Four effery?"

"Fair, fat, flatulent, forty. See somebody like her who can't eat pork chops without belching or bloating and has pain in the right upper quadrant, that's the first thing you think of, cholelithiasis—gallstones."

They sipped at their respective beers.

"Kind of surprised to see you," she said. "You don't usually do much socializing."

He shrugged. "Bobby's a patient. He invited me." He took a deep breath, blew part of it out. "Truth is, I was kinda hoping I'd see you here."

She noticed that his Texas accent deepened some when he said that. He was, she realized, nervous. She still liked having that effect on men. She could have made it easier for him but decided to see how he did on his own. "Oh? How come?"

He gave her a small grin, an acknowledgement that he knew what she was doing. He wasn't some teenaged boy who was going to balk at the first hurdle. He said, "You're good company. I like talking to you."

That pleased her, too, maybe more than it should have. She wasn't looking for another relationship with a man, at least not one that involved any kind of real effort. Yes, he was maybe a cut above her last lover, a logger named Derek Fleur who, it turned out, had a wife and five children waiting for him back in Canada. That one still burned if she touched it. All she wanted to do was lay low until the casino got built, get a high-paying job there and take it easy.

Then again, Scales wasn't bad company himself and she didn't have any plans to join a nunnery any time soon. Talking didn't hurt anything.

"Thanks," she said. "You're not bad yourself—for a white boy."

They both grinned.

The salmon was, Scales decided, the best he'd ever tasted. The mussels weren't bad, the crab outstanding. It would be easy to make a pig out of himself.

He sat at the outdoor picnic table and watched the sparks from the dwindling fire shower up as somebody lobbed an empty mussel shell into it. Jay sat to his left, doing a fair amount of eating herself. Healthy appetite on that woman.

He stared at the fire. Another handful of shells hit it, more sparks erupted upward and into the night. It was after ten, he still hadn't gotten used to it staying light so long in the summers here, but the night had finally settled in. People laughed, talked, sat or walked around, eating or done.

Watching the sparks fly, Scales had a memory surge:

When he was five or six, his family took a trip to his great-grandparent's farm in Oklahoma. All four of the children and both parents went. Tom Junior would have been about twelve, Eliza, ten, Sassy, seven and little Annie a year younger than Scales, probably four.

The place was somewhere near Tulsa, about eighty acres, and his mother's-father's-father had been working it for sixty years. The old man had to be eighty, though he looked to Scales as if he were a thousand, and his great-grandmother looked even older. She wore her hair in a bun and had old lady shoes, black squarish things under a blue-gray print dress that almost touched the ground.

He couldn't remember much about the place. He thought they grew corn and wheat, had a big truck garden and a few cows. What he most remembered about that trip were the bullwhips, the snake and the chimney sparks.

The bullwhips hung on the back outside wall of the house, inside the screened porch, two of them. They were black, plaited leather, twenty feet long, his great-grandpa said, made them himself, and he used to use them on the plow mules, before he got a tractor. The whips were old and cracked, they'd been hanging on the wall for years, coiled around a big nail, but they still had that leather smell if you got close enough.

The snake had been lying on a dirt road that led to the stream. Scales and Sassy and Anne had gone exploring and they saw it. Sassy and he had left Anne there to watch it while they ran back to tell Momma.

"Momma, momma, we saw a snake!"

"That's nice, Ricky. Where is Annie?"

"We left her to watch the snake," he said.

"Dear Lord!"

Momma jumped up and Scales didn't understand at the time why she'd been so excited. They'd told her not to touch it or anything.

By the time Momma and the rest of them got there, the snake had crawled off and Annie was sitting in middle of the dirt road in her pink dress and matching underpants, crying.

"Did it bite you?" Momma asked.

"N-N-No. But it ran away and I couldn't catch it!"

It was a lot funnier forty-odd years later than it had been at the time. His mother had not been happy with him and Sassy.

And the third thing he remembered was after dark, when the old folks had cranked up the fireplace—it got chilly there, even in the early summer—and they had gone outside to sit in the porch swing. Scales wandered out into the yard and looked back at the house. There was no place else around and it was pitch black except for the stars and lights of the house. Sparks boiled up the chimney and spewed into the night, whirling and shifting, glowing orange fireflies soaring high. Scales had never seen anything like it. Most of the tiny sparks flew up and vanished, but some of them floated lazily down to the ground before they winked out.

That would have been in the mid-fifties. The night sky had been sharper then, not so much light pollution, especially way out in the country. It was his first memory of the stars, too, come to think of it.

His great-grandparents both died before he was fifteen. He would have liked to have gone back to visit them more, but they never did, and when he was older, he realized how interesting their lives must have been. His great-grandfather had been born a few years after the War Between the States—sometimes called "The Recent Unpleasantness" in Texas but never "The Civil War." He had seen the advent of the automobile, electricity, indoor plumbing and telephones. His great-grandmother had come of age in a time when an uncovered ankle was a sexual perversion.

He always regretted that they didn't live long enough for him to realize what real history they could have passed on.

Sparks from the fire danced into the night sky . . .

"Where'd you go?" Jay said.

He blinked, looked at her. "Oklahoma," he said.

She didn't say anything for a moment and he decided to tell it to her.

After he was done, she nodded. "Family is important," she said.

She drank from her beer. "For me, it's always been my nanna, my mother and sisters. I never knew my father, he was gone by the time I was born." She looked at him. "I have three half-sisters, all younger than me: Mirabella, Samantha and Joan. All married and nine children among them. Mirabella still lives on the reservation, Samantha lives in Guam with her husband, an Air Force lieutenant, and Joan lives in New Orleans with her second husband, a riverboat casino blackjack dealer."

He nodded. "I've treated Mirabella's children. Her husband is Sam McClean?"

"Yes."

"When Nanna got sick, I came home to help my mother with her. She died in '89. Liver failure. She drank too much." As if to emphasize that, she took a sip of her beer. "Decided to stay."

"Hey, Scales. Got any of them armpit bandages left?"

Scales turned and saw Ray Jenkins standing there. Jenkins was a year or two older than Scales, had a ponytail to his shoulders and a full beard gone mostly gray. He wore surplus camo fatigues, and combat boots, a web-belt with a K-bar knife and a holstered .45 on it. Probably had a grenade or two in his pockets, too.

Scales smiled. "I'm keeping the sweatiest one for you. You need to come in?"

"Yeah." He glanced at Jay Hughes.

"My chopper is in the shop but the morning is pretty clear. Drop on by anytime."

"Copy, Scales. Semper Fi."

"Semper Fi, you fucking jarhead."

The bearded man grinned. He turned and ambled off.

Jenkins was a Vietnam vet who never made it all the way back to the World. He did his tour, came home, bummed around for a year or two before he moved up here. He had a semi-permanent camp in the woods south of the reservation, his hootch, he called it, and mostly he stayed in the forest. Nobody bothered him. There were a few like him still out there, hiding most of the time, never quite able to get over what happened to them as young men. Local people knew where they were and they tended to stay clear of them. The vets went armed and could mistake a logger for a Viet Cong in the wrong light. Jenkins had been in the woods for more than two and a half decades and it wasn't likely he was ever coming out. One of the walking wounded from McNamara's War. And Kennedy's and Johnson's and Nixon's war . . .

Jay said, "Armpit bandages?"

He nodded. "Yeah. I was a Navy corpsman in Vietnam. Like a medic. Detached to a Marine unit. Charlie—the Viet Cong—would shoot at anything that moved American, but he particularly favored officers, radiomen and medicos. They taught us to keep our insignia hidden, our sidearms under our shirts, and to avoid hauling medical bags when we went into the bush. Never let anybody call you 'Doc' or 'medic' or 'corpsman' either, Charlie learned what that meant pretty quick. I packed most of my gear under a cut-up shirt I wore as a vest. Meds, bandages, whatever. It was a joke with the Marines, crotch bandages, armpit bandages, because of where they were carried."

"Doesn't sound like fun to me."

"Only reason Ray comes to see me is because he knows I

was there. A big part of him stopped moving forward somewhere in the jungle. He's alive but he couldn't get past it."

"Stupid thing, war," she said.

"Amen."

He nodded again. He was full, had drunk three beers
and was relaxed and comfortable. Twenty years ago, he
would have been trying like hell to get her to leave with
him, to find any spot private enough to get into her pants.
Now, he still felt the desire, but not the urgency. He said,
"I think maybe I better head home before I'm tempted to
eat or drink any more." He tossed his empty beer can at an
oil drum lined with a black plastic leaf bag, was pleased that
it went in.

"Good idea. I'd hate to have to arrest you for drunken
driving."

He stood, smiled at her. "You going shooting tomorrow?"

"Might."

"Maybe I'll see you there." He thought about it for a
second. Said, "I'll probably be there around nine."

She raised her beer can, offered a silent toast.

He turned and went to find Bobby to offer his congratu-
lations and to thank him for the food and drink. He hadn't
asked her out. It wasn't a date or anything like that. Just a
casual mention of what time he'd be at the gravel pit, that
was all.

He sure hoped she'd be there, though.

As she watched Scales amble away, Hughes took a final
sip from the middle of her second beer, then got up to put
the half-full can into the oil drum nearby. Scales liked her.
It showed, and if telling her he was going to be shooting at
nine in the morning wasn't an invitation, she didn't know

anything about men at all. She couldn't claim to know much, even after being with dozens of the suckers, but she knew male interest when she saw it.

Did she want to pursue it? Maybe not. If she happened to show up at the pit at the same time he did, it wouldn't really mean anything. He hadn't asked her out, just mentioned what time he'd be there. If she didn't go, that didn't mean anything either.

Right at the moment, she was disposed to give it a pass. He was a nice enough guy on the surface, pretty sharp, but once you got to know somebody a little better, you tended to find out all kinds of things that didn't show on first look. Sometimes they were good things. More often than not, they were bad.

Of course, that was what a new man was all about, the finding out, wasn't it? Could be very disappointing, but then again, it could be like happening upon a Picasso at a garage sale. You just never knew until you dug through the old boxes and looked.

She gave herself a wry grin, a small one. She'd rummaged in a lot of old boxes in her time and the Picassos were few and far between. Mostly you found matadors on black velvet. But if you didn't look, you'd never know.

The party was still pretty quiet. No fights, no mean drunks lit up. Maybe she should head home while she was still ahead.

SIX

"—six!"

Oh, but that rep went up hard. Scales let the weight settle to his chest, took a deep breath and shoved, expelled the air forcefully as if trying to blow the barbell to the garage's damp rafters. The heavy bar inched up slowly. His triceps quivered and it was all he could do to keep his back flat on the bench. Come on, come on—!

". . . seven!" he said. He locked his elbows, okay, a bit of a cheat, but not much, took another breath, unlocked his elbows and fought gravity's unrelenting grip on the iron as it settled to his chest again.

One more. One . . . more . . .

Up . . .

You could grow trees it was taking so fucking long, *come on, up! up! go up, damnit!*

Halfway into the bench press the bar stopped. God reached down, put his hand on the bar, said, "Sorry, Ricky, can't let you do it."

Hell with that. He cheated, arched his back, grunted and shoved. Messing with the wrong guy here, God.

The bar moved a hair. Stopped again. God chuckled. "Oh, really?"

His arms started to shake.

Wasn't going to, was . . . not . . . going . . . to . . . go. And not nearly high enough to rack, either. Shit.

He didn't have any choice. He let his left arm relax slightly. The bar tilted sharply and the plates on that side, a hundred and thirty pounds worth, slid off the end. The weights crashed into the thick rubber pad put on the concrete floor for just that purpose but *blang-blang-clanged!—loudly*—against each other anyhow. Two fifties, a twenty-five and a five.

It was like a fat kid leaping off one side of a see-saw. Now the other side dropped, pivoted the forty-pound bar up and over, jerked it free of his left hand and dumped the other plates.

Crang, clong, clack!

Jesus Fucking Christ!

Scales caught the now-empty bar on the rebound and racked it. Sat up. Pulled the towel from around his neck and wiped his face. Okay, some noise but that was your safety when you didn't have a spotter, you left the collars off, let the weights fall on the nice pads instead of having the bar pin you to the bench like a bug. They didn't like you to do that in a commercial gym and he didn't much like doing here, either. Then again, more than one home gym lifter had been badly injured or even killed when a bar came down on his chest or throat with the collars keeping them neat and snug on the bar. Rubber pads were a lot cheaper than a casket.

He ought to get a machine, then he wouldn't have to worry about it dropping on him, but he liked the free-weights.

Thing was, they didn't like him as much as they used to. Seven lousy reps with three hundred pounds. Shit. Five years ago, he could do eight with three seventy-five, and ten years before that, he could push four hundred for a triple.

Those days are gone, Scales. The new car smell has worn off. You're driving a beater now. Thank whoever is in charge that it still runs at all.

He slid off the bench and began to pick up the fallen plates. He stacked them back on their stands. He could still move respectable weights in dumbbell rowing or deltoid flyes or calf raises. He could curl one-ten for reps, but he'd never lusted after monster biceps so he'd never pushed that. People always wanted to know how much you could bench, how much you could squat, how much you could deadlift. There was a time when it mattered to him what he could answer. Then that went away. Now, it bothered him again. Well. His bench was down, he only used light weights for deadlifts to spare his lower back, and he didn't do squats any heavier than body weight, his knees wouldn't take it.

Sure, he was stronger than most men his age, but once upon a time, he'd been stronger than most men any age.

Better hobble on into the house, old man, before you fall down.

He went to the kitchen, opened one of the bottles of new vitamins Reuben had brought and shook one into his hand. He went through the other supplement bottles and added pills and caps until there was a big clump in his palm. Tossed them all into his mouth and washed them down with a couple of swallows of iced Coke. Patch, patch, patch.

It would be nice to have a hot tub to soak in, but he'd have to settle for a shower. He glanced at the clock over the stove. Seven o'clock. He could clean up, put in an hour at the computer and half that on the charts and get to the quarry by nine. He needed the time; shaky as he was now, he wouldn't be able to hold the gun still long enough to hit anything.

Christ, it was hell getting older. Better than the option, but still . . .

Showered, shaved and feeling closer to human again,

Scales sat in front of his computer, tapping away at the ergonomic keyboard. He was a Mac guy, and the heart of his system was a G5. He didn't have many vices, at least not expensive ones. Rent was free, food for him alone was cheap. He sent some money to the girls, even though he didn't have to anymore. A couple of visits to Honey a month. There was money left over from his pay that he banked. The simple life was cheaper. But the computer, ah, yeah, that was a *need*. The once-blazing speed of its processor was slow compared to what was out there now, but that was always how it went. It was fast enough for what he did. He had a laser printer, a color monitor, a fax modem and a scanner hooked into the system, and the modem was still faster than his phone lines and most of the online services could stand. Someday, he'd get broadband . . .

At the moment, he was logged into the Doc-in-a-Box bulletin board in Los Angeles. This was a medical professionals' board with a whole bunch of online software you could access. He had an 800-number to avoid long distance charges, but at $25 per, the hourly charges were high. Fortunately he had been able to convince Reuben that he needed it. With the scanner, he could upload an ECG tracing and have the DIB BBS's cardiology program read it and give him an opinion. There was also a pretty good differential DX program online. You gave it the age, sex, signs and symptoms of a patient and it took you through a Q&A session, at the end of which it gave you a percentage diagnosis. He'd been doing medicine a long time, but now and then, it didn't hurt to check and make sure he wasn't screwing up. A lot of it was as much art as science but it was amazing how much medicine was cut-and-dried when you got right down to it. There were only so many common diseases and if you got enough information, it would usually point to a couple. When you hear the sound of hoof beats, you don't look for zebras.

Right now he was spending Reuben's money on a real-time chat that had nothing to do with medicine, save that the other people logged into it were mostly doctors, nurses, PAs or NPs. It was pretty amazing, that you could have a couple dozen folk all gathered in a cyberspace room at the same time, typing their comments back and forth, with some of them in L.A., some in New York City and some in Tampa. Every now and then, they got visitors from halfway around the world. Each of the speakers had a screen name and it appeared in front of any comments he or she made. Right now, they were telling stories:

> *BillySol:* So first thing was, this patient didn't do his enema. But he didn't tell us. Came in, we put him ass up on the table and lit up the long cold finger.

Long cold finger was medicalese some places for a proctoscope.

> *Mammary:* Sounds messy. I've been there. :)
>
> *BillySol:* Oh, you don't know the half of it. So he starts to rumble and my nurse starts using language her teachers at the Catholic school never taught her.
>
> *BillySol:* So I yell at her to get the damned suction pump going. We're filling the bottle with brown and looks like we're going to stay ahead of it, barely
>
> *BillySol:* but all of a sudden the motor seizes up. Blue smoke pours out of the sucker, it's grinding metal and we lose suction

Normally people would be crosstalking, but BillySol's story was interesting enough so the others were willing to listen.

BillySol: Guy on the table groans and lets go. I mean he was <<<spewing>>> feces. Got it all over my lab coat, my nurse was trying to plug him up with a towel, stuff was spattering on my new Italian shoes.

Scalpel2: LOL, Billy.

Fever: ROFL, BillySol. 8D

He was still learning the shorthand for computer boards but these he knew. LOL was "laughing out loud." ROFL was "rolling on the floor laughing." and the little symbols when you turned them upright usually made faces. 8D was a laugher.

BillySol: It gets better. My tech was passing by in the hall. Smart ass kid, about thirty. He plays guitar. So at lunchtime, he writes a song for me. *Proctoscope Blues.* I uploaded a sound file to the library. You can listen to it. It's pretty good.

Scales: Probably not much of a market for it.

Fever: Oh, I don't know, I'd probably pick it up. Proctoscope Blues . . . Sh*t on my shoes.

BillySol: You heard it already?

Scales grinned. He had to log off if he was going to get his charts done. With the scanner, he could put them into the computer and with the huge hard drive Dr. Reuben had coughed up for, you could store an awful lot of them there. More than there were people in these parts.

71

Scales: I gotta run, guys. Talk to you later.

There was a flurry of good byes. Scales waited until they were done, then logged off the BBS and shut off his modem. A lot of people left those on all the time, but he was paranoid enough so he didn't want to take the chance. Nobody could invade your computer if they couldn't link to it.

This stuff was seductive. You could spend forever flitting from home page to home page, learning all manner of things you didn't need to know. All visual, just point and click the mouse. He'd never seen himself as a computer nerd but some nights, he spent hours online poking around. What happened when you didn't have anybody around to help you have a life . . .

He started going through the charts. The first one was a patient who'd come in complaining of feeling tired all the time. Nothing in particular wrong, he said, I just don't have any energy. Can't keep up with the kids when they come to visit. Common enough in today's world, but this particular patient was an 89-year-old Makah with sixteen great-grandchildren. It had been all Scales could do to keep a straight face. Physical exam was unremarkable, the old boy was in pretty good shape. He took a blood sample and a urine specimen. The urine was clear except for a few casts and the blood hadn't come back yet, but Scales didn't expect it would be abnormal. He'd given Great-Grandfather some of the new vitamins, talked about how potent they were to ratchet up the placebo effect, and sent him home.

Next case . . .

In her bedroom, Hughes packed her shooting gear. Her

mother yelled at her from the kitchen: "Jasmine, you eating breakfast?"

"No," she yelled back.

A moment later Molly Maxwell Hughes came into the room, wiping her hands on a dish towel. "You gotta eat, girl. You gonna blow away."

Hughes grinned. "Wishful thinking, Mama. I'm one-fifty naked."

"Yeah, but you tall. Five-eight."

"Five-seven, Mama."

Mama was five-four and probably outweighed her daughter by twenty pounds. She still wore her hair long and it was still mostly blue-black, only a few strands of gray in it. Hughes figured she put a rinse in it but her mother swore she didn't. "You still look skinny. You ever gonna get a husband, you need to have some meat on your bones. Men like women with a little padding."

"Men like anything with a hole and a pulse," Hughes said. She shoved her extra speedloaders into the bag. "Some of them don't need the pulse."

"Bad men. Good men want more."

"I know about bad men," Hughes said. "I'd say they outnumber the good ones about a thousand-to-one."

"Fleur wasn't so awful."

"I'm sure his wife agrees."

"He might have left her if you'd pushed him a little."

Hughes turned and shook her head. "Mama, I wouldn't want a man who would cheat on his wife. If he did it to her, why wouldn't he do it to me?"

Her mother shrugged. "Men are men. They are how they are. You have to overlook a few little things."

Hughes laughed. "Little things. Like Fleur's five children?"

Mama shook her head. "You set your standards too high, Jasmine. Your sisters have done all right."

Hughes didn't say anything. Done all right? Joan's husband, the river boat dealer, liked to use his hands for more than playing cards. Hughes caught him slapping Joan once and told him if it ever happened again, no matter where they were, she would find him and put a bullet through his dick. Samantha's Air Force husband was a womanizer who had given her the clap after they were married and lucky it wasn't something worse. Mirabella's husband, fifteen years older than she was, spent most of his days drunk or stoned or both. Fine catches—if you set your standards at male and breathing.

"I'll eat a big lunch," Hughes said.

"You going to see that doctor?"

Hughes turned away from her packed bag to stare at her mother. That was the trouble with a place as small as the reservation. You couldn't sneeze without everybody for fifty miles knowing when and how wet it was.

"I might."

Her mother grinned. "Doctors do all right. I know you don't have any love for them but that Scales seems okay."

Yes, he did seem okay, but she wouldn't admit that to her mother. Instead she said, "He's not a doctor, he's a Physician's Assistant."

Her mother shrugged. "Whatever. He's a good-looking man, strong, got a job. You could do worse."

"Bye, Mama. I'll see you tonight."

"Be careful, little Kwenetchechat."

Hughes smiled. Kwenetchechat was the old tribal name. It meant "People who live on a little spit of land that juts out in the ocean," or somesuch.

"I will."

As Hughes left the house, she thought about it. Mama was right. She could do a lot worse than Scales. Not that that meant she couldn't do better, too. *We'll just see how it goes.*

He saw her truck when he arrived at the pit and it made Scales smile.

The shooting was okay and when it was done and they were packing up, Scales took the risk.

"You want to go get a cup of coffee?"

She hesitated a moment. "Sure. Why not?"

He followed her back to the main drag. She pulled into the small parking lot of Art's Cafe's on the highway and he parked next to her. As they entered the place, it started to rain. In a few seconds, the outside washed to monochromatic gray. Hard to believe it was summer here, cold and wet as it was.

If there was an "Art" Scales had never met him. The woman behind the counter was Bertha, she was the cook, and as far as he could tell, owned the place. There was a skinny girl of about nineteen waiting tables, and while the place had cleared out this late, there were still ten or twelve people sitting around nursing coffee. There was only one other restaurant on this part of the reservation.

"Morning, Bertha."

"Morning, Jay, Doc. You want some breakfast?"

Jay exchanged glances with Scales. He shrugged. "Sure."

They sat in one of the four booths, scanned the single page menus. Scales saw a man he didn't recognize at one of the tables with two teenage boys. The man looked fifty, had what was left of his hair cut in a tight gray crewcut, and a face that had seen better decades. He smoked a Camel from a pack on the table in front of him, wore a khaki jacket over a powder blue shirt and a dark blue tie. He laughed a lot and it was always a quadruplet—heh, heh, heh, heh. From what little Scales could hear of his conversation, he was some kind of artist and trying to get the boys to pose for him. Nude. They weren't real interested but were stringing the guy along.

"What'll it be?" the skinny waitress said. She was Indian, dark, lots of white showing in her eyes, dressed in jeans and a T-shirt that said, "Save the Makah—Kill the Whales" on the front.

"Hey, Becca," Jay said. "I'll have three eggs over easy, sausage patties, whole wheat toast, hash browns, OJ."

Scales cracked a small smile. Big girl, big appetite.

Becca scribbled on her pad. Glanced at Scales.

"Farmer's omelette," he said. "English muffin."

"Coffee?"

"Please," Scales and Jay said together.

Scales looked at Becca's T-shirt, the kill-the-whales message was on the back, too. "Greenpeace must love that," he said as he watched her go to put their orders in.

"You didn't hear? Tribal Council wants to harvest five grays this year. Chairman Markishtum is trying to get the International Whaling Commission to endorse the plan, to get National Marine Fisheries to sign off on it, too."

Scales looked at her. "Five? Never happen."

"They're back up to maybe twenty thousand and off the endangered list."

"You're serious. The feds'll never go for it. That's real bad press. Didn't you see *Free Willy*?"

"No. I didn't see 'Free Bossie' or 'Free Porky,' either. That's your cultural bias. Before the white man came, eighty percent of what the Makah ate was whale meat. We have it written into our treaty with the United States that we can hunt whales—we're the only tribe that has that provision; technically, we don't even *need* the government's permission."

"Really?"

"Oh, yeah. It was a big deal among my people, whaling. There was a whole lot of ceremonial stuff attached to it, special boats and harpoons and rituals all wrapped together. It was at the center of who we were two hundred years ago. The Council figures it would help instill a sense of solidarity in the tribe if they could get back into it again."

"You believe that?"

She shrugged. "Yes and no. I think a lot of the young men would love blasting something that big with an explosive harpoon; it would keep some of them off the streets. It would help the tribe financially. National Geographic or somebody will pay a nice chunk for the film rights. It will draw tourists, both to watch the hunt and eat the results— whale steak is supposed to be pretty good. Probably get a lot of protesters and that would make for more news. You know the old Hollywood saw: 'Say anything you want as long as you spell the name right.'

"I don't think it would stop tribal alcoholism and if they're looking for a trip down memory lane, they need to go whole hog: cedar boats without motors and hand-thrown harpoons and sometimes the whale wins. Of course Greenpeace thinks that's worse than power harpoons. People moon about the good old days but yesterday is like virginity, once it's gone, it's gone. If I had to steam bentwood chests or carve totem poles for a living, I'd starve and so would ninety-nine percent of the tribe. Better to get the land swap worked out, build a casino and skin the white man for his cash. Then we can buy lobster and champagne and new pickups and wave at the poor when we go out for a ride. 'Living well is the best revenge,' the tribe needs to figure that out."

That speech was the most words he'd ever heard her string together.

The coffee came and Scales tasted it, hoping but not too much. It was thin and watery commercial grind and had been on the heater way too long. He made a face.

"Not up to your standards?" Jay said.

"I like it at least strong enough so you can't see the bottom of the cup. Ideally, you should be able to stand a spoon up in it."

"Not going to find a lot of that around here."

"I make it that way at home. I'll fix it for you some-time."

She didn't speak to that and he hoped he hadn't moved too fast.

She said, "So, how is the medical biz?"

"Better than it ought to be," he said. "I've got several patients who ought to be sick who aren't."

"You complaining?"

"Nope, not me. Just interesting. Sometimes it goes that way, you get a surge of wellness. Not too often." He paused. "How about law enforcement?"

"About the same. Drunks to get home before they kill themselves, some kids swiping stuff off boats or in the stores, a fist fight now and then. Some domestic calls, wives and husbands fighting. Nobody stabbed or shot or even beaten badly in a while. Sure isn't L.A. and I'm happy that it isn't. Nice and quiet and dull."

There must be a god in charge of listening to such comments, Scales thought, because the little hand-held CB unit on Jay's belt crackled once and a clear voice said, "Deputy Hughes?"

She plucked it the radio from her belt and keyed the send switch. "This is Hughes, go ahead."

"This is Ben Jackson. We got a wreck just outside the reservation, past the turnout about a mile out. Cadillac over the side into the Sound."

"Anybody hurt?"

"I dunno. All we can see is the tail lights and they're under the water. Raining like hell. Don't know how long ago it happened, could have been a while. Bastrop is trying to climb down and see if he can get the driver out."

"I'll call the state boys," she said. "And I'm on the way." She looked at Scales. "Looks like I'll have to take a rain check on breakfast."

"No problem. Maybe I'll tag along. Might be able to help."

"Why not?"

They stood and headed out into the rainstorm.

SEVEN

By the time Hughes and Scales arrived at the accident scene ten minutes later, a wrecker from Sekiu was on the way. It was going to take the State Patrol a while to get there, the nearest cruiser was just outside Port Angeles; nobody from the county had hauled any prisoners out recently and there hadn't been any other pileups serious enough to send a state unit this way. Bastrop, a thin and bony hatchet-faced clerk at the hardware store in Clallam Bay, had gone into the frigid waters but the Cadillac's doors were locked and he couldn't get enough leverage to break a window. It was murky—the Cad was in about twenty feet of water and had kicked up a lot of bottom muck when it hit—but he had seen the outlines of two men in the car. There wasn't any air in there with them, as far as he could tell. They must have been under for a while.

He'd surfaced, climbed back to Ben Jackson's pick up, got a hammer and a flashlight, then dived back to where the nose-down car waited. He smashed the driver's window and tried to unlock the doors but the goddamned electric locks must have shorted out or something and he almost drowned trying to get the goddamned door open. Couldn't. It didn't matter, both men were sure as hell dead. The driver was floating around a little, he'd gotten his seat belt off, but the passenger was still strapped in. Both air bags had gone off on impact.

"Time them bags deflated, they would have been sinking real fast," Bastrop continued. He was wrapped in a blanket

80

from the back of Hughes' truck and shivering from his swim.

At least the rain had slackened. It was down to a drizzle.

"Should have rolled the windows down first thing," Jackson said.

Hughes nodded. Everybody around here knew that. With air inside, the water pressure against the doors would be too great to shove open, would only get worse the deeper you sank. If it happened you went over the edge into the Sound, first thing was to get the windows down so the car would fill up with water and equalize the pressure, then you could shove the door open—if it wasn't sprung. If it was, you could get through the window. You'd have to hold your breath and not panic but once you were out of the car, you'd be okay.

"Panicked, I'd say," Bastrop said.

A few more curious drivers stopped and pulled over. Hughes gave Jackson a flare and put him out in the road to help move traffic along that wanted to get somewhere instead of stopping to gawk.

The wrecker arrived, Stan Knight at the wheel. He pulled over to the turnout and stopped. Hughes looked at Bastrop. "You're already wet, you know where it is, you want to go down and attach the cable?"

"Sure, might as well."

"I appreciate it."

She looked at Scales. He looked a little agitated. "Something?"

He shook his head. "Just wondering if the water is cold enough for the mammalian dive reflex."

She raised an eyebrow. "What, like in the movie *The Abyss*?"

He nodded. "Based on fact. Really cold water can effectively suspend animation for a while. Half an hour, forty-five minutes. Maybe longer. Kids who've fallen through the ice, like that. I don't think the Sound is cold enough this time of year."

"They might have been down there a long time anyway."

"We can try CPR, take them back to the clinic at the reservation, see if they can do anything."

But when the groaning winch managed to get the Cad high enough so the water started pouring out from under the hood and the shattered window, the two inside the drowned car looked awfully pale. Scales and a couple of men muscled them out and stretched them flat on the gravel, began CPR, pressing on their chests, using plastic mouth tubes to blow air into their lungs.

The winch groaned louder as the Cad came up the slope the rest of the way and dropped onto its tires with a sodden squish.

The drowned men burbled as the air came back out of them unused.

Hughes recognized them as the same two who'd been at the museum the day before, the slick boys from back east.

While Scales and three others worked pumping and breathing—one, two, three, four, five and breathe—she worked her way around them and dug wallets from the slick boys' hip pockets. She opened the wallets and got a couple of surprises: First one was California Drivers Licenses, not what she'd expect from men from a gaming concern in New Jersey Then there were the names: The two dead men—and she was fairly sure, just as she was sure everybody else was sure, they were dead—were named Mr. John NMI Smith and Mr. John NMI Jones.

Somebody must have had fun doing that.

Aside from the licenses, there was a soggy and smeared

rental agreement for the Cad from Hertz in Seattle, a likewise soaked hotel bill, and a couple of thousand dollars in
hundreds and fifties, with the odd small bill folded in. Each
wallet had an American Express Gold card—the names
were different but the numbers were the same on both
cards. Other than that, no pictures of the wives or kids, no
phone numbers or AAA memberships.

Warning bells went off, psychic alarms she hadn't heard
since she was on the job in L.A.

Something was very much wrong with this picture.

If these two were even half-legitimate salesmen from the
pinball and slot machine guys in New Jersey, she would eat
the damned corpses.

Behind her, Stan Knight said, "Uh, Jay, you want to
come take a look at this?"

She turned. Knight had pried open the trunk of the
Cadillac. Water sloshed from it and cascaded over the
bumper and soaked the already wet ground.

Inside the trunk bobbing in the seawater was another
body.

Scales shook his head after five minutes and knew whatever miracles had been passed out locally here of late, these
two hadn't gotten in line in time. Their pupils were dilated
and non-reactive, there was no response to CPR and even if
he'd had a defib unit, it wouldn't have done any good. He
knew dead when he saw it. These two had crossed over. To
be sure, he used a trick a Chinese doctor had showed him in
Vietnam. He reached up and pinched the right eyeball of
the one he'd been working on.

The eyeball stayed pinched.

He'd worked up a sweat, despite the misty rain still
falling. He wiped his face with the back of his hand, leaned

back on his heels and said, "Give it up. They're not coming back."

Those helping with the CPR stopped what they were doing.

"Scales," Jay said. "Come here a second, would you?"

He stood. His knees creaked and he noticed the soreness in his shoulders. CPR took it out of you. He walked to where she stood by the rear of the Cadillac.

In the trunk was his AIDS patient, Jimmy Lewis.

He checked for a pulse. Nope.

He stared at Jay.

"Look at his neck," she said.

He saw the bruises.

"I'd guess he was dead before they hit the water," she said. "He's already stiff."

Scales nodded. Pulled Jimmy's shirt from his pants and looked at his back. The post-mortem lividity showed he'd been dead long enough for some of his blood to settle and pool where he'd been lying on his side in the trunk. He hadn't drowned like the other two.

"Holy shit," he said. His voice was quiet.

"Yes. We got a problem here. Two dead guys with bogus IDs." She waved the wallets at him. "And the body of a local man in the trunk which they probably caused to be there. And their briefcases? Each one came equipped with a pistol. Doesn't sound much like two pinball videogame machine salesmen from New Jersey, does it?"

"Why would anybody want to kill Jimmy Lewis? He's got AIDS, he didn't have more than another six or eight months left."

"Maybe he gave it to the wrong person. Maybe he made a pass at one of them and they were homophobes." She shook her head. "I don't know. But we've got a crime scene here and it's already fucked up enough so the State Patrol is going to chew my ass." She turned. "Okay, everybody back off. Nobody comes close to the car or the bodies until the state boys get here." She pulled her cell phone. "I'd better call and warn them they've got more than a traffic accident waiting for them. Probably ought to give the Clallam County Sheriff a call, too. Jesus."

Scales nodded. Yeah.

EIGHT

By the time the accident was cleared away and the bodies hauled off, it was almost noon. Scales headed back for the clinic, Jay being busy talking to the state troopers—and the deputy not long behind them—who'd showed up. The rain had stopped, though the sky was still tarnished pewter.

The way the clinic was set up, the driveway looped off the main road and around to the garage in the rear. As he used the electronic door opener, Scales thought he caught a flash of something in the woods behind the house. He pulled the car into the garage, parked, alighted, then walked back out onto the driveway and stared at the woods. It was a patch of mixed evergreen and alder, with a few stubby bushes thrown in, and the yard sloped up slightly from the woods for a hundred feet before the scraggly lawn reached the driveway. He stared, didn't see anything. But his scalp prickled and the back of his neck got goosebumps.

Something was there, even though he couldn't see it—or them.

After a moment, the bushes shook, scattering droplets that sparkled in the sunbreak. Scales felt a small jolt of fear. Bears had been known to come up and rob garbage cans and even though they were relatively small, a couple hundred pounds of hungry black bear was larger than he wanted to wrestle with.

It wasn't a bear, though.

It was Jenkins.

The vet ambled across the yard, his boots sinking into

the wet grass. He grinned.

"You got sharp eyes, Scales. You shouldn'ta been able to see me."

"I didn't see you. I felt you."

"I hear that."

"How long you been there?"

"A little while. Don't mean nothin'."

"Come on in."

Scales unlocked the door and shut off the alarm system. The alarm was hooked into a national net but by the time a cop from anywhere got here, the thieves could have loaded everything he owned into a van and hauled it away. Swiped his stove, and come back for the smoke. His hope was that the noise and the neighbors would scare them off. He didn't have a whole lot of good drugs but there were a few injectibles and some pills worth swiping. He kept the ones that didn't need to be refrigerated in a fireproof lockbox under the dirty laundry in his hamper. He figured most dopers wouldn't think to look for it there. His computer was locked with a password, it wouldn't start unless you knew it, and he'd pasted a sign on the side that said just that. Maybe they wouldn't take it if they knew they couldn't sell it.

"What can I do you for?"

Jenkins laughed. "Ain't no big thing, got a touch of crotch rot."

" 'Tis the season. C'mon."

They moved into the exam room. "Okay, drop 'em, let's take a look."

Jenkins unbuckled his hardware and set it carefully on the exam table, then unbuttoned his pants and let them fall, pulled his underwear down at the same time.

Scales looked. Tinea cruris, all right, classic jock itch,

you didn't need to be a dermatologist to DX this one.

"I believe I've seen enough of your sorry white ass," he said.

Jenkins laughed and pulled his clothes back on.

Scales went to his sample drawer, opened it, found a spray can of Lotrimin powder and a tube of Lamasil. He tossed then to Jenkins. "You know the drill. You're going to have to wash more often, change your shorts more often and try to keep your privates clean and dry."

"Oh, sure, no problem. I'll have the maid in to do my laundry three times a week instead of just the once."

Scales shook his head. "Coat it with the powder a couple times a day, alternate that with the cream. Should clear up on a few days. It doesn't, come back."

"Roger that, Scales."

"Anything else I can do you for while you're here?"

"I could use some weed—just until my crop comes in. Them nice Commie Red seeds I planted ought to make for some good smoke."

Scales laughed. "I bet. They don't send me samples of that, sorry."

"Guess I'll just have to wait, then. Check you later, man."

Scales raised one hand in a still wave. He never charged Jenkins for visits, the man needed his disability check for supplies and the samples were free anyhow.

Jenkins started to leave, but paused. "Weird about them Air America dudes goin' into the drink, ain't it?"

Scales blinked. The "Air America" reference was to one of the CIA cover operations in Southeast Asia during the war. He didn't ask how Jenkins knew about the accident, the man had eyes and ears everywhere even though he lived in the forest.

"What makes you think they were company men?"

"What else? Come out to kidnap poor ole Jimmy to experiment on. I mean, they created that AIDS shit, didn't they? Everybody knows AIDS ain't nothin' but a bio warfare bug that got loose in the wrong place. Got to figure every once in a while they pick up one of the victims and check 'em out. You can't trust Uncle, man, he lies."

Scales kept his face neutral. This was one of the reasons why you didn't want to sneak up and surprise somebody like Jenkins in the woods. All he had with him was a sidearm but he had heavier artillery stashed somewhere and if you spooked him, he'd probably crank it up. "Way I heard it, the disease came from monkeys in Africa."

"Sheeit, man, that's just where they had the lab set up, 's all. You wouldn't want that gettin' loose in the World, but out there in the boonies with the natives, who gives a shit?"

"Maybe."

"Maybe nuthin'. You watch your ass, Scales. You do right by me. I don't want to see 'em fuck you up like they did ole Jimmy. They didn't have to kill him, he woulda gone along peaceful."

Despite the paranoia rap underlying it, Scales heard the rings of something else in Jenkins' voice. "How do you know that? That he would have gone with them?"

"I saw 'em take him down. Too far away for pistol, though." He patted his .45. "Time I got there, it was done and they were in the car and gone."

"When did it happen?"

"Early this morning. Jimmy, he was just a stick, couldn't have put up a fight if he wanted. Dudes strangled him." He shrugged "Fuck it, we all goin' down sooner or later, it don't mean a thing."

"You want to talk to the cops?"

"Ain't no way. They'd ship me to a bughouse, you know that. What I saw don't change it. They grabbed him, squeezed him dead. Now they're dead, probably taken out from orbit by one of the killer satellites, blew 'em right into the drink. Telling the cops won't bring any of 'em back and that just puts me higher up on their list. You can't trust nobody works for Uncle, it's all wheels inside of wheels. You keep that in mind, Scales."

With that, he was gone.

Scales thought about it for a moment. Jenkins was probably right. It wouldn't do any good for him to tell the law what he'd seen. The killers were history a few hours later than Jimmy, what did it matter?

Why they had killed him and taken the body, now, those were questions he'd like answers to.

The better part of a week went by. He took care of his patients, managed one trip to the gravel pit—didn't see Jay there—and a trip to Forks.

Life ground on.

Reuben arrived bearing gifts. He had a trunk and back seat full of medications this time and Scales went out to move it all into the clinic.

"Nice haul," Scales said, as he stacked the last of five boxes in the storeroom.

"Yeah, I twisted a few detail men's arms. Told them about my poor PA out in the woods who had no meds and all these welfare patients who were broke. Got some antibiotics, some BP meds, hormones, a few NSAIDs, some suppositories."

"I appreciate it."

"I ever tell you about my favorite suppository patient?"

Twelve or fifteen times, Scales thought, but he said, "I don't recall."

"Guy came in, throwing up, so I gave him some anti-nausea suppositories, told him to use one q.i.d. He comes back in next day, says, "Jesus, Doc, for all the good these horse pills are doing me, I might as well be pounding 'em up my ass."

Scales laughed politely. He'd had patients insert rectal or vaginal suppositories without removing the aluminum foil wrapping, but none so far who had taken them orally.

Reuben went into the kitchen and found himself a beer. "Hard work, watching you move boxes." He took a big swig, drained a quarter of the bottle. "Anything special this week?"

"Nope. No miraculous cures, nobody died. Did you check the bloodwork on Timmy Joe Canton?"

"I did. You might need to get some glasses, Ricky, m'boy. His white counts are back up and the CBC says he's still a pretty sick little boy."

"I did a diff, it looked fine."

Reuben shrugged, sipped at the beer. "What can I tell you? I'll fax you a copy of it when I get back to town."

Scales nodded. He was sure his diff had been done right but the course of Timmy's disease could be jagged. He couldn't fix it.

Reuben drank two more beers, signed charts, left.

Scales saw his last scheduled patient around five. Katherine Stroud's chronic bronchitis had flared and she needed to get a new script for an inhaler. She knew what she had, he knew, and she was in and out in five minutes.

As Stroud was leaving, Jay Hughes pulled her truck into the driveway.

Scales smiled as Jay stepped out of the truck, nodded at

Katherine, then ambled up the drive toward the clinic. He met her at the door.

"How's it going, Jay? This a professional visit?"

"In a manner of speaking."

"Come on in. You want a cup of coffee?"

"Sure."

She followed him into the kitchen. He opened the freezer, took a bag of coffee beans out. He bought them whole from a catalogue and ground them in an old fashioned hand-grinder he'd picked up at a shop in the Pike Place Market in Seattle. He cranked the grinder, dumped the powder into a paper cone, poured distilled water into the coffee maker and hit the switch.

"Lot of work," Jay observed, watching him.

"Not really. If you're going to drink the stuff, might as well do it right."

The water began to drip into the freshly-ground coffee. The smell was one of the joys of the whole process. Scales inhaled, appreciated the aroma. "What's up?"

"I've been poking around Jimmy's death," she said. "I don't have any jurisdiction, the state boys, the deputies, even the FBI are all over it and don't need my help, fuck you very much. But he was one of my people."

Scales nodded, let her talk without interrupting.

"So I called in a few favors, got a couple of old buddies to play with the cop computers. According to FBI fingerprint records, Smith and Jones were former private eyes from L.A., under different names. Lost their licenses a couple of years back."

Scales raised his eyebrows. The coffee burbled into the pot.

"Jimmy didn't owe anybody any money. As far as anybody around here knows, he never went farther south than

Portland in his life. He came home from Seattle a year ago and hasn't left this area since."

Scales nodded.

"Look, I don't want you to compromise any patient confidentiality or anything, but he was dying of AIDS, right?"

Scales shrugged. He wasn't going to hurt Jimmy by telling her what everybody knew. "Yes. His immune system was knocked way down. He'd had several opportunistic infections—candida, pneumonia, Kaposi's. His CD4—a kind of white cell—count was one-fifty. It was pretty far along. He had maybe six, eight months left, if that. Cocktail didn't work on him. That happens."

"His mother said he was feeling pretty good lately."

Scales nodded again. "You get small remissions. Good days and bad. It's kind of like a rubber ball. You drop it, it hits, bounces up, falls again. Each time the rebound is a little lower. Eventually it stops."

"Coffee smells good," she said.

"Almost ready. Why don't you have a seat?"

She gave him a brief smile, moved to the table, settled into a chair.

"Cream or sugar?"

"Black."

He took a couple of mugs from the cabinet, put them onto the counter. Waited.

"What I can't figure out, what makes no sense, is why two thugs would drive a thousand miles from L.A. to kill a man dying of AIDS," she said. "And then try to sneak off with the body."

"I wondered about that myself."

"I can come up with some theories. Maybe Jimmy gave the disease he had to some rich man's kid and he wanted revenge. Or maybe he saw something while he was running with the wrong crowd in Seattle and somebody wanted to make sure he didn't say anything."

The last of the coffee was running through the filter. Scales moved the pot from the heat, put the filter into the sink. He poured two cups and moved to the table, passed one mug to Jay.

She took it. "Thanks." Sipped it. "It's very good."

Scales sipped at his. She was right. He gave good coffee.

"I know somebody in the coroner's office," she said. "If I get a copy of the report on Jimmy, would you take a look at it and translate it for me?"

Scales took another tiny sip of his brew. Should he tell her about Jenkins? He considered it, decided not to. If what Jenkins had told him was right, Jimmy's cause of death was going to be asphyxiation—he'd been choked to death. He didn't think she'd need any translation for that, but he said, "Sure. No problem."

"Thanks." She drank a bit more. Said, "I talked to one of your patients on the way here. George Swell."

Swell was the eighty-nine-year-old great-grandfather who had recently complained of tiredness.

"He's slowing down some," he said.

"Really? I stopped and offered him a ride a couple of miles from here but he said he'd rather walk. Said he'd hiked out from the reservation."

Scales stopped with the mug halfway to his lips. "He walked from the reservation? Jesus, that's almost fifteen miles!"

She smiled. "You white people got no stamina."

Scales frowned. Last week, George Swell didn't have a lot of stamina himself, to hear him tell it. Amazing how resilient the human body was.

Jay finished her coffee. "I'd better be going," she said. "I need to make a pass through Sekiu to see if any of my people are getting D&D. Thanks for the coffee and letting me bend your ear."

"Any time," he said.

He watched her walk to her truck. A very handsome woman, Jay Hughes. He looked at his watch. Time to go play in the gym. If he hurried, he could get his workout done before the news.

NINE

Somebody had once told Scales that the Latin phrase *Nisi defectum, haud reficiendum* meant, "If it ain't broke, don't fix it," and that had always been a major tenet of Scales' personal philosophy. It dovetailed nicely into western medicine's own bit of Latin, *Pecunia non olet*—literally, "Money doesn't smell," but meaning, "Don't look a gift horse in the mouth."

As he sat in his office before his patients were due to begin arriving, Scales once again considered those bits of wisdom. They'd always served him before and he was perfectly happy to continue to let them. The recent spate of patients who were doing a lot better than they should, well, who was he to argue with a little miracle now and then? Better to keep his mouth shut, smile and take credit for it. Rick Scales, PA-C, heals the sick, raises the dead, the impossible takes just a little longer. Take a bow, boy.

Thing was, it was getting a little hard to do that. What he was staring at was a copy of the coroner's report on James L. Louis. Just as Jenkins had said, and the bruises on the dead man's neck had indicated, Jimmy had been throttled to death. Fine, no big surprise, nothing for him to translate for Jay, all clean cut and straightforward.

But:

According to the attachments to this document, all of which looked to be copies of a fax and little blurry but still quite readable, James L. Louis' bloodwork was all perfectly normal and that was fucking impossible. More, there were no signs on the physical exam of Kaposi sarcoma, thrush, miscellaneous rashes or anything else that might point a finger at the dead man's having been in the final stages of AIDS.

These miracles were getting a little big to swallow.

Now, he hadn't seen Jimmy in almost a month, but Scales knew one thing: Somebody had fucked up. They'd mixed Jimmy's exam in with some other corpse because no way, no how could this be right.

Yeah, there were people who had been infected with HIV who had managed to cheat the reaper for twelve or fifteen years. Patients who meditated and medicated and controlled their diet and exercise to the nth degree, who managed to stave off full blown AIDS and somehow keep half a step ahead of death. Jimmy wasn't one of them, though, he had the entire complex. According to this, and except for being dead, he'd been in better shape than Scales.

Scales looked at the report again. Before he said anything to Jay, he wanted to check it out a little more. He picked up the phone and punched in the number. It rang twice.

"This is Howard Reuben."

"Dr. Reuben, Rick Scales."

"Hello, Tex. What can I do for you?"

Scales explained about Jimmy.

"What are you doing with that report anyway?"

He explained about Jay Hughes wanting to do something about Jimmy's death.

"Hmm. It does seem strange, doesn't it? Tell you what, let me make a couple of calls and see if I can clear this up."

"I appreciate it. If I've come up with a cure for AIDS, you're going to have to give me a raise," Scales said.

Reuben chuckled. "I'll get back to you, Ricky."

Scales cradled the phone.

Scales was about to break for lunch when the phone rang.

"Medical Clinic."

"Ricky, m'boy."

"So, do I get that raise?"

"Afraid not. Turns out you nailed it right on the head: somebody's secretary in the coroner's office blended two reports together. You're looking at the bloodwork for one of the guys in the front part of the car."

Scales nodded. "I figured it was something like that. Well, you could give me the raise anyway."

"I already pay you too much. Nice try, though."

"Hey, thanks, Dr. Reuben, I appreciate it."

"That's what I'm here for, to back up my staff. Tell your overzealous cop friend that poor Jimmy must have pissed off the wrong people and they killed him for it. You know these dope addicts and deviants, they get into all kinds of bad places. What made her start poking around in this anyhow?"

"He was a Makah," Scales said. "As far as anybody could tell, there was no reason for a couple of Los Angeles bad guys to come up here and kill him. She was curious. Hell, so was I."

"Los Angeles bad guys? How do you figure that?"

"Jay ran it down, the killers were in the FBI computer, she has contacts."

"Well, I'm not one to tell you how to run your life, but better you should stick to treating the sick. The world doesn't need another Sherlock Holmes. Let the proper authorities handle it. If anybody official found out you had a copy of the coroner's report, you could get in trouble."

"I'm off the case as of now," Scales said.

"Glad to hear it, son. See you later."

Scales went back to have lunch.

Hughes could have called but decided to pass by the clinic to speak to Scales in person. It was six p.m. when she pulled into the driveway, and the fit of sunshine that had blossomed threatened to keep the rain at bay. With any luck, it would last for at least the rest of the day.

She didn't see Scales but the garage door was open and when she walked around the back, she spotted him. He was lying on the weight bench in the garage, doing presses. She stood there silently until he finished.

He racked the weight, sat up, wiped at his face with a towel and smiled.

"Hey, Scales."

He nodded at her. "Jay."

"What are you grinning like a baboon for? That happy to see me?"

"Of course," he said. He slid off the bench. He was wearing gym shorts and a T-shirt, both soaked with sweat and plastered to his body, which, she had to admit, looked pretty good. "Plus I just benched three-forty for eight reps."

"Is that good?"

"It is for me. I haven't been able to do that much in years."

"Maybe it's your second childhood."

"I hope so. Come on in, I'm done."

He led her into the house. "Want coffee?"

"Nah, I'm on my way into Clallam, gotta stop by the market and buy groceries. You get a chance to look at that report?"

"Yeah. Looks as if they choked him to death, just like the bruises on his neck showed."

She nodded. "Anything else interesting?"

"Well, yes and no. Somebody at the coroner's office screwed up the report."

"How's that?"

"Part of the stuff attached to it belongs to one of the other guys in the car."

"How'd you figure that out?"

"Jimmy had terminal AIDS, the bloodwork on the report belonged to somebody who didn't. I checked it out through Reuben, he got in touch with a buddy in the coroner's office and sure enough, the things got mixed together."

Hughes was disappointed. She didn't know what exactly she hoped the report would show but whatever it was, this wasn't it.

He wiped his neck and face with the towel again. "Phew, I need a shower." After a second, he said, "You're not going to get in any trouble for poking around in this, are you?"

"Me? I don't think so. Why?"

"No reason. Hate to see the feds drag you away in chains, that's all."

"I wouldn't worry about that too much."

"Any other progress?"

"Not really. My buddies in the L.A. cop shop can't backwalk the two killers very far. No records of employment since they were drummed out of the P.I. biz, no income tax or business stuff. One of them got a couple of parking tickets that are still outstanding but the car he was in was a rental. They don't sound like model citizens. It's pretty much a dead end. Only thing that makes sense is some kind of drug connection. Jimmy ran with the IV crowd in Seattle. Maybe he was in the wrong place at the wrong time, saw something he shouldn't have seen."

"It's been a year since he was there," Scales said. "You'd think they'd have come looking for him before now if they were worried. Whoever 'they' are."

"Maybe they didn't know where to look."

He shrugged. "You're the cop."

She sighed. "Well, I used to be. Nothing like trying to act like one when you've been away from the game for awhile to show you what you've forgotten. Truth is, the state boys and the feds have more resources, they are in a better position than I am to run this down. Thing is, he wasn't one of theirs. Priority won't be real high."

He nodded.

"Why am I boring you with this?"

"I'm never bored when you're around," he said.

Uh oh, Careful. It sounds like he's about to put a move on you, sister. You ready for that? "Why, thank you, sir."

"My pleasure."

She waited a few seconds but the pass didn't get thrown. It was a little disappointing.

"Well. I'm going to run on into town. Can I bring you anything?"

"Nope, I'm fine. Sorry I couldn't be more help to you with this thing."

"Not your fault," she said. "See you around."

She pulled the truck out onto the highway and drove toward town. She kept the window down to enjoy the sunshine and the incoming breeze smelled fresh, the air washed clean. Somewhere not far off a chainsaw *renh-renh*ed, slowing and speeding up as it chewed through whatever it was biting.

Jimmy's death bothered her for a lot of reasons, not the

least of which was that it was the first murder of a local by an outsider in a pretty long while. There were occasional domestic arguments that got out of hand, a few violent rapes or muggings, but white men coming in specifically to kill a tribesman was unheard of—at least in this decade. It had been a long time since the Spaniards had unlimbered their cannon from offshore to blast away at villages for some real or imagined insult.

Something about this whole thing didn't fit, no matter how she tried to stretch the rationalization to cover it.

Which was too bad, because from where she sat, there wasn't anything else she could do to solve the murder.

Well. No point in beating up on herself for it.

She pulled into the lot of the Clallam Bay Grocery and parked next to an RV with two dogs sitting in the front. Dogs looked like a red Chow and a German Shepherd and the way they sat watching the store, their master or mistress must be inside. The dogs watched Jay get out of her truck, but neither barked at her and both quickly turned their attention back to the store.

Dogs had it easier than people. Nobody expected them to behave like anything but dogs, they didn't have to figure out anything as complex as a first degree murder. There were times when Hughes would have changed places with one of those critters in the RV's seat. Just to be able to sit in the sunshine waiting for her master to return so she could lick his hand and be happy to do it.

She sighed, and went into the store.

TEN

Timmy Canton missed his appointment on Wednesday. Scales called the boy's mother but got the machine. He left a short message and hung up.

He saw two patients, one of whom had a splinter in her finger that took all of thirty seconds to remove, the other of whom needed a refill on her birth control pills, no exam necessary. Good thing he had all those years of practice to handle such major medical chores.

His fourth patient, Tom Inch, didn't show up for his appointment.

Batting fifty percent today, he thought. Great in baseball, not so good in the medical field. He shrugged. Not something he could control.

A rain cell blew in about midmorning and drummed wet fingers on the shake roof, a soothing, lulling background sound.

It was still raining, though slacked to a drizzle, when Old man Handel came by during lunch to deliver the mail. Scales was at his computer. He logged off the web.

Handel also brought the local gossip, and in it, an explanation as to why Timmy Canton had missed his appointment.

"You didn't hear?" Handel said. He must have been pushing seventy-five but he was still delivering the mail in a beat-up truck that looked almost as old as he was. "Cantons won a contest. A two-week all expenses paid trip for the whole family to Hawaii." He pronounced the word "how-why-yuh."

"Really?"

"Yep. Beach hotel on Maui. Room service, rental car, tours, the whole shebang."

"Must be nice," Scales observed.

"Yep. Although me, I'd have waited until the winter to go. Summer here, summer there, what's the difference?"

Scales glanced through the window at the gray-on-gray wet sky.

Handel said, "Aw, they get rain in Hawaii. Lots of it."

"Yeah, but it's warm rain. And there isn't mold growing on everything."

"You Texas guys can't stand a little weather?"

"I grew up in Tornado Alley," Scales said. "Come late spring we sometimes got three-four inches of rain in two hours, complete with lightning that could bring the dead back and wind that'd peel the barnacles off a battleship. I saw a car dealer's lot once had two hundred cars with the windshields all busted out from baseball-sized hail. Don't talk to me about weather."

They both laughed.

"Better get on my appointed rounds," the old man said. "See you later."

Scales' first appointment after lunch was a follow-up on Harold Gaines, a sixty-six-year-old alcoholic with cirrhosis. Gaines had finally stopped drinking a year or so back but it was too late. His liver was shot. It was massively fibrotic and he had most of the classic signs and symptoms of bad liver disease: big spleen, enough ascites so he sloshed when he laid down, portal hypertension, nausea, impotence, assorted aches and pains and clay-colored stools. Scales had the latest round of blood tests back and according to them, things had not gotten any better. Gaines was anemic, his blood didn't coagulate worth shit, liver enzymes were up, bilirubin was up, serum albumin down. Big surprise. Current treatment was rest, a good diet and vitamins, including vitamin K for the bleeding, diuretics for the excess fluid. Gaines' brain still worked and he didn't have any major esophageal problems but he was getting pretty yellow and there was a fifty-fifty chance he'd be gone in a couple of years. There wasn't much else to be done about it.

The Reaper always won.

Gaines arrived.

"Hey, Doc."

"Afternoon, Harold. How are you feeling?"

"Not so bad, not so bad. Went fishing this morning, caught a nice twenty pound sea bass. One of them red meat kind."

Scales grinned. Salmon season was over and sea bass didn't come in red.

"Still on the wagon? Here, let's weigh you."

Harold stepped up onto the scale and Scales waited for the almost obligatory Scales'-scale comment while he fiddled with the balance.

Harold didn't make it this time. Instead, he said, "One year, two months, three days sober."

Scales looked at the chart. "Lost a few pounds. Down to one-ninety-six."

"Thought maybe I'd dropped a little."

"Come on into the exam room and let's check your pressure, draw a little blood."

"You want me to pee in the cup this time?"

"After we take a look."

Harold climbed up onto the exam table and unbuttoned his shirt. Scales made a notation on the chart and when he looked up at Gaines, his *Augenblick* kicked in:

Harold Gaines wasn't sick.

Scales didn't say anything. His talent was almost never wrong when it came upon him, but it had to be wrong this time. Yeah, you might come back from lung cancer or leukemia, might get a remission, but nobody spontaneously healed a mostly-dead liver. You could get by on just a little bit but once it was gone, it was gone. Plus he was looking at bloodwork results that were less than a week old and that would have to be one hell of a recovery. Impossible.

And yet, Scales couldn't shake the certainty. Gaines was not sick. His color was better, he had lost eight pounds of excess water and his affect was not nearly as flat as it had been.

Well. A physical exam should help clear up his unease.

When he scratched down Harold's belly and listened with the stethoscope, he expected to hear the change when he got to the edge of the enlarged liver where it usually was. But he didn't hear it. And when he palpated, he couldn't feel any enlargement, either.

Holy shit. Where did it go?

He finished his exam then drew a couple of tubes of blood. "Okay, now go pee in the cup."

He could manage a urinalysis here, at least he could dipstick it and run a drop under the microscope to see what he could see. And he could ship the blood off and ask for a quick turnaround. Other than that, there wasn't anything he could do. Or should do. He was just a PA, not even a doctor and certainly not an internal med specialist.

Maybe he ought to call Reuben . . . ?

Nah. No point in doing that yet. Wait until the labwork got done.

Gaines came back with the little plastic cup. He swirled the straw-colored liquid around a little and smiled. "Looks a little thin," he said. "Want me to run it through again?"

Scales returned the smile. At some point, he'd told Gaines the old med student joke: Bring a glass of apple juice that was supposed to be urine into the lab, make a comment about it looking or smelling funny, then drink it—and mention that it tasted funny, too. The variation was to squash up a Tootsie Roll and pretend it was a stool specimen. No lab tech who'd been on the job more than a few weeks fell for those old gags.

"I think it'll do. You can head on home. Anything weird comes up, I'll call you."

"Ten-four, Doc. See ya next month."

After he left, Scales went into the lab and set the urine on the counter. It was a pale yellow, clear, no clouds or sediment. He fished a dipstick from the brown bottle and dipped it into the liquid, pulled it out and set it across the cup's rim. He used a pipette to get a drop of the pee for a slide. He fiddled with the slide and cover, shoved it under his microscope, ran a quick scan. No casts, no crystals or fat globs, no mucous, RBCs, tube cells or bacteria floating around in it, either. So Gaines' kidneys seemed to be working better than usual but that was no big deal.

The dipstick was a bigger deal.

According to the little colored patches on the plastic strip, there wasn't any bilirubin, glucose, hemoglobin and only a trace of urobilinogen in the specimen. No nitrates. No white blood cells.

Well, damn. Maybe the bottle of dipsticks had gone bad? He found a new bottle, opened it, repeated the test.

Got the same results.

He poked around a little more.

The specific gravity was 1.01, right in the middle of normal. PH was 6.1.

Scales shook his head. Looked at the chart. A month

ago, Gaines had all the usual pointers for liver disease in his urine. Now he didn't have them.

Just what the fuck was going on around here?

Jay Hughes leaned back in the office chair she'd bought at an auction in Seattle. It was a big oak office chair with arms, the kind her teachers had all sat in when she'd been in school. It had wheels, a big spring that squeaked like a monster movie door opening and was very comfortable despite its lack of padding. She had all her official stuff set up in a trailer the tribe had furnished her, but the cheap chair that came with it was a back killer and she'd brought her own in. This chair was forty, maybe fifty years old and a lot nicer than the makeshift office.

Well, at least the phone worked and they allowed her to make whatever calls she thought necessary. At the moment, the call was to Don Griffith, a man she'd gone through MP school with a long time ago. And whom she'd shared a bed with for a few months, too. Don had stayed in the service, risen the hard way to the rank of Major, and wound up in Army Intelligence. He'd gone for advanced training, gotten his college degree along the way and was now stationed in a "special unit" at Sixth Army headquarters at the Presidio in San Francisco.

"Well, I'll be damned. Sergeant Hughes! How you been, Jazz?"

Hughes grinned. He'd had potential, Don had, but while the sex had been okay, there wasn't any real fire there—something both of them had wanted at the time. They still exchanged Christmas cards, and she'd stopped in to see him a few years back on her way to L.A.

"I can't complain, Don, wouldn't do any good if I did. How's the family?"

"Jeri is about to get promoted to vice-president, Bill won the science fair, Mary Lea is working at summer camp as a counselor."

Hughes shook her head. He had kids in middle and high school. It didn't seem like it could have been that long ago that they'd been checking bars for drunken soldiers together. Drunken soldiers, drunken tribe member, she was an expert in drunks.

"What can I do you for, Jazz?"

"I got a little problem," she said.

She told him about the killing and the mysterious pair who'd died in the wreck.

"And you want to know more about them," Don said.

"You know people," she said. "It's not really my case but I can't just let it lie there."

"You never could," he said. "Always wanted to see if you could get it to stand up one more time."

They both chuckled.

"I'll see what I can do, Jazz."

"I'd appreciate it, Donny."

After she hung up, she wondered if she was doing the right thing, messing around after she'd been politely advised to fuck off.

Thing was, she realized, she missed being a cop. It wasn't the same here. Sure, that fat city job at the casino loomed, and she was the tribal law, but it didn't have the promise—or maybe the threat—the job had in L.A. It was safer—but she had come to realize, it was also boring. Her days had a sameness to them, and the murder and accidental deaths had broken that sameness in a way she found more than a little interesting.

She'd wanted to lay low, take it easy and she had—but now? What did she want? To get back into the game?

Yeah, that was exactly it. She wanted to get back into the game. Not just for the sake of the dead man but for her own satisfaction. A long, long time ago in a galaxy far away, she'd thought of herself as a warrior. Time and circumstance had worn that image away so little was left, but now and then, for just a moment, she could remember what it felt like to be full of great notions and raw bravery. To know she could stand tall against the bad guys and give as good as she got.

Maybe it was time to see if there was anything left of that warrior she'd once thought she was.

Yeah.

ELEVEN

It was almost seven-thirty and Scales had shut it down for the day. He was in the kitchen, considering what to cook for supper. What to thaw in the microwave.

The phone rang.

"Medical Clinic."

"Scales? Jay Hughes."

"Ah, the thin blue line. What can I do for you, ossifer?"

"I've got some information I want to bounce off you. You want to go grab a beer, maybe a bite to eat?"

"Sure. Better yet, why don't you drop by here? I got a few beers left and I was just fixing some supper. I can do steak and fries. Might find some broccoli or something to go with it."

"That sounds good. See you in about half an hour?"

"I'll be here."

After he broke the connection, Scales found himself grinning. So the lovely Jasmine Hughes was dropping round for dinner.

All of a sudden he felt nervous.

Christ, Rick, it's only a beer and supper, what are you getting all het up about?

Could work into something more, that's why. She might want to jump your bones. You wouldn't fight that too hard, would you?

He shook his head at himself. Well, no, he wouldn't fight too hard. Then again, he wouldn't worry too much about having to beat her off with a stick, either. He thought of himself as a nice enough guy, not too ugly, in pretty good shape for a man whose eyebrows were getting bushy. Most women didn't cross the street to get away when they saw him coming; then again, neither did they switch sides of the road to get a closer look at him. He was fairly average-looking in his estimation.

But you got a great personality . . .

He laughed aloud at himself. Yep, get to know me, women become my love slaves. Want to go in the back and see the harem?

He laughed again as he pulled two sirloin steaks from the freezer and put them in the microwave to thaw. Be ready to cook about the time she got here.

He looked in the refrigerator, saw he had most of a twelve-pack of Henry's left. He wasn't a heavy drinker and didn't think Jay would be either, long as she was driving.

She doesn't have to drive. Get her loaded and she can stay here.

Once again, he laughed at himself. Get a grip, boy. You're more than half a century along, not fifteen. Act your age!

But he hummed part of an old Carole King song as he wiped the counter tops clean with a sponge.

Hell. He had a smile on his face. Maybe he was as beautiful as he felt.

He heard her truck arrive thirty minutes after she called. He had two mugs frosting in the freezer, the steaks were thawed and ready to go. He had peed, washed his face and hands, combed his hair, swiped at his armpits with a wet washcloth and a little Mennen and put on a clean shirt. About as presentable as he could get under the circumstances.

Jay came toward the house carrying a brown paper sack.

He smiled at her as she entered the house and put the sack onto the counter in the kitchen. "Brought a loaf of French bread and a six-pack," she said. "Henry's okay?"

He grinned. God, the woman even drank good beer. His belly knotted inside him in that lurchy sensation he got on a roller coaster's first drop. A blend of fear, anticipation and excitement.

"Let me put the steaks on and the fries in."

"Don't let me get in your way."

There was something different about her and after a second, it came to him what it was: She was wearing makeup. Not much, just a hint of pale lipstick and maybe a light dusting of powder or something on her face. No perfume.

His hands suddenly felt damp.

Easy, boy. It don't mean nothing. No more'n you changing your shirt.

He pointed her toward the kitchen table. "Have a seat."

She ambled to the table, pulled out a chair, sat.

He opened the freezer, took the two icy mugs out, brought them and the beers to the table. They twisted the caps off and poured.

"So, what's up?"

She sipped at her beer. "Well. I called an old friend of mine who's in Army Intelligence. He's been around a long time, knows all kinds of spooks and feebs. I asked him to do some checking on the two dead guys in the Cad."

Scales nodded, sipped at his own cold beer. "And . . . ?"

"Turns out our boys have done a little freelance work for a couple of agencies. It was contract-labor, the kind of thing you might not want somebody from your agency getting caught doing."

He raised an eyebrow. "Shady business? Our government? I'm shocked."

"Yeah, I can see that. We're not talking wetwork, no murders or anything, but probably some semi-legal drug deals, bodyguarding, maybe illicit courier stuff. The feds are always getting into bed with big time crooks, selling planes to Colombians to try to nail them smuggling, laundering money, like that. They use a lot of unskilled informants, but occasionally they want somebody in the field who isn't carrying official ID but who is good enough to do the job."

" 'If you're caught or killed the Secretary will disavow all knowledge of your actions?' "

She smiled through the beer mug. "According to my contact. High risk stuff but the pay is real good."

"So what does it mean?"

She shrugged. "I don't know. These boys were more than they appeared to be. It would be real interesting to know who hired them."

"You have anything else?"

"My friend is still looking, but so far, no. Other than that, just the traffic tickets."

Scales nodded. Yeah, she'd told him about those. "You got addresses on those tickets?"

"Addresses?"

"Town, street, block, like that? I've got access to this terrific program on the web, it can find a street anywhere in the country, draw you a map, then it uses linked phone, zip code, and reverse directories to fill in the businesses and houses in the area, tells you all kinds of things."

"You're one of those computer nerds? No, come on."

He laughed. "We're living here in the future, Ossifer Hughes. Everything is on a computer somewhere. You give me a name and if they've got a listed phone number any-where in the United States, I can give you the city and their home address without having to leave my office."

"Lord. Big Brother."

"Actually, it's more like millions of little brothers. The net is still pretty much unregulated, though the feds are trying like hell to catch up."

"I didn't bring it with me, but I can get that informa-tion."

"Fax it to me or drop it by and I'll see what I can do," he said.

After the second beer and about the time the steaks were done, Hughes thought Scales was a pretty attractive man, all things considered. He was bright, he was being helpful—though she didn't think knowing where two cut-rate spooks got a parking ticket would do much good—and from the look of the sirloin, he could cook meat okay. He'd made her laugh a couple of times and that was always a good sign.

They toasted the French bread, microwaved broccoli, and sat down to eat. The steak was medium rare, just as she liked it, and the frozen fries were plank style and passable. She was hungry and they both ate several bites in silence.

She decided she could risk a personal question without being thrown out of his house. "You were married, weren't you?"

"Yeah. Didn't work out. Been divorced since forever."

"Kids?"

"Two daughters. Shannon is twenty-one, going to school at Ole Miss, an education major. Bethany is nineteen, working as a checker at a supermarket in Dallas. Hasn't de-cided what she wants to do when she grows up yet." He paused, chewed a bite of steak, washed it down with a swig of beer. "We keep in touch, see each other a couple of times a year, but we're not real close. Janet—my ex—remarried twelve, thirteen years ago. Real Estate salesman in Fort Worth. Seems like a nice enough fella, the girls like him okay."

She didn't say anything to that.

"How about you? Ever married?"

"Nope. Came close a couple of times, never could quite get it together. No kids. I wanted 'em once, but . . ."

He became very interested in cutting a slice from his steak. He did it with surgical precision and pointedly did not ask the next question.

She sighed. "When I was fifteen I ran off to become a hippie," she said. "It was a little late, the sixties were long over, but the flower children hadn't all bailed from places like the Haight. I wound up in San Francisco. Discovered drugs, sex and rock and roll but not birth control. I got pregnant. I had an abortion and the guy must have not washed his hands. I got an infection that scarred something bad enough so I couldn't get pregnant again."

"I'm sorry."

"It was a long time ago. I got over it. I knocked around for a few years. One day when the rent was overdue and I was broke, I found myself thinking maybe I could sleep with the guy who'd offered me fifty bucks to do so, he wasn't all that ugly. I figured, what the hell, I'd been with a boatload of men for free, what would one more for money matter? It was a scary thought. Instead, I marched into an Army recruiter's office and joined up. Did six years, made it to buck sergeant in the MPs. Army taught me a trade, just like they promised. I got out, spent a few months blowing my saved up pay, then signed on with the LAPD."

They looked at each other. She saw it in his eyes. He was

116

not only interested, he actually liked her.

What the hell. It had been a while and he seemed like an all right guy. He wasn't married and he wanted her. They'd both been around the block a few times.

She said, "We better not eat any more of this, good as it is. We don't want to be bouncing around on full stomachs, do we?"

He smiled, a truly happy looking expression. When he spoke, he sounded like a cowboy actor: "No ma'am, we surely don't."

Scales had boxes of condoms in the clinic, he passed out dozens every week to patients, only not a single damned rubber was in the bedroom.

He and Jay were on the bed, half undressed and kissing and he had an erection so hard he thought he might cut himself on the inside of his zipper. The idea of getting up and going downstairs to rummage around in a box did not appeal in the least.

"You got distracted," she said, kissing him on the throat.

"Uh, yeah, well, thing is, my, that is—the goddamned condoms are downstairs."

She laughed, a deep, throaty sound. "Not to worry. I'm a modern woman." She leaned over him, her breasts resting on his stomach, and reached for her purse on the floor next to the bed. He heard it click and in a second she was back. She waved the foil-wrapped package. "Ta dah!"

"I'm impressed."

"Let's see if it's big enough."

"Hope so. It's as big as its gonna get, sweetie."

"I meant the condom, goofus. I know that's big enough. Feels like a nightstick poking me in the solar plexus."

She unzipped his jeans and his erect penis came out into its own.

"My, my. I think that will do nicely. Here we go." She peeled the foil off he condom and rolled the latex onto him. Before he could move, she bent and slid him into her mouth. She moved up and down a couple of times, stopped and pressed her lips hard against him just behind the head.

"Oh, yeah," he said.

After a few seconds, he said, "Turn around." His voice was tight and a little hoarse.

She complied. He slid her jeans down and she lifted one leg so he could slide them off. Her panties followed.

She had thick pubic hair, black and kinky, and a wonderful musky smell. He slid his tongue into her, tasted the salt of her, began to nibble gently on her.

She moaned around him.

This wasn't going to last long.

It didn't. When he felt her start to climax, he began to pump into her mouth harder and he finished five seconds behind her. They both shook with hard spasms and finally he pulled his face away so he could breathe. She fell over onto her side.

"Oh, man!" she said. "That was great."

"Boy howdy."

She laughed, spun around to lie next to him.

" 'Boy howdy?' Shee-it, you southern boys sure have a way with words."

She still had her shirt on. He came up on one elbow, unbuttoned her shirt, slipped it and the unhooked bra off. Looked at her full-length nudity.

"A little worn," she said.

"Bullshit. You're beautiful. A grown woman."

"Not so bad looking yourself," she said.

Amazingly, his erection was undiminished. "Stay right there," he said. "I'm gonna run downstairs for a second—unless you've got another rubber in your purse?"

"Nope, that's the emergency love-glove, I'm not that modern a woman."

"I'll be right back."

She looked at him. "Maybe you better bring the whole box."

They laughed.

He was back in thirty seconds and he did bring the whole box. A quick change and he was ready again. This time, he entered her from the front, propped himself on his elbows and they rocked slowly.

"Anything in particular you'd like?"

"What you're doing is fine," she said. "We'll try something else later."

It felt great. Better than great. He was so hot he thought he was going to stroke out and melt. He held off as long as he could before he began to drive himself into her harder and faster. She urged him in deeper, both hands on his ass, her legs high, heels on his back.

He raced to his second climax in three minutes. It was so intense he could hardly stand it. For a brief moment, he lost track of where he was, of who he was.

He became one with the Void.

When he came back, he thought sure he was done for the night.

He was wrong. Five minutes later he was semi-erect, and a minute after that he was inside her again. He'd never felt anything so good as this woman next to him, around him, with him.

For the next three hours they made love. He brought her to orgasm twice more and she coaxed two more from him.

He hadn't come four times in one night in fifteen years.

After the last one it was almost midnight and he could hardly move.

"Wow," he said. "I have to tell you, that was the best I ever had. I felt like I was fifteen again. You're something."

She snuggled into his sweaty armpit, bit him. "Yeah. Me, too, you."

"So, you want to get married?"

She laughed, her breath tickled the hair under his arm. He hugged her to him. Oh, yeah. She was really something.

TWELVE

It started to rain just before dawn. Scales heard the gentle tapping on his roof and allowed it to bring him slowly out of sleep. In a few minutes it went from tentative to a downpour.

Jay lay sprawled over about two-thirds of his queen-sized bed, mouth open and snoring quietly. He smiled at her.

He slid carefully from the bed, padded naked to the bathroom. God, he felt terrific, like he was twenty. Just the thought of Jay naked in his bed began to arouse him again as he urinated. Jesus.

He went into the kitchen, made a pot of coffee, stretched a little while he was waiting for the drip to finish. It took a few minutes. He stared through the kitchen window, watched the water pour off the overhang and stream in intermittent ropes to the ground. The daylight grew brighter even through the thick liquid lenses.

The coffee pot filled. He poured a cup and walked back up the stairs to the bedroom.

As he entered the room, the rain stopped abruptly, as if a tap had been turned off. More gray light filtered through the curtains. He sipped coffee—too hot—glanced at Jay, then moved to peer out into the back yard.

The yard undulated.

Scales grinned, blew on his coffee and stared through the gaps in the bedroom curtains at the lawn.

From the bed, Jay said, "What are you watching out there?" She sounded wide awake.

121

He turned to look at her. God, what a magnificent woman this was in his bed. "Sorry, I didn't mean to wake you. Coffee?"

"Please."

He padded down to the kitchen and fixed her a cup.

Back again, he sat on the edge of the bed and handed her the coffee. She sat up, allowed the sheet to fall away from her nude body. Sipped tentatively at the brew.

"Thanks."

He stared at her breasts.

She smiled. "Looking at my sagging hooters? They don't stand up like they used to."

"What does? Who cares? They're beautiful. So are you all."

Another exchange of smiles.

"So, what was so interesting out there?" She waved at the window with her free hand.

"Slugs."

"Slugs?"

"Yeah. I grew up in the south so we had crawly things, but I'd never seen anything like what happened here a little while after the rain stopped. First time I saw the whole yard crawling with a thousand of those suckers leaving a carpet of slime behind 'em, I thought I was having a flashback."

"You did acid?"

"Sure. During the war. The Marines had plenty of it. Wouldn't have thought you could get LSD in the Southeast Asian jungles, would you?"

She took another drink of coffee. "When I lived in the Haight, I wore purple shades, smoked a lot of dope, dropped whatever psychedelics were around. Acid, mescaline, mushrooms. Got high and waited for the Age of Aquarius to get there."

She stared into the distance, through the walls and back through time. "The peace and harmony bus must have had a flat tire along the way to my place, so I eventually left on foot. Strange journey—from flower child to cop."

He leaned over, kissed her shoulder. "They're all strange journeys. Come on, I'll show you my slug garden."

"Pit stop first," she said.

He strolled to the window, sipped at his coffee as she headed for the bathroom.

This time when he looked out, there was a very wet man hiding in the bushes behind the house. Or at least trying to hide there. At first he thought it was Jenkins, but even though the guy was probably fifty yards away and the light wasn't all that great, he could tell it wasn't Jenkins. This guy wore a green jacket but also blue T-shirt and jeans and a dark blue baseball cap, all of them soaked. He didn't have a beard, either.

Scales stared through the small gap between the curtains.

"I think the big banana slugs are the best," Jay said from behind him. She moved toward the window. "Though the leopard slugs are not bad."

He held out one arm to stop her. "Move slow," he said. "Come up behind me."

"Boy, you really aren't from around here. Slugs don't spook that easy. Don't go looking for a stampede."

"There's a guy crouched down in the bushes at the edge of the yard," he said. "He's watching the house."

Jay moved over behind him and edged slowly toward the narrow aperture in the curtains. "See, to the left?"

"I see him. You know who he is?"

"Nope. I was thinking it might be one of the vets who camps in the woods but he doesn't look right for that."

"No, he doesn't."

She moved away and he saw her reaching for her clothes.

"What are you doing?"

"I'm a cop, remember? I think I'll get dressed and go have a word with our visitor down there. At the very least he's trespassing and a peeping tom. Or maybe he's psychopathic axe-murderer."

"He can't see anything," he said. "He's not even looking up here." Although he'd probably seen Scales walking around naked downstairs making the coffee, there were a few windows uncovered on the ground floor.

"Not for lack of trying." She hooked her bra and slipped her shirt on.

Scales shook his head. Well, shit. This sure wasn't how he'd hoped the morning was going to go.

He put his cup on the bedside table and started to pull his jeans on.

"What are you doing?"

"Putting my pants on."

"Probably be better if you stayed here," she said.

"I'm supposed to let you go out there by yourself?"

"I have a gun," she said. "In the kitchen or somewhere on the floor downstairs, I think."

He smiled at that.

"Besides, I am a cop. This is my area of expertise. I won't try to sew people up, you don't pass out speeding tickets."

He thought about that for a second. She was right. Then again, it was his yard. What if she hadn't been here? Back where he came from, if you spotted somebody skulking around your house, you didn't call the police, you got your shotgun and went to find out who and why.

"Okay," he said. "I bow to your experience. I'll stand behind you."

"I knew you were smarter than you looked."

But by the time they'd gotten dressed and circled around from the front to sneak up on where the man was, he was gone.

Jay poked around in the bushes for a minute, squatted and looked at the ground where the guy had been crouched.

"Looking for clues?"

"Maybe he dropped his wallet. Or a diary."

"You a funny woman. I could get used to you being around."

She stood, wiped her hands on her pants. "You have any enemies?"

"My wife's divorce lawyer. I shoved him into a wall once."

"Think that was him?"

"I doubt it. He'd be hard pressed to find his ass with both hands. I don't think his attention span is sufficient to remember me and if he did, figure out how to get here."

"Let's see if the peeper had any wheels."

He followed her to the driveway and up to the highway, but there wasn't any sign that a car had parked off the pavement anywhere nearby recently.

"He's going to get awful wet wandering around on foot out in the woods," he said.

"Huh," Jay said. "I wonder what that was all about."

Scales shrugged. "Probably one of the vets we don't know about. No harm, no foul. You want me to fix you some breakfast?"

She glanced at her watch. "I'd like that, but I need to get to work."

He felt a moment of gut-constricting panic. She was leaving.

"Uh, listen, I really enjoyed having you."

She looked at him, raised her eyebrows.

"I mean, no, really. Can we do it again?"

Her eyebrows went higher.

"Jesus, you aren't going to make this easy, are you?"

She smiled. Reached out and took his hand. "Okay, cowboy, I hear you. I had a fine time myself."

"Call me about that ticket thing," he said.

"I will."

"Call me just for the hell of it."

She leaned forward, kissed him lightly. "Thanks. I will."

He sighed. Nodded. "Yeah. Me, too."

He watched her walk to her truck, get in, drive away.

Man, oh, man. First woman he'd been with in a long time he hadn't paid for the privilege and damned if she wasn't the best he'd ever had and more fun than a stadium full of clowns.

But the guy in the woods bothered him. He went back into the house and pulled his shotgun out of the bedroom closet. It was an old Savage 12-gauge pump. The barrel was too short for it to be much of a hunting weapon, it was more like a riot gun. He'd had it for years, took it when he went camping in case of bears or human predators. He wiped dust off it, found a box of #4 buckshot in the bottom of the closet and loaded five shells into the gun but didn't chamber a round. He set the piece on its butt next to the bedroom door, leaning against the corner. He wasn't planning on shooting anybody but it was better to have it and not need it than to need it and not have it.

As Hughes drove away from Scales' house, she found herself grinning stupidly and slapping her hand on the steering wheel. Who would have thought that two people as old as she and he were would have burned so hot? And

126

more than that, would have been so comfortable the first time together? It was great. And it was also a little scary. It would be all too easy to fall into a relationship with Scales and she wasn't sure she was ready for that. She'd been down that road too many times not to know that the shiny, wide and smooth highway usually narrowed to gravel and rutted dirt real fast. Real easy to slide right off and into the ditch.

But, oh, boy, with sex that good? Hell with the road.

She drove toward the reservation. She needed to shower and change clothes, otherwise she was going to walk around smelling like sex all day.

Mama would know all about it, of course. Hughes' truck had been parked out in front of Scales' clinic all night, somebody would have seen it and sure as hell somebody would have mentioned it to her mother by now. Mama would be thrilled. She didn't think a woman could be complete without a man, preferably a husband. Hughes had known a couple of lesbian cops in SoCal who would have argued that, but the truth was, she did feel better when she had a new fella around, at least at first. Honeymoons were great, it was only when those were over that things got dreary.

Well. One romp did not a relationship make.

Then again, more romps were definitely a possibility. As long as it was that much fun, definitely a possibility.

"Medical Clinic."

"Hey, Doctor Feelgood."

He smiled into the phone. "Hey, Jay. How are you?"

"A little sore, actually."

He chuckled. "Oh, yeah? I can fix that. Hair of the dog."

"I don't think it was the dog's hair that did it."

He took a deep breath and let it out slowly. This was fun.

"Listen, you told me to call you with that ticket stuff."

"Yep, I sure did. Lemme get a pencil . . . okay, shoot."

She rattled off the street address.

"Got it. It won't take but a few minutes to check this out."

"You want to call me back?"

"Why don't you come by after work? I'll give it to you in person."

She laughed. Put on a thick and fake southern accent: "My, my, Doctor Feelgood, how you do go on. I believe I hear a double entendre there."

"Yes, ma'am, that's a fact."

"About six-thirty okay?"

"That would be just fine."

" 'Jest fahn?' you said?"

"Yes'um."

"See you then, cowboy."

Before he could log on to his computer check out the address, the phone rang again.

"Medical Clinic."

"Rick Scales?"

"Speaking."

"David Sperling, med tech at Independent Bio."

Ah. IB was the lab in Port Angeles, the one that handled all of Reuben's clinics. He didn't know this particular tech. "David. What's up?"

"You asked for a rush on Harold Gaines' bloodwork. I tried to fax it to you but I couldn't get through."

"Damned fax is probably not working right again," Scales said. "Give me a quick run down and you can just send it in the mail if I can't get the machine running."

"No problem." He started rattling off the values and Scales wrote them down. It took only a minute or so.

According to what Sperling said, the numbers were consistent with extensive liver damage and pretty much in the same ballpark as what Scales remembered the last bloodwork had been.

He frowned but said, "Hey, thanks for calling."

"No problem."

After they hung up, Scales looked at the results. Something was wrong here. How could Gaines have a clean urine and PE and still have blood this dirty? Either his clinical skills had gone to hell or these numbers were wrong. Seemed to be a lot of that going around these days, him being in error or the labs getting patients mixed up.

Which was it?

Probably that he was getting senile and losing it. But just to be sure . . .

He clicked on his patient listing on the computer screen. There it was. He had his modem dial the number, switched to voice as the phone started ringing on the other end. Slow, but cable wasn't out this far yet.

"Hello?"

"Harold?"

"You got him."

"Rick Scales."

"Howzit goin', Doc?"

"Fine. Look, I need you to stop in when you get a chance. I need to draw some more blood."

"What's the matter, the vampires got a tapeworm?"

"Somebody dropped a tube," he lied.

"Oh, great. Makes me feel good about my medical care."

"Stop by any time, you don't need an appointment."

"Okay. I can probably make it in tomorrow. See you then."

Scales broke the connection and stared at the phone. What he had in mind wasn't illegal but he felt a sudden stab of guilt anyway. Well. He could live with that. Better than thinking he was losing his mind.

Now, to find out where the bad guys overparked.

He connected with the map server, managed to find an empty slot, punched in his request. It took a little while for it to come up. The street and block pulsed in blue, the other streets were in red. He hit the zoom command and zeroed in until he had a small section magnified. It took a few more minutes for the cross directory function to add the buildings and ID them and those wouldn't show up on screen, only in the retrieved file. When the screen announced that it had finished, he sent the file directly to his printer, then logged off the net.

When the file got done printing, what he should have was a map centering on Westwood and Westwood Village. The marked street was south of the UCLA campus, north of Wilshire Blvd. There would also be buildings sketched in, each marked with a number that should correspond to a directory listing attached to the map.

Scales grinned. He loved technology.

THIRTEEN

Naked and propped up on two pillows against the bed's head board, Hughes took a sip of now-tepid beer and looked at the computer printout. It was pretty amazing that Scales could get all this just by dialing up some computer somewhere and asking it. Nice of him—not that it looked to be worth all that much. There didn't seem to be any listing for "Hired Killers" or "Cut Rate Secret Operatives."

Scales came back from the bathroom, also naked, carrying a mug half-full of beer. "See anything you recognize?" he asked.

"Nope. Just a bunch of names."

He slid onto the bed, squeezed her thigh gently. "Well, actually, I know a few of them," he said. He pointed at the list. "That one is the corporate headquarters of a place that makes home cholesterol tests, and that one is a branch of a big drug manufacturing company, they produce a lot of vitamin products. This one down here publishes a bodybuilding magazine."

She grinned at him. "Very helpful. Neither of the two dead guys looked to me like they were worried about their fat or vitamin intake or exercise regimen."

He shrugged. "Sorry. It was a shot."

"Thanks, I appreciate it. If I were down in L.A., maybe I'd knock on a few doors and see if I could get anybody to recognize a picture. My guess is the feds won't bother. We're probably looking at a dead end. I've run out of things to check."

He set his beer down on the table.

She looked at him, saw that his interest in printouts had given way to something much more erotic. "Jeez, you sure you're fifty-something? I thought sure that thing would be ready for a nap by now."

"Can't help itself," he said. "Your overwhelming beauty combined with your razor-sharp brain call to it. Or you got super pheromones or something."

Absurdly, that made her feel good. It was nice to believe she had that kind of power. Over the hill, maybe, but not at the bottom just yet.

"Well, come here."

"Yes, ma'am."

Another wild night with Jay and Scales could see how he could get used to those real quick. She was gone to work and he was in the shower, barely awake and very relaxed. After they'd made love, he'd slept as if he'd been comatose and if she hadn't heard the alarm this morning, he'd still be asleep.

He soaped his half-raw penis and wondered if it was too early to ask her to move in with him.

Was he ready to make that kind of decision?

Maybe not. Big decisions were not his thing. He didn't like to think about them, didn't like to make them. Especially did not like being wrong when he did step up to the line. He'd done that way too many times and it was depressing to think about being wrong again. Maybe it was better to let things flow along of their own accord and see what happened.

At noon, Hughes sat in her truck in the parking lot at the museum, eating and watching the tourists come and go.

The sun was out, the sky was clear and achingly blue, and a lone eagle wheeled in big circles overhead, looking for some lunch of his own. Things were relatively quiet and on days like this with the air warm and clean and dry she could remember why she liked being here. A hundred years ago, two hundred years ago—and except for the modern buildings—this spit of land would probably have looked much as it did today. It was postcard country, the end of the world, and it was home.

She finished the ham and cheese sandwich, washed the last of it down with sips from a plastic bottle of Coke. She needed to drive to the Inch's house and talk to Mina. The girl had called in to report that her father hadn't come home from Port Angeles last night and nobody had seen his truck around anywhere. Probably old Tom had gotten lucky, he sometimes trolled the bars between Clallam Bay and PA looking for female company and every once in a while he scored. Which proved that lust, if not love, was surely blind.

Other than that, the day had been typical. There were a couple of minor theft complaints; fishing tackle, an old outboard motor; a domestic argument that had apparently ended when Marian Leewook crowned her husband with a cast iron pot—no permanent damage to either skull or skillet—and a loose dog that had nipped a couple of people. Plus the usual quota of tourists whose RVs had flat tires or engine trouble and who were waiting for AAA to send somebody. Real mean streets out here . . .

She finished the Coke, screwed the cap back on the empty bottle and dropped it on the truck's floor. Pretty soon she'd have to clean this sucker out.

Ah, the exciting life of a tribal cop.

Well, it had been a little more interesting on a personal

level lately, the thing with Scales. Entirely too much fun and something of a worry. So far, it had been fine, but she was already wondering where it was going to go. Did she want it to go anywhere? That bright new honeymoon shined like a big, fat, glowing pumpkin, casting its orange and golden light on everything. She knew that couldn't last but as long as it was up and gleaming, why not enjoy it? As she got older, the carpe diem, be-here-now philosophy grew more and more attractive. Life was full of dangers. Some tourist in a big RV might plow into her when she left the parking lot and turn her into bloody paste. Hell, a big meteor might drop on her out of the clear blue sky, squashing all her tomorrows in a heartbeat. You never knew. Be-here-later was risky. The shit you swallowed for breakfast today so you could eat caviar next week might be your last meal and then wouldn't you be sorry you'd done it? You couldn't live your life as if each sunrise were going to be your last one, the intensity of that would cripple you; still, you could enjoy what came your way. And she did enjoy Rick Scales, more than she had any man in a long, long time. Yeah, he might turn out to be a brass-plated bastard six months or two years from now, but if she held off living unless she got a guarantee, she'd damn sure never live at all.

She smiled at herself. Amazing what a good lay did for your life-philosophy, and what rationalizations you'd come up with to justify throwing caution into the nearest garbage can so you could get laid again. Still, when something was this good, it made you wonder if there was something bad lurking in the shadows waiting to mess it up. About whether it was too good to be true.

When the FedEx guy came by, Scales had his labwork

ready, including a fresh blood sample from Gaines. The FedEx guy glanced at the packages, did a quick take when he saw the Gaines sample. "You got the right address on this one? Don't you want it to go to Independent Bio with the rest of these?"

"Nope. Medley Labs is right."

The guy shrugged. "Nooo probleemo, Batman. See you later."

He left.

Scales had two patients waiting so he didn't have time to worry much about his decision. If he were wrong, all it would cost him would be a few bucks for checking it out and nobody would ever know. If the bloodwork results on Gaines were anywhere close to the last test, he'd know it was him and not the lab screwing up. He'd have to start paying a lot closer attention to his exams and his own lab stuff, he'd have to be not so sure of himself. Which, when you got down to it, wasn't a bad idea anyhow.

Back in Texas and New Mexico, Scales had known a lot of guys who rode motorcycles. Most of them had been in accidents, even those riding for years. One guy whose broken leg and collarbone Scales had set had told him why he thought the experts got into wrecks. "Now, your newbie, he pays attention when he's on two instead of four," the biker had said. "He fuckin' knows people are out to get him and he rides on the defense, he's always lookin', always figurin' how to get out of the shit when it hits. And it's gonna hit, it's just a matter of when, he knows that 'cause that's what everybody's ever cranked a starter has told him. But after a few years, after he's at home in the saddle, he starts thinkin' he's on a real vehicle and not an overgrown bi-sickle. He gets to thinkin', 'Hey, I know how to do this.' That's exactly when the little old Q-tip granny who can't hardly see over the damned steering wheel of her big Cad and who thinks he can stop that motorsickle on a dime anyhow nails him.

"I was doin' forty when that one pulled out broadside in front of me and that's just what she said: 'Why didn't you just stop?' Sheeit. Lucky I didn't get kilt."

Yes. You ought never to be too certain you're right, Scales realized. And probably that was all it was, he'd gotten cocky after doing this all these years and he wasn't checking himself enough. Still, he had to know. He'd stuck a note in with the sample, along with his personal check for the cost, asking them to call him before they mailed or faxed the results. If he were wrong, that phone call would be the end of it. He'd have them flush the sample and eighty-six the paperwork, nobody would ever know he'd gone around Reuben's lab.

And if he were right? If it was the lab's fault and not his?

Well, he hadn't gone too far down that road yet. At the least, it would mean somebody in Reuben's lab was a fuck-up and he'd have to pass that along. If you couldn't trust your lab, you would eventually do some damage to a patient based on the wrong results. Reuben would have to know, he had a whole bunch of doctors running their stuff through Independent.

If that was what was going on, maybe it was just one tech asleep at the switch. Bad technique, sloppy work, an unfortunate accident, straighten him out or fire the son-of-a-bitch and that would be that.

There was another possibility, one he hadn't wanted to think about too much because that fork led down a real ugly path: What if somebody had done it on purpose?

If you were going to build a house using logic as one of your tools, you had to at least consider it. He didn't think anybody else had been on that grassy knoll in Dallas but if he'd been in charge of the investigation, he would have damnsure checked every lead out. You didn't look, you sure couldn't see. If a thing wasn't done by accident, then it was done on purpose.

He couldn't for the life of him think why somebody would deliberately jigger medical results that way. What possible reason would anybody have to want the PA treating somebody to think the patient was sicker than he really was? That made no sense at all.

Well. No point worrying about that bridge until he came to it. Best to take care of the patients in house and deal with later when it came round.

He went to remove a triple pronged fishhook from Sam McCaffe's shoulder.

Hughes got a call from Arlo Henderson, a trooper she knew in the Washington State Patrol.

"Arlo. What's up?"

"You said you were looking for a green pickup?" He rattled off the license number of Tom Inch's truck. "Belongs to an old Makah from out the reservation?"

"Yeah?"

"It's in the Bear Claw's parking lot."

The Bear Claw was a bar on the highway just outside of Port Angeles. Not the kind of place you'd take your mother—unless she was a good boxer or looking to get picked up for a one-nighter. Or maybe both. The bar had been cited repeatedly for promoting prostitution, serving alcohol to underage patrons and was well-known for its fights. A particularly bad brawl had started there last winter, had taken half the deputies in the county to break it up and had put nineteen people in the hospital before it was done.

The Bear Claw had gone through three owners in five years. It was not a place where you sat under ferns listening to new age music while you sipped your white wine spritzers.

"I don't suppose you stopped in and asked about Tom Inch?"

"As it happens, I did. Nobody remembers seeing him, least the bartender and none of the barmaids do. But it was a busy night, pay day. He could have been in, left with somebody. He's been known to do that before."

"Thanks, I appreciate it."

"Happy to do it. Why don't you let me buy you a beer sometimes, Jasmine? I'm not bad company."

Arlo tried to get her to go out with him nearly every time they talked. "What would your wife think about that, Henderson?"

"We wouldn't have to tell her. If it didn't show up on *Oprah*, she'd never know."

She laughed. "Next incarnation, maybe."

So Tom Inch probably had found a willing partner, though it was not like him to stay gone for more than overnight without calling Mina. Hughes would give her a call and pass that on.

She thought about calling Scales, inviting him out to dinner, but decided against it. Maybe it would be better to stay home tonight. No point in rushing things. He'd probably still be there tomorrow. A little more caution wouldn't hurt and she was past the days when she would fling herself off a cliff and hope the water below was deep enough to keep her from breaking her neck. Once upon a time that had been oh-so-thrilling and the risk unimportant; now, she might not be wise but she wasn't quite as stupid as once she had been. She hoped. She wanted to be with him but like her Mama used to tell her, she was big enough to where what she wanted wouldn't hurt her. She could call him tomorrow and keep an eye out for meteors meanwhile.

FOURTEEN

"Medical Clinic."

"Dr. Scales?"

"That's PA Scales. Or just 'Rick.' "

"Ah. This is Brent Roth at Medley Labs. You sent us a blood sample." The man sounded excited. Must be a slow day to get thrilled about delivering routine blood test results.

"That's right, Mr. Roth."

"Call me 'Brent.' Um. Anyway, I hustled it along. I can give you a verbal and then fax or snailmail the paper work."

"Sounds good to me. Shoot."

Scales heard computer keys clicking softly in the background. "Okay, first, on the SMA, we got albumin, 4.2; alkaline phosphatase 100; SGPT 40; SGOT 21; BUN, 12 . . ."

Scales tapped the numbers into his own computer as the man continued to rattle them off. He could see there was a problem. The SMA—sequential multichannel analysis—tested a bunch of chemical substances in the blood and the amounts and proportions of these chemicals told a clinician all kinds of things about the patient.

So far, these numbers were telling Scales that, according to his blood, Gaines was in great shape for a normal, healthy, thirty-year-old male. Which was flat out impossible for a sixty-six year-old man with terminal liver disease.

Sodium, bilirubin, cholesterol, protein, uric acid were all normal, too.

Well, shit.

Brent read off the results of the CBC and those numbers were also WNL—within normal limits—except for a viral shift in the white cell count.

So. Scales was right. Gaines wasn't fucking sick at all, unless maybe he had the flu—

"—know you didn't ask for it, but something looked hinky, you know? So we ran a couple more tests, no charge. Didn't have much blood left but we found some real interesting stuff. We're getting some weird reactions on enzymes—this guy's got very high levels of something that looks like tumor factor, telomerase. And the AIDS test went off, well, sort of—we've never seen a reaction quite like it. Kind of positive and kind of not. It's like he's got HIV but that isn't quite it."

Scales shook his head, not understanding. "Go on."

"Guy's got the DHEA of a twenty-five-year-old. Apoptosis residues are practically zip. The glucocorticoids are all out of proportion and dismutase and catalase enzymes are sky-high.

"Barry—he's our itty-bitty man—got all interested and went to the U where he cranked up the electron microscope and poked around. Found a big, fat, complex virus like nothing he's ever seen infecting some of the leukocytes. Barry thinks this virus is all full of folded proteins, coiled-coil, leucine zipper kind of thing—at least that's what he figures from the shape, he can't see the proteins, he'd need X-ray crystallography to be sure and we don't have anything like that around here.

"There are some very strange combinations of hormones and bugs and God knows what else in this guy. Seems to be some other things going on we can't pin down, they don't make any sense. What's his problem, medically speaking?"

Scales ignored the question and threw out one of his

own. "I'm just a country PA. What does all this mean?"

There was a pause. "We don't have a fucking clue. Barry is smarter than the rest of us combined—he was a hotshot postdoc at Stanford but he blew it off and headed north to get away from all the academic bullshit—and he doesn't know. If he can't figure out, none of the rest of us can. Something is stranger than hell about this blood sample. Could you get us some more? We'd like to play with it, no charge or anything. Can you tell us about this guy?"

Scales felt a coldness touch him, a stomach-lurching, over-the-first-drop roller coaster sensation. "Uh, look, Brent, let me get back to you on this, okay? I need to check something out first."

"Sure."

"And hold off on that paperwork for a day or two, until I get back to you. I, uh, might want it sent somewhere else."

"Got it. But do get back to us, okay? I haven't seen Barry this excited since Nixon died."

Scales cradled the phone and stared at his computer screen.

What in the fuck was going on?

Scales had a light afternoon, nothing major scheduled, no big accidents, and as he wrote prescriptions for hay fever and backaches, he went over the thing with Gaines again and again. How could somebody with a dying liver, one too far gone to possibly regenerate, how could he be getting over that? And what was all this crap in his system? He was out of his depth here, supposed that most doctors in family or general practice would be as well. But it didn't take a genius to figure out something was, as Brent had put it, hinky. And it wasn't much of a hop to leap to the conclusion that whatever strangeness was going on in Gaines with all these enzymes and hormones and crap could have something to do with it. But what? How?

Scales ushered Monica Jackson to the door, told her to use the suppositories he'd given her and avoid straining at stool.

The fact that he'd had several of these unusual remissions lately, well, those took on a different aspect, too.

And what about Jimmy Lewis? His AIDS patient whose autopsy had come back negative for signs of the disease—until Reuben straightened that out.

Of a moment, Scales had a nasty suspicion. Reuben knew something about all this and he was making sure Scales didn't know.

That's kind of paranoid, isn't it, old son?

Maybe. Maybe it's just coincidence that the autopsy screwed up, that the bloodwork on Timmy was at odds with Scales' physical exam, that he had an alcoholic with a rotted liver whose tests showed him to be in better shape than Scales himself was.

A lot of coincidences.

Jesus. What did it mean?

He had to talk to somebody about it and his sudden distrust of his boss made that call the wrong one to make. But who else could he tell?

Hughes leaned back in the chair, backed it up onto two legs and stared at Scales. "Okay, let me run through it to make sure I've got it right. First you had a patient come in who had terminal lung cancer and it went away. Then another patient with leukemia had a similar sudden and dramatic remission. An old man who was tired turned into a major hiker and a guy with a bad liver got well. And there is some question as to whether a murdered man who had

AIDS still had it when they cut him open for the autopsy."

"It sounds pretty wild when you lay it out like that," he admitted.

She nodded. "It does. But there are some other things working here. Tom Inch has disappeared, we have his truck but nobody who saw him leave it there. Your leukemia patient went to Hawaii with his parents and nobody around here knows exactly where they are staying. Lewis got himself killed and the body is still being held for tests. I haven't seen George Swell around but maybe that doesn't mean anything. He sometimes goes off camping in the woods for a couple of days. That leaves Harold Gaines. Can I use your phone?"

"Sure."

"You have Harold's number handy?"

He got it for her.

She called. No answer and Harold didn't have a machine.

"He could be out to dinner or having a drink," she said.

"Better not be drinking," Scales said.

"Okay, let's say statistics may have caught up with you. You happened to get your lifetime dose of miracles all at once. But here's the thing—right now, we can't lay our hands on any of these people. If I poke around and it turns out that Harold Gaines has taken a sudden trip and nobody knows where, that will really bother me."

Scales sighed. "This is all too weird."

"Maybe not. Maybe it is just coincidence. Stranger things have happened. But let's suppose, just for the sake of argument, that it isn't chance. That these things are all related. What would explain them?"

Scales shook his head. "Nothing medical that I know of. Some bored god decided to toss a few miracles my way.

Something is going on in Gaines' blood, according to the new lab. I guess what I'd want to check out would be if anybody else in this group had similar things floating around in their systems."

"Can you do that?"

"Not unless I can draw more blood and I can't get it if I can't find them."

"Hmm."

He said, "What are you thinking?"

"I'm wondering if this ties in with Jimmy Lewis's death. And if it does, how? There's a lot of gristle to chew on here."

He nodded.

"Look, let me think about this. There are some people I can reach out to who owe me. I'll poke around and see what falls out." She stood.

"You could stay for dinner," he said.

She hesitated a second.

"Or not," he added quickly. "I don't want to be pushy here, Jay. I don't want to screw this up, whatever it might be with us."

She smiled at him. "Thanks. I kind of promised my mother I'd have supper with her and I'm already late. Rain check?"

"Any time, ossifer."

Mutual smiles. God, she felt like a fool grinning so much at him. "I'll call you in the morning."

She moved to hug him, and the good night kiss was warm enough so she didn't want to leave after it began but she pulled away. Shook her head at him. "Hold that thought," she said. "We'll get back to it tomorrow, okay?"

The insistent ringing brought Scales out of a bottomless

sleep. He grabbed at the phone, saw the bedside clock: It was 2:17 a.m.

"Yeah, what?"

"Doctor, there has been an accident out the highway near the reservation. One of your patients, Harold Gaines, he is hurt very bad. You better get out here quickly." The speaker was a deep-voiced man with some kind of foreign accent, German or Austrian, maybe, like Arnold the Governator . . .

"Who is—?"

The speaker hung up.

He was still half asleep when the name finally sank in. Harold Gaines!

Scales got dressed, grabbed his emergency bag and the powerful diver's flashlight he'd bought for rainy night work, and headed for the bedroom door. As he got there, he noticed the shotgun leaning in the corner.

Back when he'd been training in Texas, a country doctor he knew had been robbed. Guy got an emergency call late one night and when he went out to check, somebody stuck a gun in his face and took his medical case. The cops caught the guy later and it turned out to be a doper looking for some quick morphine and Demerol. Scales had never really worried about that kind of thing even in the city, he had always been careful about paying attention to his surroundings when he had to go out on call. He carried his medical stuff in an old day pack. And he'd never worried about it here, he didn't get called out that often. But with that prowler in the yard and this mysterious caller, maybe it was better to be safe than sorry.

He grabbed the shotgun and headed for the stairs.

The early morning darkness was warm and muggy, overcast enough so there weren't any stars showing. He drove at a steady fifty on the straights and slowed on the curves, and when he was a couple of miles from the reservation, he began looking for signs of an accident. So far, he hadn't seen another vehicle.

He spotted Gaines' truck. The pickup, a fairly new red Chevy, was wheels up on a sandy spit fifty feet below the road. The shrubs and grass were torn up where the truck had gone over the embankment. Scales pulled his Toyota over and stopped.

He was getting out when he saw the glint of light across the road.

There was a stand of thick bushes and a couple of small evergreen trees there, dimly lit by the peripheral wash of his headlights. And something shiny in the bushes.

It probably was nothing, just his paranoia flaring again, and Harold Gaines might be dying down there in his truck.

But—where was the caller? Except for the truck and his car, there wasn't anybody else around. Wouldn't they have stayed to help? Or at least called the volunteer fire department or somebody? That was odd.

If he was wrong, he was going to feel pretty stupid, but as he alighted from his car, he slid the short-barreled shotgun out with him and let it hang down by his leg. If there was somebody hiding in the bushes, his body and leg would block it from their view.

He hurried toward the overturned truck.

The climb down was easy and he made it quickly, even trying to keep a shotgun out of sight.

Gaines was in the truck, seatbelt holding him upside down in place. Scales put his bag and the shotgun down and reached inside, pinched Gaines' neck with his thumb and forefinger over the carotids.

No pulse.

He'd have to get him out and see if he could pump him back—

He sensed the motion behind him, remembered why he had brought the shotgun. Scales jerked his hand away from the dead man, dropped and swept up the shotgun, jacked a shell into the chamber.

The man coming down the hill was twenty meters away and if he heard the clack-clack of the shotgun he didn't slow his descent.

The temptation was to shoot, just shoulder the weapon and cut loose, but it might be a passerby who'd seen the wreck and wouldn't that be great? To blast a Good Samaritan with a twelve-gauge? Oops, sorry, pal.

He held the shotgun with his right hand and reached for his left back pocket. The flashlight there was black plastic about six inches long, held four C-cells and had a wrist lanyard so a diver could wear it like a big dangling bracelet. It also had a krypton bulb that threw a very bright beam.

Scales pointed the light at the dark figure and flicked the switch with his thumb.

The circle of brightness caught the oncoming man right in the face and he wasn't expecting it. He put his free hand up to block the glare.

There was plenty of illumination to show the pistol in the man's other hand.

Scales raised the shotgun and fired it. The recoil was too much for his awkward grip and he nearly lost the weapon. He did lose the flashlight, it fell at his feet. The boom slapped hard at his ears and the bright flash of the belching gun destroyed his night vision with the orange and yellow flare.

He heard the man yell, "Motherfucker!" and heard the *pap-pap-pap* of the handgun—it didn't make much noise— saw the muzzle flashes sparking at him.

One of the bullets hit the truck with a metallic chunk!

Scales, dived, rolled to his right and came up into a crouch. He jacked another shell into the chamber, snapped the shotgun up and fired. He had only a vague idea of where his target was. He dived and rolled again, hit hard in the darkness and slid part way down the incline in a shower of gravel and sand before coming to a stop. He rolled prone, faced up the slope on his belly and elbows, shotgun pointed that way.

It was very quiet.

A minute later, he heard the sound of a motorcycle starting. The rider caught rubber in two gears as he drove off, no lights Scales could see.

After five minutes, Scales dared to move. He inched his way up to where his flashlight lay, still on. He flicked it off, then started up the slope toward the road. He worked his way around in a big half circle to his left. The hill was steeper and he had to tuck the light back into his pocket to manage the climb. When he got to the road, he didn't see anybody. His car was where he had left it. He held the flashlight under the shotgun so that the barrel and beam would be aligned and thumbed the switch. He swept the beam back and forth.

Nobody.

He went back to his car. Looked around carefully, didn't see anything amiss. He opened the door, slid into the driver's seat.

It was another five minutes before his heart and lungs had settled down enough for him to dig his cell phone from the glove box to call Jay Hughes.

He waited for her to answer and blew out another in the series of big sighs.

Man, oh, man, oh, man!

149

FIFTEEN

Scales had gotten over the worst part of his fright by the time Jay arrived. He had three shells left in the shotgun and he had backed his car around with the front at a right angle to the road so he could see traffic coming from either direction. Jay's truck was the first vehicle he'd seen. It was pushing three a.m. when she pulled over. She had her right hand on the butt of her revolver and the other hand held a big aluminum flashlight like a javelin when she stepped out of the truck.

"Scales?"

"Right here," he said. He stuck his left hand out of the car window and waved. He got out of his car. He left the shotgun on the seat.

She drew near. "Okay, what have we got?"

"Harold Gaines down there in his truck, dead. It looks like an accident but I wouldn't bet a plugged nickel it was. As I was going down the hill somebody sneaked up behind me with a pistol. Had a silencer on it."

"Silencer?"

"It didn't make much noise when he shot at me."

"He shot at you."

"Three or four times. Of course, that was after I shot at him."

She stared at him.

"Gaines is in his truck, deader than last week's crab dinner, some guy who was hidden in the bushes sneaks up behind me with a silenced handgun? Damned right I shot at

150

him. I don't think I hit him, I didn't see any blood up where he was. I did see some shell casings from his piece. 9mm, I left them where they were."

"Okay, run it through from the top. Take your time."

He noticed that his hand was shaking a little and he put it into his pants pocket as he told her what happened. She didn't interrupt, let him finish, then said, "I don't like this, I don't like it at all."

"You and me both."

They stood there for a minute. "Well, we're going to have to call the county and state boys in, no way around that. But the thing is, how much of this are we going to tell them?"

"How much?"

"You want to lay it all out like you just told me, that's okay. If you want to limit it to being called and finding Gaines in the truck, that's cool, too."

"Why wouldn't I want to tell it all?"

"Well, here's the deal. You tell them, and assuming they buy it, you all of a sudden have to answer a whole lot of questions, the feebs come out and poke around again, don't find anything, then leave. Stirs up things, muddies the water, doesn't accomplish shit."

"And if I don't say anything, then what?"

"Maybe you and I can find out something outsiders can't, now that we know we have something to look for."

Scales sighed. Shook his head. "I dunno, Jay. This is like one of those movie things where the good guys take off on their own and the audience sits there screaming at them for being stupid."

"We can always call in the law," she said.

He looked at her, saw the hint of a smile. "You want to solve this thing, don't you?"

151

The grin manifested. "Yeah, I do. Whoever this is, they're dumping in my yard. I don't like it and I figure I'm the one ought to do something about it."

He considered it. Took a minute. "All right," he finally said. "We'll try it your way. If it gets out of hand—"

"I'll reach for the nearest cell phone."

He nodded. "Which might work out here or not. Okay. What now?"

"It's tampering with evidence, but—go see if you can find those empty shells. Anything else around that might spook the investigating officers?"

He thought about it. "I picked up my fired empties. I don't think the dirt'll show where I missed the guy. Oh— wait. I think one of his shots hit the truck."

"Let's go see."

They couldn't find a bullet hole in the truck's body. There were some fresh scratches on the undercarriage, in- cluding a long gouge close to the rear axle. "That's prob- ably it," she said. "If you weren't looking for it specifically, you wouldn't think it was done by a bullet. This is a one-car accident. They won't notice it."

"Okay."

The two of them pulled Gaines from the truck.

His neck was broken and he had a cracked skull that looked a lot like the impression a steering wheel might make. Absolutely he was dead.

With the body laid out on the ground next to the flipped vehicle, Scales went to collect the empty handgun shells.

Even as he did it, he worried that he was being extremely foolish. The state and federal cops would probably cut his nuts off if they knew he was removing the 9mm brass. Then again, Jay wanted to do this, a lot, and he was willing to give her the chance. He wasn't sleeping with the state and federal cops and he didn't owe them anything.

"I got 'em," he said.

"Here, I'll hang onto them."

He passed the brass to her. The shells were nickel plated and gleamed like chrome when she shined her light on one of them. "Winchester. 9mm Luger," she said.

"Yeah. I saw that."

She shoved the shells into her pocket.

"Why don't you go on home? I'll put in the call and wait," she said.

"Guy might come back," he said.

"If he does, I won't miss," she said.

Touché.

He was tired and adrenaline-depleted and wanted nothing more than to crawl into bed and sleep for a few months, so he didn't fight it. "All right."

"Maybe you better keep that blunderbuss handy, though," she said. "It makes a big noise."

"Not to worry, I'll keep it where I can reach it."

After he was gone, Hughes moved around the site, looking for more evidence. Scales might be right, this might be terminally stupid but she was pissed off enough not to care. The State Patrol and the FBI and the BIA didn't have their IQs automatically elevated twenty points when they joined up. Sure, some of them were all right, some of them even real sharp, but most weren't any smarter than anybody else. She'd give it to them that they wanted to outwit the bad guys and clear their cases, even the not-so-swift ones. But they couldn't have much of a handle on this situation. And besides that, the agent who drew an assignment way the hell out past where the sun went down would definitely not be first in his or her graduating class. Out here, it was the second-string, unless it was some VIP who got tagged. Harold Gaines was no VIP and for now, better thought a traffic accident. Hell, even if she and Scales left the casings and told them the story, the dead man and the shooting weren't necessarily connected. Could have been some passing robber stopping to take advantage of the darkness and the situation to pick up a wallet and watch.

Silencer? You sure about that, Mr. Scales? It was dark and the man was shooting at you, wasn't he? That would be a hard call even by a trained officer, given those circumstances. How long has it been since you were in the Navy? Twenty-five, thirty years?

She knew better, she felt it in her bowels, all this crap with Scales meant something, but an outside cop probably wouldn't see it that way. They were used to citizens seeing conspiracies behind every rosebush, she'd felt that way herself when she'd been on the job in L.A. A pigeon crapped, and crazies came out of the sewers screaming it was a Communist/CIA/Aliens-from-Outer-Space plot!

When she got her part of this cleared, she would go see Scales and they'd see what else they could come up with.

When Scales pulled into his driveway and around back, he saw that the back door to his house was open.

He killed the engine but left the lights on and sat there for a second, looking around. He didn't remember turning the alarm system on but he sure as hell closed and locked the door, that he did know.

Well, Scales, m'boy, it seems as if you had visitors. And maybe they're still there, hey?

He killed the headlights and left his car in a hurry, the shotgun held against his right hip. He had a shell already chambered, and he fished his light out and lined it up with the barrel again, ready to switch it on.

He made it to the door and peeped inside, then flattened himself against the outside wall.

That won't help much, sucko, a round from a 9mm will punch right through the Sheetrock and wooden siding to tag you.

That was true, a frame-house wasn't much protection against a fast bullet, especially a jacketed round.

But it was cover if not protection and if somebody was in there, better they wonder where he was rather than know.

He dropped into a crouch and scooted around the door jamb and into the house. ER and storage were on the left, the kitchen and lab on the right. A plug-in nightlight at the other end of the hall past the bathroom on the exam room wall was the only light on this level, except for the stove hood appliance bulb. Thirty-two watts total.

He crouched by the door for two minutes, listening. If somebody was inside, they were being very quiet.

There were a few ways to do this. He could stand up and start switching on lights, making a shitload of noise and hope if there was an intruder he'd scare them and they'd get the hell out.

Given that somebody had already tried to pot him, he didn't put much faith in that option.

He could turn around and haul butt back to his car and use his cell phone to call for help.

That one didn't set well, either. He'd already had to call Jay once and he didn't want her to think he was the world's biggest wimp.

He could creep down the hall, checking the rooms as he went, and if something moved, he could blow it away.

This was his house and he knew it better than any un-invited company. Anybody who jumped out and went booga-

booga was going to be very close—and very sorry.

It took five minutes to clear the first floor, his heart thumping like crazy as he opened closets and doors, shotgun ready to cook.

Another five minutes and the upstairs proved to be empty.

Now he clicked on every light he could reach.

Another pass showed that he'd been robbed. Somebody had broken into his storage cabinet and dumped drug samples all over the floor. His fridge was missing a couple of vials of injectable pain killer and one of Valium. And they'd found the stash under the dirty laundry and stolen the lockbox.

He'd have to go through the boxes and see what else was missing, do an inventory.

At least they hadn't swiped his computer.

He went to the doors, locked them, set the alarm system, except for the motion sensors. Might as well check to see what got ripped off. Tired as he was, sleep wasn't part of the equation just now.

Any other time, he would have assumed some doper had broken in and stolen the drugs but given all that had happened, no way was he going to believe that. The theft was just a cover for the real reason.

But—what were they covering? What was the real reason?

SIXTEEN

By the time Scales finished his quick inventory it was dawn. Ghostly fingers of gray light began to poke through the cloud cover, slow-starting another damp summer morning. The thief had taken all his narcotics and some other low-schedule pain and hypnotic meds, that would be expected with a druggie. But they'd also taken a box of antibiotics, some inhalers—and all of his vitamin capsules.

What, was the guy an asthmatic crook with scurvy?

A truck pulled into the driveway. Scales reached for his shotgun, saw it was Jay, put the weapon back down. He went to let her in.

"You having a party?" she said. "Every light in the place is on."

"Somebody had it without me," he said.

He explained about the theft.

Jay frowned. "Lord, it's been a long night. How about some coffee?"

"Sure."

As he puttered in the kitchen, she sat at the table watching.

"Look, I'm assuming all this is somehow tied together," she said. "Problem is, I can't for the life of me figure out what it means."

He poured the water, flipped the on switch. Went to sit across from her. "I don't know," he said. "I don't have a clue."

They heard a car rumble out on the highway, slowing

157

down. Scales got up and walked to the front door, Jay behind him. He cracked the door and looked out in time to see the paperboy's '65 Chevy speed up and the morning paper sail from the car and into a puddle next to the driveway.

"Little bastard does that on purpose," Scales said. He opened the door and trotted out. The early edition of the *Peninsula Daily News* was in a plastic bag but that wouldn't keep it dry in a light rain, much less at the bottom of the deep puddle in which it lay. He fished the paper out, slung water from it, headed back to the house.

Jay stood in the doorway, hand on her holstered revolver, watching.

Jesus. He hadn't even thought about it, he'd just barged right out there to get the fucking paper. *Non-survival thinking, Scales, you idiot.* Somebody had taken a shot at him only a few hours ago, several shots, and here he was walking around as if it hadn't happened. That had always pissed him off when he read detective novels or watched that kind of movie—that the private eye would get attacked and then go on about his business as if his brain had shorted out and the attack had been forgotten. The guy would have a gun but he'd leave it at home when he went out, never figuring that if somebody had cut loose on him once, they might do it again. Stupid.

Just like you, pal.

Yeah, Jay was there and armed, but she might not be next time.

He gritted his teeth. Until they got this all sorted out, he wasn't going to get more than a few steps away from his shotgun.

Jesus. That was scary. The idea that he would walk around like some survivalist in the woods, armed to the teeth.

As he walked, he peeled the plastic bag from the mostly-wet paper.

Soggy or not, the headline caught his attention: FIRE DESTROYS MEDICAL LAB.

Medical Lab?

By the time he got back to the door, he'd reached the part of the story that identified the place. Just under that, there was a notation that two employees of the lab were missing, names withheld pending notification of next of kin.

Witnesses said there was an explosion before the fire that totally destroyed the building.

"Holy shit."

"What?"

He wasn't aware he had spoken aloud. He pointed at the soaked paper. "Explosion and fire in Port Angeles last night. The lab I was talking to yesterday. They're the ones I told you about, did the bloodwork on Gaines."

The two of them looked at each other.

Hughes didn't like coincidences, especially when they were piled this high and deep. Something was going on here, something big and dangerous and she needed to figure out what.

She sat across from Scales, drinking coffee, brooding about it.

"Okay," she said. "Let's assume, for the sake of argument again, that this fire is because of the work the lab did on Gaines."

"Man," he said.

"Maybe it wasn't. But if it was—then the question is—how did the arsonist or bomber or whoever the hell it was, how did he connect them to you?"

Scales shook his head. "I don't know. Nobody but the

UPS guy knew I sent the sample there and the only person I talked to about it was you—well, and the tech who called to give me the results of the test."

She frowned. "I didn't tell anybody. And who would the tech tell that would matter?"

Scales chewed at his lower lip for a second. Said, "Somebody from the lab went to the university to use their electron microscope. Maybe he mentioned it there."

"Possible, but even if somebody is keeping tabs on what you do, that's a reach." She stood.

"What?"

"Let's go upstairs. I want to look at something."

He followed her up the stairs. She went into his office, sat down at his desk, picked up the phone, which had been old when he moved in here. She unscrewed the mouthpiece on the receiver, dumped the little metal speaker thing into her hand, turned it over and looked at it.

He started to say something but she waved him quiet. Put the phone back together. Went back down stairs, led him out into the backyard.

"What, you think my phone is bugged?"

"Almost certainly it is," she said. "I don't have the expertise to be sure but that little piece is easy to replace with one that does more than the original. Or it could be connected to a line somewhere. And there might be other listening devices in the clinic."

"Come on."

He didn't want to believe it and it wasn't that easy for her, either. "You have a better explanation?"

He stood there for a second, the early morning light showing his consternation. "No. But—but—why?"

"That's the question, isn't it? We'd better find out."

"How?"

"You said you suspected maybe your boss had some knowledge of all this."

"Yeah?"

"Well, what say we go and talk to him?"

Scales wanted to take his shotgun but Jay went to her truck's lock box and came back with a little black leather belly pouch. "Here," she said, "this is a lot easier to haul around."

He unzipped the pouch. Inside was a shiny snub-nosed revolver. He took it out. It had black rubber grips on it.

"S&W Model 60," she said, "stainless steel, Chief's Special. It's loaded with Cor-bon +P jacketed hollowpoints. Kind of a scaled-down version of my service piece, J-frame instead of a K-frame, .38 special instead of .357, holds five instead of six. If you have to shoot it, it will make a big boom and it will kick some. Hold to center of mass and pull the trigger until the threat falls down. There's a speedloader with five more rounds, here in the little front compartment."

"Not legal for me to be carrying it like this, is it?"

"I'll get you a permit, they're easy to come by in this state. Meantime, it's better twelve men trying you than six men carrying you."

"I hear that."

He put the little belly pouch on, adjusted it.

"Let's go find your Dr. Reuben."

State highway 112 was a twisted, curvy road that looped around in hairpins through the trees on the way to Port Angeles. In places, the macadam had washed out and the road one-laned. At one point, a bridge had crumbled and a wooden arch had been hastily constructed over the gap.

Amazing that it would support a log truck.

It wasn't that far but the drive took a while.

Jay drove and Scales tried, unsuccessfully, to raise Reuben, using his cell phone. Reuben wasn't in his office, wasn't answering his private unlisted line at home, nor his own cell phone.

"This unusual?" Jay asked.

He shrugged. "I dunno. I don't call him that often. He wasn't scheduled to work today, so maybe he went to play golf or something."

They passed through Joyce, a wide spot on the road, just west of the Lower Elwha Reservation and about nine or ten miles out of Port Angeles. The sky threatened but the rain held off.

Reuben had a big two-story brick house off Eunice, not far from Webster Park. It wasn't the best neighborhood in the world but the house had been redone and expanded. Probably worth a quarter mil, and if it wasn't a castle, it was nicer than most homes in the area.

Jay pulled the truck to a stop on the street. She and Scales got out and strolled to the front door up a sidewalk bounded by rows of bright and colorful flowers: roses, pansies, something that looked like an iris, something else blue and puffy.

Scales rang the bell. Reuben lived alone, had a housekeeper who came in once a week to do cleaning and laundry, but that was, he said, on Saturdays.

No answer. He rang it again.

"Looks like he's out," Scales said.

"Let's check around back," Jay said.

They walked around the side of the house. There was a detached garage at the end of the driveway and a chest-high wooden gate between the garage and corner of the house, blocking access into the back yard.

Jay peeped into the garage. "He have more than one car?"

"Not that I know of."

He moved to stand next to her, looked into the garage through one of the little oval glass windows. Reuben's big brown Mercedes was there.

"Your boss a hiker?"

"Hardly. He bitched about having to walk across the room to the fridge for another beer."

"Maybe he caught a ride somewhere with somebody." She moved away from the garage to the gate. "Not locked, just a metal latch." She opened the gate.

The back yard was small, had a neatly trimmed lawn and several bushes and medium-sized evergreen trees. A large oak shaded one corner of the lot and there was a hammock in a metal frame squarely in the shade.

A short set of steps led up onto a small wooden deck bounded by wooden rails. A hibachi sat on a stand, a bag of Match Light charcoal behind it. An uncurtained sliding glass door behind the deck revealed a breakfast nook and part of a kitchen.

The door was unlatched. Jay slid it open partway. "Yo, anybody home?"

No answer.

"Maybe we should wait out here," Scales said.

"Probably you're right—uh oh."

"What?"

She shoved the door wide and stepped inside, pulled her revolver as she did so.

What the hell—?

He followed her, unzipped the belly pouch and dug the little gun out.

He saw the hand extended from behind the kitchen counter and a couple of steps revealed the rest of the man lying on the floor.

Reuben.

"I'll check the house," Jay said. "See about him."

She moved off in a crouch, gun leading. Scales tucked his own weapon back into the pouch and hurried to where Reuben lay.

He could have taken his time, though.

Howard P. Reuben, Johns Hopkins, class of '55, was as dead as they got.

SEVENTEEN

Jay went back to where Scales stood next to Reuben. She looked at Scales and he shook his head. History, like she figured when she first saw him lying there. *The dead have a kind of . . . vacant appearance. The body looks the same—but there's nobody home anymore.*

"Looks like somebody went through his desk and closets and dressers. Threw a lot of stuff onto the floor. Any ideas as to what killed him?"

"Somebody cracked his skull. They hit him with something big and heavy. I don't know if that was what did it, they might have smothered him after he was down, but he didn't feel it if they did. The whole back of his head is caved in. That was enough to have done it sooner or later."

Jay blew out a rubbery-lipped sigh. "When?"

Scales shook his head again. "I don't know. He's still warm, blood hasn't settled a whole lot. Not too long. Less than an hour, I'd guess." He took a deep breath. "What now? We gonna walk away from this like the one last night?"

"No. Local cops get here, first thing they'll do is shoe leather the neighborhood. Somebody probably noticed my truck. Might even have jotted down the license number. We have a good reason to be here, since you worked for him. We call it in—we didn't kill him. First, we poke around for a few minutes."

"Won't that disturb the crime scene?"

"We won't leave any fingerprints." She pulled a set of

rubber gloves from her back pocket.

Scales raised an eyebrow.

"For dealing with bleeding suspects or accident victims," she said.

She figured they could squeeze five minutes in before they had to report it. That could be a long time. Could be pretty short, too, especially when you didn't know exactly what it was you were looking for.

All she knew for sure was that this was way over the line to be a coincidence. Too many bodies piled up.

Jay slipped the latex gloves on and looked at Scales. Maybe he had an idea of what they should be hoping to find.

They didn't happen to turn up any terrific evidence, though. Scales shook his head. "I don't see anything that looks like a clue to me."

"Me, neither. Okay, let's call. We'll use the cell phone. Let's get our stories straight. You came to town and as long as you were here, swung by to pick up some drug samples Reuben had for you, you don't know what they were. We got here and found him. End of story."

"Why are we here? Why are you here?"

"You and I, we have a . . . relationship. We were going to spend the day playing hooky from work, have a nice lunch, check into a motel and screw our brains out after you saw Reuben."

"Now there's an idea."

"You should have brought it up sooner. And let's paraphrase that, okay? As far as you know, Reuben didn't have an enemy in the world, you can't understand why anybody would want to kill him. Must have been a burglar looking for drugs."

Scales blew out a big sigh of his own. "Yeah, okay."

"Better give me the belly pouch. I'll put it in the truck. I'll walk you out, I left the phone under the seat."

"Okay. Look nervous when we go out. Run to the truck and make the call in a hurry—in case any neighbors are watching, you should look rattled."

"I am rattled."

"It doesn't show."

They started for the sliding glass door. Scales paused.

"Something?"

"That stack of boxes by the door. Those are drug samples."

"So? We are pretty sure this wasn't some doper did this."

"No, what I mean is, the company name. There on that empty one laying there."

"What about it?"

"They make those vitamins I gave you."

"So . . . ?"

"You remember the dead guy in the Cad, the one who got the traffic ticket?"

"I seem to recall that." Her voice was dry.

"Well, Medical Frontiers was one of the companies located near where he got the ticket. I remember it from the computer map and directory search I did."

"And . . . ?"

"And whoever broke into my house last night swiped all the vitamins I had left. I thought it was odd at the time, they took some heavy drugs, some inhalers and all the vitamins."

"I don't see the connection."

"I'm not sure I do, either, but it seems weird that one of the guys who killed Jimmy Lewis was in the vicinity of the same company who made the vitamins that got ripped off from my house."

"That's a stretch."

"Why is that the only empty box there? I bet it wasn't empty before whoever killed Reuben got here. Look around, he kept a neat house. Even with all the stuff rummaged through, you can see that. He wouldn't leave trash just laying there—unless he didn't have time to toss it out. Or unless somebody else left it there."

"Hmm. Well, we can talk about it. Right now, we should call the police. You ready?"

"Yeah."

It didn't take long for the Port Angeles Police to show up, and a couple of deputies in plainclothes right behind them. One of the deputies knew Jay.

"Officer Hughes," the deputy said. "What do we got here?"

Jay moved off with the deputy who knew her while Scales talked to the city cops. The other deputy went into the house. Scales told it just like he and Jay had agreed.

It was ten minutes before an ambulance arrived, and another thirty minutes before the state police sent somebody with cameras and gear to survey the crime scene.

The cops all seemed satisfied with the story, they didn't hammer at it once they were done. They did split up and begin knocking on neighboring doors.

"Hell of a thing," the deputy who knew Jay said. His name was apparently Berg. "Man like that, just getting to the point where he could enjoy his money, kilt by some psycho."

Scales and Jay murmured their assent.

"I heard you had a guy croak out near the reservation last night," Berg said to Jay.

She shrugged. "One-car traffic accident. Rolled his

truck, probably drunk. Nothing like this."

"Still, two in less than one day. Must be some kind of record for you."

"Hey, I did a few years in L.A.," she said. "Times we had to use a bulldozer to clear away bodies just so we'd have room to park the squad."

Berg and one of the city boys laughed. Cop humor. It was a lot like medical humor, well to the dark side. It helped keep you sane when you were knee-deep in gore.

"Well, I don't think there's anything else we need," Berg said. "You know how it goes. We'll call if we remember anything we forgot to ask."

"Ten-four," Jay said.

After they were in her truck and moving, Scales said, "So now what?"

"You got any of those vitamins left?"

"The bottle I stuck in my kitchen for my personal use."

"Yeah, I got the one you gave me. Haven't tried any of them yet. I think maybe we ought to take a look at them."

"Why?"

"Might be something in them somebody doesn't want us to know about."

"What—heroin? Microfilm? Dinosaur DNA?"

"I don't know. But we've got five dead people connected to this thing that we know of. I don't want to see six. Or be six. Here."

She returned the belly pouch with the gun in it.

At Scales' house, they found the bottle of vitamins in his kitchen. Scales opened the bottle and poured the capsules out onto the counter. They were standard gelatin caps with a brownish powder inside them, all the same. "I don't see—" he began, but she shushed him. Nodded toward the door.

Outside in the yard, Scale said, "What?"

"People have been into your house. Maybe they didn't come to take something but to leave something. I suspect your phone is bugged. Maybe there are other ears stashed away."

"What, a microphone under the toilet seat? Great."

"There's a way to find out. I've got an uncle who is an electronics nut. Unless there are wires leading from your house out into the woods, any bug not rigged to a phone will have to send out a radio signal, or maybe IR, like a TV remote. There are ways to detect them, even if they don't work until they hear a voice."

"You see a lot of that in L.A.?"

"I go to the movies. I'll talk to my uncle. Plus I can maybe do a little background check on Reuben."

"Won't somebody notice you poking around?"

"They'll put it down to cop curiosity if they do. We're all nosy bastards. I was involved, I got a right to know."

"And what am I supposed to do in the meantime?"

"Go on about your business. See your patients, have lunch, work out, whatever. Keep that pouch close to hand."

Scales nodded. He heard that.

After Jay was gone, Scales wandered around the house, feeling like a bacterium under a microscope. Since he didn't have any patients scheduled until the afternoon, he had time to stew in his own paranoia.

But it isn't paranoia if they really are out to get you, is it? Right.

What did this all mean? He went to movies, too; he read Stephen King. That was the part he had to figure out. Figure out the "why" and maybe that would give you the who-where-what-when- and how.

He tried to remember what the tech had told him about Gaines' bloodwork.

Something about very high levels of tumor factor, telomerase. And the AIDS test was weird and he had—what was it?, elevated DHEA. What else? Aptosis? apoptosis? something, residues diminished—whatever the hell that was. Something about a virus infecting some of the leukocytes? Glucocorticoids and dismutase and catalase enzymes—this was all way out of his league.

But it had to mean something.

How could he find out?

Abruptly his niece came to mind. Dana. She was Harvard Medical and in the thick of a residency back where the science was still a required part of her training. Maybe she would know something, or at least could point him in a direction. He wasn't much of a detective, he couldn't do forensics, but he could do research. You didn't have to know everything if you knew where to look it up.

He took the cell phone out into the yard and put in the call. Maybe somebody could overhear that conversation if they wanted, but they'd have to have a scanner set up to decode the digital sig, and somebody monitoring it to do it. Fuck it.

He didn't expect to get her. Doctors seldom answered their own phones and usually didn't return calls until the end of their work day, that was another reason to have a nurse or a good assistant, to screen that stuff. He'd leave a message.

"Dr. Hart," the voice that answered the phone said.

"Dana? This is Rick Scales."

"Uncle Rick! How are you?"

"Just fine. How about you?"

"Fine. Busy. Let me guess—Grandma told you about my

friend from 'Packy-stan?' You calling to tell me to break it off?"

"Not me. Go for it."

"Thanks, Uncle Rick, I thought that would be your advice. If you aren't supposed to convince me to mend my wicked ways, to what do I owe the honor?"

"Well, I've got a little problem."

He kept it brief and as to the point as he could, and he left out all the stuff about killings. That would get to her mother and eventually Dana's mother would tell her mother and then he'd be getting a worried call from Momma wondering what was going on—and why didn't he ever tell her anything?

Dana listened to as much as Scales could remember.

"Offhand, it sounds like some kind of immune system work," she said. "Cancer research, AIDS, RA, like that. It's the sexiest thing going in medical circles right now, everybody and his kid sister wants a piece of it. It's not my field, but I can ask a couple of people I know if you'd like, see if it rings any bells."

"I'd appreciate it, Dana."

"No problem. I'll give you a call if I get something. Say hello to Grandma for me if you talk to her."

"I will."

Scales shut the cell phone off. The cancer remissions, the AIDS patient, that fit with what Dana said.

Oh? Exactly how does it fit, Mr. Wizard? What is it we're talking about here?

Scales frowned at his inner voice. He had no idea.

He looked around. The sky was gathering for another shower and he was alone out in the back. This was crazy, all of it. Nothing like this had ever happened to him before and he didn't like it worth a damn. He wanted to get into his car and drive somewhere far away, find a room and hide in it until whatever the fuck was going on went away.

He shook his head. He didn't want the responsibility for this. He wanted to forget it had ever happened. But—who else was there? Jay, but she didn't really have the medical background to figure it out. And this was all centered around him. If somebody had killed Reuben because he maybe knew something he wasn't supposed to know—and he sure as hell had known something—then they could come for him. He wanted to run. On some level, that was what he had always done when faced with big decisions, run. Taken the path of least resistance, drifted along, a leaf blown by the winds of fate. That's what he wanted to do now.

But he couldn't. He had to know what it all meant. It scared him. Given the circumstances, the weight of the little gun in the belly pouch under his belt was very comforting, even if he hated the need for it. He thought his war was over a long time ago. Maybe wars never really ended until everybody who'd been in them was dead.

Man. Who would have ever expected any of this?

EIGHTEEN

Hughes had a lot of "uncles." Most of them weren't her mother's brothers, but that didn't mean a whole lot. The one who knew about electronics—Uncle Joe—was a cousin a couple of times removed but he was family and family was where you went when you needed help. He was dragging sixty in his wake, had gone steel gray and tan-wrinkled but was still as sharp as a box of needles.

She told him what she needed.

He rummaged in a big drawer in his workshop, came up with a little box about the size of a pack of cigarettes. It was black plastic and had an LCD read-out on it.

"Not much more than a field strength meter," he said, "got a beeper and a diode. Used to call 'em hound dogs. If something is transmitting on a frequency it can pick up, you'll get a peep and a blinking red light and you can run it down with the meter or the sound or light flashes. Closer you get, faster everything will go. Most of the cheap common bugs are FM, you can get 'em with feedback over a radio if you tune it right, but this'll get the ones on un-common bands, too. If they're using IR? That'll have to be line-of-sight, so check outside the house, you can eyeball those."

"Thanks, Uncle Joe."

"No problem, kiddo."

He didn't ask and she was grateful but she had to say something.

"I'll tell you about it after it's done."

He nodded, gave her a ghost of a smile.

Scales' clinic was just ahead. Hughes scanned the road in her mirror as she got closer, glanced to either side of the road. Anything that looked as if it didn't belong there was certainly going to get her attention.

Didn't appear to be any strange cars with gun-wielding drivers in sight.

She'd stopped by her mother's and picked up the vitamins Scales had given her. Mama was out, probably out at the new "resort" playing bingo. Scales was probably right, somehow this was tied to the drug company, though she didn't think it had anything to do with vitamins, unless is was vitamin "C"—the kind that went up your nose.

A lot of illegal drugs got moved by supposedly legitimate companies, the profits were big enough to tempt usually honest people who wouldn't shoplift a Snickers bar. And it wasn't all recreational stuff like weed or coke. The latest wrinkle was a booming business in steroids, from Europe or Mexico, for high school jocks who wanted muscle with less effort. Some nasty side-effects to those things; guys growing tits, women's voices going down two octaves, terrible acne. She remembered a case a while back somewhere in the Midwest where the male half of a bodybuilding couple went into a 'roid rage and started beating his wife. She took a shotgun to him. All that testosterone made a user edgy.

Problem with drugs, legal or otherwise, was that most of them did things other than they were designed to do. She'd been a hippie and had run and played in the chemical fields herself, but she'd been lucky. And all drugs were not created equal. Smoking a joint and raiding the fridge was not the same as snorting coke and taking the family for a drive on the freeway. On the job in L.A. she'd seen a fourteen-year-old bicyclist on speed try to outrun a bus and lose, and an angel-dusted woman knock three male officers twice her size on their cans when they tried to cuff her. You had to be careful with drugs and some people just didn't have the wherewithal to do it.

Must be getting old, she thought. Next thing, I'll be talking about how crappy the music these kids today listen to is . . .

She pulled the truck to a halt next to the garage and stepped out. The scan for trouble was quick but getting to be automatic. Just like being back in SoCal. She thought she'd left that behind when she came back here. Then again, she couldn't really say it was so bad, not just in this moment. It added something that, until she bumped into it, she hadn't really noticed was missing.

Scales heard Jay arrive, checked to make sure it was her. They smiled at each other as she came to the door. She waved a little plastic thing at him. "Electronic Black Flag," she said.

The device in her hand started to beep and flash a little light. She walked to the downstairs phone in the kitchen and the beeps and light got faster. She unplugged the phone and took it out into the garage.

"Got your car keys?"

Scales dug them out of this pocket and gave them to her. She popped the trunk lid of his car and put the phone inside the trunk.

Back in the house they did a room-by-room search. Not counting his cell phone, there were three phones in the house—the one in the kitchen, one in his office, one in the bedroom. All three had something in them that made the device Jay had beep and flash. They put all of them into the trunk. Other than that, the house seemed to be clean—at least the little toy she carried shut up.

Outside in the yard, Jay said, "Uncle Joe says there could be non-radio cameras or listening devices hardwired to a line but they'd probably be connected to the power or phone. They probably didn't have enough time to get that done, but we should check a few places they could reach."

She led him to where the electrical lines went into the meter, to his circuit breaker, and where the little satellite dish connected to his TV. They didn't see any wires that didn't belong.

"Okay, so now we can talk inside."

He blew out a sigh as they went back into the kitchen. He started making coffee. "I have to tell you, this makes me very nervous."

"I hear you. What do you want to do?"

"Do?"

"I mean, we could bundle this up and give it to the feds. I don't much like the way they operate but the FBI isn't stupid. They've got experts who could play with the bugs, take the information we have and put a lot more heat on it than we can."

"If they believe us."

"There's that. What we've got so far is mostly a lot of weird shit and some way out theories."

He watched the water start to drip into the coffee pot. "You have a theory?"

"Well. I don't know about your patients getting well but my guess would be illegal drugs of some kind."

He nodded. "If somebody is feeding my patients something that can cure cancer or AIDS, you can believe it is illegal—or at least not on the FDA's approved list. Do you have that bottle of vitamins I gave you?"

"Right here."

"Let's have a look."

She poured the contents onto the kitchen table. They all looked like the ones in his bottle—no, wait. He reached down, picked up a capsule.

"This one is different," he said.

She took it from him, compared it to another cap. "Looks pretty much the same to me."

"Look at the color. The stuff inside this one is slightly darker."

She held the suspect cap up to the light with a second cap next to it. "Yeah, you're right. What do you think?"

"I think maybe what's inside that isn't vitamins."

"What might it be?"

"I don't have a fucking clue."

They stared at the capsule.

"Question still stands. We could bail out, hand it off to the state and federal boys and let it go. Up to you."

Scales stared at the capsule, then at Jay. "Up to me? Why me? You're the cop."

"It's your toy. You brought it to the party. You want to take it and run or give it away, you have to decide."

Scales inhaled slowly, blew the air out in a pale sigh. Well, here it was. The smart thing to do would be to let go of this whole mess before it burned his hands any more than it already had. Walk away and wait to read about it in the paper. Ten years ago, five, even one, that's what he would have done, no questions. It was what he had always done before. Sometimes he muddled through but most of the time he avoided making major decisions for as long as possible—or ever. Time would wash over it and him and when it had passed, some kind of default was usually achieved. Like a pocket veto, doing nothing had its consequences, even if he didn't have to make the active choice. It had gotten him by.

Maybe that's why you're at such an exalted height at this stage of your life, hey? Backwoods medicine and all by yourself.

Well, not exactly by himself. Jay was an unexpected surprise—

And how long will she stay with you once she realizes you're more crawfish than hero?

He took another deep breath. "Let's not give it up just yet," he said.

NINETEEN

"Okay," Jay said. "We stay with it."

"Pardon me for asking, but—how?"

She said, "You know what Willie Sutton said when they asked him why he robbed banks?"

Scales shook his head.

" 'Because that's where the money is.' "

"Los Angeles," Scales said.

"Yes."

He nodded. He wrapped the altered capsule carefully in several layers of Saran Wrap, tucked it into the watch pocket of his jeans. Maybe they could find some way to analyze it later. Maybe his niece would know somebody.

Maybe he would win the lottery.

TWENTY

"So how do we do this, Ossifer Hughes?"

"You have any patients about to kick off, somebody who won't make it if they show up here and you're gone?"

Scales thought about it for a moment. "No. Nobody who can't make it out to the reservation or to the NP in Sekiu."

"Fine. Pack a bag. Toothbrush, couple pairs of jeans, maybe some shorts—it's hot down there this time of year. I'll do the same and meet you back here in an hour or two. Lock it up and go. Don't leave a note on the door, nothing."

"Probably piss a lot of people off," Scales observed. "But until they get Reuben's death sorted out, nobody is going to fire me."

"I can take an emergency leave," she said. "Tribe won't kick too hard. And while they won't say anything to out-siders, I won't tell them where I'm going."

Scales blew out a breath. "So what then? We catch a flight to L.A.? Ride down on the Coast Starlight?"

"Nope. No planes, trains, buses. No kind of public transportation. We don't want anybody to know where we're going. No matter what they've picked up on their bugs, if we just disappear, they won't be sure where we went. Can you get any cash?"

"I got a few thousand saved, yeah."

"Make a withdrawal," she said, "because I don't have shit in the bank. All you'll have to do is pay for food and gas—I'll get us a ride."

He raised an eyebrow at her, but she shook her head. "Pack. I'll explain when I get back."

It didn't take him long to finish packing. He threw five days worth of clothes and toiletries into a bright red nylon bag he'd bought at Costco a few years back. As an after-thought, he zipped his .22 target pistol into a gun rug and packed it and four boxes of CCI MiniMag ammo among the T-shirts and socks. He still had Jay's little snubnose .38 in the belly pouch but given everything that had happened, he felt better having the second gun. And felt strange that he felt better.

He considered taking his shotgun. He worried about leaving his computer behind but it wasn't really portable. Too bad he hadn't gotten a PowerBook and a dock.

Yeah. Too bad he *hadn't* won the lottery, too.

It took only a few minutes to get ready, and he had time to sit and think while he waited for Jay.

On the one hand, this felt surreal and—not to put too fine a point on it—stupid. To take off, leave his job, his re-sponsibilities, his life, such that it had been, just like that— well, that didn't seem very bright.

On the other hand, people had broken into his house, bugged his phones and shot at him, not to mention all the shit going on with his patients, plus the killings and all. He didn't think things were going to drop back to idle and just go away. Not unless he did something. And in a strange way, he felt better than he had in years, despite the turmoil. Right or wrong, at least he had made a decision.

Mama was very unhappy. Hughes listened to her express the unhappiness as she packed her old duffel, filling it with jeans, shorts, and a pair of nice slacks. Even a cotton dress and her one pair of heels, two-inchers. Have to iron it before she could wear it, though.

"—don't like this at all, Jasmine. What is it you can't tell your own mother? Are you running off to get married to this doctor? It's too soon for that."

Hughes tossed an unopened pair of panty hose into the bag. God, she had brought those back from L.A., hadn't had occasion to wear them in all that time. She hoped they hadn't rotted or something.

"Because there's nothing you could say that I couldn't understand."

Hughes found her favorite running shoes, added them to the collection. Three pairs of white socks.

"Jasmine?"

She turned to face her mother. "Listen, Mama, I'm not running off to get married, I didn't do anything illegal, and I can't tell you where I'm going. All I can say is, it is police business."

"Jimmy Lewis and those casino people in the Cadillac? Or Doctor Reuben?"

Hughes sighed. "Yes, Mama, it has to do with them. I'm on an undercover job, okay? Nobody can know about it."

"Hmm. Why didn't you just say that in the first place?"

"I would have, if you hadn't started hammering me with questions so I couldn't get a word in edgewise."

Mama shook her head. "You children don't have no respect for your elders. The old ways are gone."

It was Hughes' turn to shake her head. "Of course they're gone. They always go, to make room for the new ways. Harpooning whales, buggy whips, typewriters, those have been replaced by other things."

"Not necessarily better," Mama said.

"No, not necessarily better. But time doesn't stop in a

nice comfortable place. Great-grandma didn't want a telephone, wouldn't have one in her house, but that didn't make phones go away. I respect you, Mama, I always have, you did a good job with us girls."

"Yeah?"

"Yes, Mama. And I love you. It's okay."

Her mother gave her a small grin. "Well, I tried."

"You did fine."

Hughes turned back to her packing. Wait until Mama figured out that she had left town with Rick Scales. She'd have a fit, no matter how much she wanted her daughter to find a nice man and settle down. When Hughes got back, she'd be hearing about it for a long time.

When she got back.

PART TWO

Ontogeny

TWENTY-ONE

Port Townsend, Washington, was a scenic little burg on the other end of the Olympic Peninsula from Neah Bay. It was slantwise across the Sound from Seattle, forty or fifty air-miles, a couple hours away by ferry. In the off-season, there was a paper mill, now owned by some German company, that was the town's mainstay. During the summers, tourists poured in and quadrupled the town's population, to snap pictures of the stately and restored Victorian commercial buildings and homes, to stay at Fort Warden or the other parks, to catch the ferry to Whidbey or Keystone. Bed and Breakfast places did big business.

The town had peaked as a major shipping port in the last century; then Seattle got the railroad and Port Townsend became a dwindling echo of itself. There was a writers' conference every summer, a wooden boat show and several excellent restaurants. The locals likened the look of the place to San Francisco in the 1890's, though scaled down considerably. Hollywood had filmed most of *Officer and a Gentleman* there a few years back. There were a lot of loggers in the area. In the seventies, herds of dope-fogged hippies migrating north had to stop here when they hit water. Many of them also stuck around, selling sand-cast candles and health food and leather goods. Until he died, the guy who wrote *Dune* had lived there in the summers—though he wintered in Hawaii.

Scales drove and listened as Jay gave him the verbal tour of their destination.

And the reason they were going to Port Townsend?

Jay had an uncle there.

They took 101 to 20 and headed north. Jay gave him directions as they got into the town proper, and they drove past a mill belching smelly smoke and down a strip that looked a lot like Disneyland's Main Street USA. It was almost noon.

"That's the ferry dock, there's the police department, city hall. Over across the street, that little cafe has a great breakfast. Turn left. My uncle is out on the point, other side of the marina."

Scales obeyed, looked at the motor- and sailboats moored in the small marina. Couple of them was pretty impressive. The road was narrow. There was a boat-builder and a sailmaker's shop on the left.

"Hang a right at the next corner."

He saw a building marked "Wooden Boat Foundation" and a dry dock to his left and several long two-story whitewashed wooden buildings ahead and to the right. There was a trailer/RV park across the road from the buildings.

"Point Hudson," Jay said. "Turn right."

There was water to their left and ahead. They cruised slowly along the edge of the resort.

"That trailer, over there," Jay said. "That's my uncle's. Park in the gravel."

Scales parked his car, shut it off. They got out and walked to the trailer. It was a single-wide, tan with gray trim. Flowers had been planted along the sides and it was on a foundation and not going anywhere without some deconstruction. They knocked on the door. A dog barked inside. Big dog, from its voice.

Jay's uncle appeared to be about seventy-five, tanned and seamed like an old pair of boots. He wore a pale green cowboy shirt with pearl snaps, a bolo tie with a big chunk of amber for a slide, stovepipe jeans and Nike running shoes. His face lit in a big grin when he saw Jay.

"Little Puke!"

They hugged, and the old man said to Scales, "She used to throw up on me every time I saw her as a baby."

"Twice, Uncle John. Two times, my mother says."

They both laughed.

"This is Rick Scales. Rick, John Temper, the second-worst blackjack player in the Western Hemisphere."

The old man laughed again. "Come in."

The trailer was neat, though there were a lot of small china statuettes of dogs and horses and blue-glass bottles and vases on homemade fir shelves lining the walls. A German Shepherd on a throw-rug raised her head long enough to look at Scales and Jay, then yawned and went back to sleep. Scales could almost read the dog's mind: *Hey, I barked, I warned you, that's my job—it's up to you now.* They'd always had dogs and cats on the ranch growing up. He liked them.

Three windows that looked as if they had been made much larger than the originals looked out at the water.

"You hungry? I was about to walk over to the Shanghai for lunch."

"Sounds good," Jay said.

The dog opened her eyes as they left, made a snorting sound.

"Katie. You guard the house and I'll bring you back an egg roll."

The dog snorted again, closed her eyes.

They followed the old man out and along the road toward one of the wooden buildings that backed up to the marina. Jay and John talked about family, who they'd seen,

189

who was traveling, who had died. They climbed a short flight of steps onto a long porch under an overhang and went into the Chinese restaurant.

The woman behind the register greeted John and showed them to a table. The place was about half full of lunch patrons. A Chinese boy of fifteen sat at the table next to theirs, cutting the ends off a mound of what looked like sugar pea pods on a spread-out newspaper. He used a big semicircular ulu knife, rolling it with smooth wrist action, decapitating the snow peas.

"Everything is good here," Jay said. "Best Chinese food west of Seattle—until you get to China."

John Temper ordered a beer and Jay and Scales joined him.

After the beer came and the old man had drained two good sips, he smiled at Jay. "What can I do for you, little one?"

"We had some trouble out on the reservation, Uncle."

He sipped the beer. "I heard. Bad business, Jerry's sick grandson in that car trunk, those dead white boys. Evil things."

"Rick and I are going to catch those responsible. We need to borrow your moving house."

The old man smiled. "Sure. It's parked over in the dry dock. We'll eat, I'll get you the keys."

They ordered, each a different dish. Shrimp, chicken, fish. You had a choice of how hot you wanted it. As promised, the food was delicious. Medium hot was enough to bring a flushed face, tears and clear sinuses all the way to Scales' medulla oblongata. He ordered another beer.

The old man watched him eat. Smiled. "You two are connected," he said. He nodded. "Deep, solid. Serious."

Scales said, "You can tell by looking?"

"Ah, yes, us old Indians, we got wisdom, we know things." He tapped the side of his head. "Psychic. Just like on the infomercials."

"Bullshit," Jay said. "You've been talking to Mama."

The old man smiled. "Well, yes, that too. You gonna settle down with this one? Make your Mama happy?"

Jay smiled. Was she blushing? Dark as she was, it was hard to tell. "Maybe," she said.

Her uncle looked at Scales. "What about it, cowboy? You going to do the right thing by my grand-niece?"

Scales smiled around the heat of the food. "Yessir. If she'll let me."

"We'll see," Jay said.

The RV was about a twenty-four footer, Scales judged, and not more than a year or two old. A class-A motor home, cab and interior continuous.

Jay led him to the door, opened it with the key the old man had given her. They climbed inside.

"Very nice," he said.

"Uncle John is the second-worst blackjack player in the Western Hemisphere. The worst player used to own this. Uncle John calls this the 'Twenty Two.' "

"Like Travis McGee's boat? The 'Busted Flush'?"

She looked at him. "You read those?"

"Sure."

She nodded. "Guy who lost this didn't miss it. Hal Fairweather, big oil millionaire from Alaska. He and Uncle John go way back, were Marines in the Pacific together, Iwo Jima, like that. John saved his butt a couple of times during the war. John wouldn't take a dime for saving his life, so Hal lets him win at blackjack."

Inside, the RV had all the comforts of home. The bedroom in back sported a big bed and closet space, a color TV mounted on the wall. The bathroom had a flush toilet, a shower stall and sink. There was a kitchen with a four-burner propane stove, a microwave oven, a sink and more cabinet space, a small refrigerator. The couch behind the driver's side folded out into a bed and the dining nook table next to the sink could be dropped down level with the benches to make another bed.

"Ever played with one of these before?" she asked.

"My father-in-law had one about this size," he said. "My ex and I used to take it 'camping' every now and then."

"Yeah, really roughing it," she said. "Rolling along the interstate with the cruise control and the air turned on—'Honey, while you're up, would you get me a Häagen Dazs bar from the freezer?' "

They smiled at each other.

"It makes practical sense in this situation," she said. "We can take two or three days to toodle on down to L.A. Nobody can watch every vehicle on I-5, we won't need to stay in hotels or eat in restaurants, we can stock up on food before we go and just stop for gas. Stay in RV parks or state campgrounds. Have a place to stay when we get there."

Scales nodded. He had withdrawn four thousand dollars in cash from his bank account, half of which he had given to Jay to hold. This sucker would guzzle gas, probably get eight or nine miles to the gallon, but it was cheaper than flying or taking the train even so. Even with food and gas and plug-in at campsites, they'd only spend maybe four, five hundred bucks. And be anonymous, no paper trail.

"Okay, what now?"

"We crank it up, drive over to the Safeway and buy supplies, then roll."

"Sounds like a plan," he said.

★ ★ ★ ★ ★

Scales was as good at picking out useful groceries as Hughes was, she noted, though he did have a tendency to too much red meat. And at one point, she saw him reading the side of a package of light potato chips. She laughed.

"What?"

"Worried about how healthy your junk food is? Come on."

"Ah, well, you know, a man my age has to watch it."

"More preservatives the better, I'd think," she said.

It took about half an hour for them to get enough stuff for a week or so in the RV. Her weakness was cookies. Whenever she traveled, she always ate store-bought cookies. She bought Nutter Butters, Devil's Food cakes and Brown-edged Lemon Thins.

With condiments and paper towels and toilet paper and all, it came to four bags worth. Scales pushed the shopping cart toward the RV, parked down at the end of the lot. Halfway there, he took four or five running steps and stepped up onto the back of the basket, riding along like a kid.

She probably would have married him right that minute if he'd asked. She laughed.

The grocery basked slowed to a halt and Scales hopped off. Turned to look at her.

"You seem to be in a good mood," she said.

"Why the hell not? I'm going on vacation."

"Not exactly."

"Between here and Los Angeles it is. Got a big fine mobile home, food, drink and a smart, beautiful woman. Why shouldn't I be in a good mood? It doesn't get any better than this."

She shook her head.

He lifted his hands, put them on the sides of his mouth, leaned his head back a little. What—?

He did the Tarzan yell, a loud yodel. Pretty good imitation.

When he was done, he grinned at her again.

"You're crazy, you know that?"

"Yeah. I know. But listen, I have to tell you, I have never felt better. Despite all the shit going down, I feel great, you know?"

She shook her head at him. Why the hell not? Might as well enjoy the honeymoon while it lasted, right?

TWENTY-TWO

As soon as they got out away from the cool breezes wafting off the narrowed portion of Puget Sound known as Hood Canal, Scales and Jay discovered that summer was still happening in the rest of the state of Washington. As they approached Olympia around four in the afternoon it was ninety-two degrees, according to a local bank's time and temp display. Not a cloud in the hard blue sky. Pedestrians and those with all the windows rolled down in their cars looked to be about half-cooked when he passed them.

Inside sixty or eighty thousand dollars' worth of air conditioned recreational vehicle, it was a pleasant seventy-two and not in the least uncomfortable. And probably costing a gallon of gas every seven or eight miles, not cheap at current pump prices. Thanks to that asshole in the White House . . .

Scales drove. There were outside rear view mirrors, plus a nice view through the big window back in the bedroom. There was also a black and white television camera mounted on the back of the RV, aimed at the road. The monitor was inset under the dashboard by his right knee. That way he could see if anybody was lurking next to the rear bumper. They had a fridge full of food and stuff packed into the cabinets but it didn't seem to be rattling around too much. Amazing.

Jay sat in the passenger's seat, a bucket captain's-chair like his own, the carpeted flat-topped hump of the motor cover between them.

"I might could get used to this," he said.

"My uncle tells a story," she said, "about why he doesn't drive this thing very much. You saw how quick he was to let us have it?"

"Yeah?"

"Says he's cruising along somewhere in Nevada, on his way back from Las Vegas. Long straight stretch of level road, late at night, no traffic. He's got the CD player on, the cruise control running. His girlfriend, Wanda—she comes and goes, I believe she is in France for a couple of weeks currently—is on the couch reading. He doesn't want to bother her, so he gets up, goes to the fridge, gets a beer. Opens it, stands there smiling at her. She glances up, sees him, looks horrified. Yells, 'Who's driving this fucker?' Until she said that, it never occurred to him there was a problem."

Scales laughed. "My father-in-law used to tell a version of the same story."

"You can see why. You can get so comfortable you kind of forget you're the pilot."

"Yeah. Sure beats dragging a U-haul trailer across New Mexico in a '63 Ford at forty miles an hour with your wife and daughters in the middle of August, though. Need to go pee? Just amble on down the hall to the bathroom while your partner takes the wheel. Wonder what the poor folks are doing?"

"Yeah. I guess being rich has its drawbacks," she said, "but it might be fun finding out what they are."

The rush hour traffic thickened as they rolled past the old Olympia Brewery off to their left.

Jay nodded at the place. "I took the tour there a long time ago. Pretty interesting. You could eat off the floor, it's spotlessly clean, they don't want anything contaminating the hops or yeasts or whatever. That's where I learned only a savage drinks beer from a bottle."

"Sounds like fun."

They were silent for a while as he negotiated the slowing traffic on I-5. There were a lot of things she could show him, he didn't doubt it. If she would.

"There are rest stops and campgrounds along here, but we can probably make it almost to the California border in another six or seven hours. Past Portland, Salem and Eugene, anyway. You get tired, I'll drive and you can go sack out."

"How about I put it on autopilot and we both go back to the bedroom?"

"I don't think so."

There was a pause, then Jay said, "I've been thinking about something. It's not my area of expertise, but that capsule we found—what do you think it is?"

He shook his head. "I don't know." He'd told her about his niece, about trying to get background on the information he'd learned from the tech at the destroyed lab. He hadn't told her he had taken some of the vitamins and that if one of those strange caps had been in the bottle, it was no longer there when he'd checked the remainder.

If there had been one in his bottle, then he had swallowed it and whatever it was designed to do, it had done it—or maybe still was doing it to him.

The thought was sobering. Still, he felt good, better than he had in a while. If the cap had anything to do with that, maybe it wasn't so bad. And maybe there would be a price to pay for feeling good later, but if there was, he couldn't do anything about it now. He had a lot of questions, and on one level, if the answers were bad, he didn't want to know what they were.

★ ★ ★ ★ ★

Hughes relaxed in the comfortable chair and watched Scales drive. Crazy as it all was, she still enjoyed being here with this man. She'd never lasted long past the honeymoon with a man before—or a woman either, if you counted that mushroom week in Mexico with Sylvia the bisexual back during the hippie road days. It might be different this time. Maybe after the bright flash died down, there might be at least a warm glow left. She could ride it along and see.

South of Eugene a few hours later, Hughes drove and Scales dozed in the passenger seat. She tried to get him to go to the back to use the bed but he shook his head. "I'll wait until we stop. Guess I'm like my ex-wife's dog."

She raised an eyebrow at him.

"Back when we were together and using her father's RV, my wife had a dog. Little terrier mix, some poodle, like that. We figured the dog would love all the room, not being cooped up in the back seat of a car with the two girls. Thought he'd crawl under the bed or the table or something. No. The rattles or the shakes or whatever scared him. Never sat anyplace but in the lap of whoever was driving or riding shotgun as long as we were moving. Even my wife couldn't coax him into the back. Once we stopped, he was fine, but rolling, he sat up front."

"I wouldn't think a few rattles would scare you," she said. "You sure it isn't my driving?"

He shrugged. "I don't much like letting the Delta pilot fly the plane when I'm on it, either. Not that I could do anything if I was up there with him, but there's this illusion of control if you're close to the wheel."

She laughed.

* * * * *

It was dark when they pulled into a rest stop not far from Ashland, Oregon and parked. They got out, stretched, walked to the stop's restroom. No point in filling up their wastewater tanks any sooner than they had to.

Scales relieved himself at the urinal. There were mirrors, but made from what looked like stainless steel. The mirrors were dented and scratched somewhat but usable. As he turned away from the urinal, he caught a reflection of somebody coming in. Or so he thought. After a few seconds, nobody arrived.

He got a sudden cold feeling in the pit of his stomach.

He took a deep breath, let it out slowly. Nerves, that's all it was. Still, he wished he'd brought the little revolver in the belly pouch. It was back in the RV, next to the passenger seat. Wasn't much point in having a gun if you didn't have it when you needed it.

He lingered for a few minutes until a trio of noisy teenagers came into the restroom. He pretended to pee until they started to leave, then followed them out.

He didn't see anybody waiting for him except Jay.

"I was beginning to worry about you," she said. "Thought maybe you'd had a heart-attack on the toilet or something. We used to see a lot of that in L.A. Old man on a pot strained too hard, croaked."

"I'm not that old."

She caught something in his voice. "Something wrong?"

He shook his head. "No. Not really. I thought I somebody was hanging around outside the restroom door."

"I didn't see anybody," she said. "Bunch of kids went in while you were inside."

He nodded. "Getting really paranoid."

"I don't see how anybody could have followed us," she

said, "but it wouldn't hurt to pay attention to our surroundings anyhow."

Back in the RV, they decided to break and eat. They fixed sandwiches, opened a bag of chips and a couple of cans of Coke. Sat at the table in front of the window. It was still pushing ninety outside even after dark, though it was a lot less humid than it had been further north. There were a dozen cars, three other RVs and a couple of trucks parked in the rest stop's well-lit lot.

"I don't think you're supposed to camp here," she said, "but the state boys probably won't bother us if we want to. Better to be sleeping here than at the wheel on the interstate."

Scales chewed on his sandwich, swallowed. "I could do that."

"We could take a shower. Try out the bed," she said.

"Yeah, I could definitely do that."

They smiled at each other.

They were both a little nervous about bouncing around too much in the RV, but they were able to restrain themselves enough for a long and slow rock. Banked a little, but still a lot of heat coming from that fire.

Afterward, they lay on top of the covers. Jay dozed off. He waited until she was breathing deep and slow, then slid carefully off the bed and padded to the RV's bathroom. It was tiny and with the door closed, not much room inside. A vent overhead allowed a cooling breeze inside.

He was on his way back to bed when he spotted somebody sitting in a car not far away, smoking a cigarette. The inside of the RV was dark, all the lights out, as was the interior of the car, a new Ford Taurus. He couldn't make out anything about the smoker but the glowing orange coal of the cigarette as it brightened and dimmed.

Scales felt an immediate stab of worry.

Jesus, Rick, it's just some guy pulled off into the rest stop having a smoke. Maybe going to catch a couple hours of sleep before he gets back on the road to wherever he's going. You really are getting paranoid.

But—what if it isn't just some guy on vacation stopping to use the john? What if it is one of the bad guys?

Scales continued to watch the smoker. The cigarette's coal pulsed, moved to the window and glowed brighter again as ash was flicked away. One more drag, then the smoker thumped the butt into the night, a small orange meteorite that arced, hit the concrete and splashed up a shower of tiny sparks.

So what are you going to do, Rick? Squat here all night watching the car?

He shook his head. Fuck this. He started back for bed and the warmth of the woman lying there.

The Taurus's door opened. The dome light didn't go on. A stray glint of light from a passing truck washed over the figure who alighted from the car. Scales got a quick look at the man's face. He realized he'd seen him before and it took a few seconds for him to remember where:

The man in the cafe on the reservation, the one with the four-part laugh trying to get something going with the local boys.

What was he doing here? And why was he walking toward the RV?

No good reason Scales could see.

TWENTY-THREE

For a second, Scales froze. He didn't see a gun or anything in the short-haired man's hand, but that didn't mean anything. The guy could have one tucked into his back pocket. He wore a long-sleeved shirt with the sleeves rolled up and the tails out over dark pants. He could have an arsenal tucked into his belt.

Jay. He needed to wake Jay up.

Even as he hurried toward the bed, his male I-can-handle-this voice kicked in. Wake her up? A woman?

A woman cop with a bigger gun than he had and a demonstrated ability to stand tall when things got dicey. Damn straight.

"Jay. We got company."

She came out of sleep fast. "What?"

"There's a guy heading toward the RV, he's been sitting in a car watching us. I saw him in Art's the morning we found the Cadillac in the Sound."

She was up and struggling into her pants. "Is the side door locked?"

"Yes."

"Can he see the door on the driver's side?"

"I don't think so."

"Go out that way, circle out and around, see if you can come up behind him." She pulled a T-shirt on over her head, reached down for her gun where it lay holstered next to the bed.

"Put some clothes on."

Scales was aware that he was naked and was already reaching for a pair of shorts. He pulled them on, grabbed the fanny pack with the little revolver in it, and headed for the front of the RV.

"Scales, be careful. Maybe he just wants to piss on our tires or something. Don't shoot, watch him, okay? No heroics, unless he points a weapon at you. Once you're in place, wait for my signal before you do anything. I'll yell out your name."

"I hear you." He duck-walked past the blinds, low, and made it to the curtain that blocked the driver's compartment off from the rest of vehicle. He peeped through the curtains, didn't see anybody, slipped through and into the driver's chair. Did a dome light go on when you opened the door? He didn't remember. He found the light control for the overhead lamp, twisted it to off. Unlocked the door and eased the handle up. No light.

Scales pushed the door open slowly, stuck his head out and glanced toward the rear of the RV. Nobody. He climbed out, eased the door closed softly, kept the handle engaged so the lock wouldn't make any noise.

He angled away from the RV, keeping it between himself and the Taurus until he made it to the dry brown stubble of grass. There were some evergreen shrubs and bushes there, and he used them for cover. The lights ended at the concrete apron but dressed only in shorts, he felt fairly conspicuous. He didn't have any tan, he was ghostly pale in the reflected light. He should have pulled on a dark shirt and long pants.

Why not a ninja outfit, as long as we're wishing?

He crouched low and moved as quickly as he dared.

Hughes held the .357 in her right hand, her flashlight in her left, thumb on the button ready to click it on. She crouched in the bathroom and watched the RV's side door. The floor was cool under her bare feet.

She heard a scratching that seemed very loud in the stillness. Somebody was fiddling with the lock. Probably trying to pick it, and it wouldn't take long if he knew what he was doing—there was a deadbolt but it was a standard cheapo model more for show than anything.

If the guy came in and was unarmed, she had him. If he had a gun out, she'd probably have to cook him. She hoped she didn't have to do that, she didn't want to deal with either the shooting or the aftermath, but she had to assume the worst. If this guy knew who they were, he wasn't a sneak thief dropping by to swipe the flatware.

At less than twenty feet if he held a piece ready, telling him to freeze might get her killed. Bad guys sometimes thought they were faster than a gun aimed at them. They usually weren't—but when it got down to split seconds, they didn't have to be. If she gave him warning, he might be able to get a shot off even if she fired first. There wasn't a lot of satisfaction in knowing that your bullet hit the bad guy a half second before his plowed into you. If you opened up first, the noise and shock should give you an advantage. Theoretically.

Her gun had come out of the holster three dozen times on the job in L.A., but she'd only had to fire it twice. She had shot two people. Both times they had been armed. Both times they had unloaded in her direction first. They'd missed. She hadn't. The first shooter had been a seventeen-year-old gangster using a cheap .25 and probably it was the first time he'd ever fired the pistol. His initial shot, it was determined later, hit the wall behind Hughes, a foot over her head. His second and third shots had been higher still. He hadn't gotten a fourth off before Hughes drilled him dead center—a lung shot—and dropped him. He survived, was convicted of a drive-by murder and filed a civil suit against her and the city, which he also lost.

She started wearing her vest after that, summer or not.

The second shooting had been a drunken wife-beater. He had a deer rifle and Hughes' vest would not have even slowed the jacketed slug; fortunately, his aim was fogged by eight bottles of Pabst Blue Ribbon. He missed her and punched a hole in the squad's rear doors, through and through. Her partner had fired and Hughes had seen the man take two hits before she added two of her own. Her partner's shots were the killing wounds, her two hit the guy in the pelvis and broke it.

She had seen a fellow officer yell at a doped-up Vietnam vet to drop his weapon and had watched in that terrible adrenaline-powered slow motion as the vet capped the cop four times, killing him, before somebody shotgunned the killer and took him down. You weren't supposed to fire without warning if you were a cop. You were supposed to identify yourself and order the man with a gun to put it down. As far as Hughes was concerned, she had used up her let-them-shoot-and-miss luck. If somebody pointed a weapon in her general direction, all bets were off.

He wasn't a locksmith, whoever he was. The lock was rattling and clicking pretty loud but the door was still securely closed. She wondered if Scales had had enough time to get around behind the guy. She also wondered if the man at the door had any friends around.

Damn, she should have warned Scales to look out for others.

Scales moved across the parking lot, now keeping the Taurus between him and the RV. He had his hand on the gun inside the unzipped belly pouch. It might have looked strange if any of the others at the stop saw him, some guy in nothing but shorts ambling across the parking lot with a black leather bag in his hands, but not as strange as it would if he had the little revolver out and glittery in the sodium lamps' yellow glow. He saw a figure crouched down by the RV's side door, working on the lock.

It occurred to him as he was working his way barefoot across the still-warm concrete and getting close to the Taurus that the crew-cut sneaker might have a partner. Scales looked around in sudden alarm, but didn't see any other watchers. The Taurus was empty, he was close enough to see that. Just to be sure when he reached the vehicle, he looked at the seats and the floor in back. Nobody lying down there.

He crouched down behind the car, scooted to the front end and peered over the hood.

Crewcut was busy with the lock. He paused and looked around, to see if anybody was about. Scales ducked. Waited a few seconds, then peeped over the hood again. Crewcut continued to work the lock.

Fifteen, sixteen yards, Scales figured. He could drive tacks at that distance with his target pistol but with the rudimentary sights on the Smith .38, he wouldn't get that kind of accuracy. Still, if he took his time and got lined up right, he should be able to hit a spot the size of his hand, certainly a head shot was doable if it came to it. Single-action, anyway. Double-action was harder and he hadn't done much of that since he'd learned with his brother back in Texas. Whatever, he could make a lot of noise and smoke and could hit the guy somewhere.

He shook his head, took a deep breath. Here he was, crouched behind a car in a rest stop next to an interstate highway considering where he was going to shoot a man. Unbelievable.

He let the air out, noticed how ragged his breathing was, tried to slow it and calm himself. Took another deep breath, held it a second, let it go. Another one. He felt a little better, a little less nervous as the oxygen flowed into him. He buckled the belly pouch on, slid it on front of himself, pulled the Smith out and held it down between himself and the car where nobody could see it. If anybody spotted him, it would probably look as if he were trying to steal the hubcap on the front wheel. He grinned at that thought.

His one experience with ripping off hubcaps had been when he'd been sixteen. He and three of his buddies, Jimmy Chalk, Steve Saunders and Larry Hollister had gone to a big bowling alley in Amarillo one hot August Saturday night. Hubcaps were still a big part of the street rod scene in the sixties and seventies—moons, spinners, wire wheels— and a set on any fast car in town might have been stolen five or six times before they got where they were. He and Larry had kept a lookout while Chalk and Saunders took their big screwdrivers and skulked into the parking lot. Saunders came back in five minutes with a set of Oldsmobile fake-wires. After ten minutes when Chalk hadn't returned, they went looking for him.

Scales and Hollister spotted Chalk. He was squatting next to an Amarillo Police car, prying the right rear hubcap free. He already had the other three caps done, they were on the concrete next to him.

Hollister spewed a loud stage-whisper: "Chalk, you crazy motherfucker, what the fuck are you doing?"

Chalk turned and grinned at them.

The hubcaps themselves were worthless, standard Detroit throwaways, but being able to say you'd swiped them from a cop car, that meant something.

Of course, at that precise moment, the two cops who belonged to the car came out of the bowling alley with cups of coffee, spotted Chalk and his screwdriver and started yelling.

Scales and Hollister headed for the trees. Scales was so scared he could never remember the actual flight; the next time he recalled, he was half a mile away in a park, trying to catch his breath. He stayed there for an hour, crouched under a big flowering bush before he worked up enough nerve to go back to his brother's borrowed pick up.

The cops were long gone and they hadn't caught any of the would-be teenaged thieves, who'd all gotten away and managed to catch rides home. That pretty much ended Scales' career in crime—

Until now.

As he watched the man fiddling with the lock on the RV, Scales realized that if Crewcut pulled a gun and threatened Jay, Scales would drop the hammer on him. He'd shoot him in the back or the head and never think twice.

Man, his life sure had changed.

Hughes took another deep breath, let it out slowly. Gripped the smooth wood of her revolver, re-gripped it, and waited.

The lock clicked. Finally managed to pick it. The knob turned, slowly, and the door opened a crack, then slowly opened wider. The man in the doorway was late-forties, early fifties, short gray hair. The hand on the door was empty and when he eased inside, she couldn't see his other hand. Was he holding a gun? She couldn't smoke him if he was unarmed. Not if he just might have a gun.

The man came in, crouched low.

Damnit, she couldn't see his other hand—!

★ ★ ★ ★ ★

Scales watched Crewcut open the door and start into the RV. He felt a moment of panic. What now? He was supposed to stay here and watch, wait for Jay's signal, but what good could he do fifteen yards away? If he couldn't even see the guy?

He took a deep breath, crawled around the front of the Taurus, and started after Crewcut, moving in a low crouch, knees bent, the balls of his feet losing skin on the rough concrete.

Hughes waited until the guy got all the way inside, still squatting so she couldn't see his right hand. She thumbed the button of her flashlight. The beam was bright, even though she was expecting it, and it splashed over the man's face. He squinted, blinded, leaned back. Swung his right hand up—

Scales was almost on top of Crewcut when the light hit the man and he backed a little way out of the doorway. There was a long moment, time dilated and spread over Scales in slow waves, as it had during firefights in Vietnam, as it had once in a traffic accident, as it had when the man with the shotgun had come at him in Neah Bay. Scales was moving, fast as he could, and he wasn't sure of what he was going to do until he did it—

He bought his right hand down from a great height like a hammer and smashed the butt of the Smith into the top of Crewcut's head.

Crewcut grunted and collapsed.

A gun fell from his hand, something black in the dim light, and clattered on the RV's step, then bounced onto the rest stop's parking lot. It made a plastic sound, not metal.

"Scales?"

"Yeah, yeah, yeah, it's me!" Scales blurted, staccato.

Crewcut had fallen into a full squat, jammed against the sink support. He was kind of wedged there, knees up by his ears, one arm caught between his body and the sink support, the other out flung and partially behind him. He was semiconscious, moaning over and over: "Unh-unh-unh-unh!"

"Help me get him inside," Jay said.

She pulled while Scales pushed and it only took a couple of seconds to stretch Crewcut out face down on the rug. The butt of the Smith had split the scalp about a centimeter and the little wound bled all out of proportion to its size. He was going to have a goose egg knot and maybe a fracture, probably a concussion.

"Ow, ow, shit, shit, shit!"

Jay had her gun pointed at Crewcut's face when he rolled over and tried to sit up. Blood ran down his forehead and into the inner corner of his left eye, dripped off the end of his nose.

"Very slowly," she said. "Or you go back down permanently."

Scales grabbed a clean dish towel and tossed it at Crewcut. "Here, press this against the cut." To Jay, he said, "There's a gun on the ground outside."

He thought about that for a second. As opposed to the ground inside?

She knew what he meant. "Better bring it in. Wouldn't want some late night stroller to see it."

Scales opened the door, stepped out, picked up the gun. It was plastic. A Glock. He stepped back inside.

Crewcut sat with his knees pulled up to his chest, pressed the dish towel against the top of his head with one hand, wiped blood from his face with the other hand.

"Turn on a light, okay?" Jay said.

Scales nodded. Clicked on one of the little overheads. Jay clicked the flashlight off.

"I think maybe you need to talk to us, friend," she said.

Despite his predicament, Crewcut smiled. "Oops. Wrong house. Sorry. I thought you were somebody else."

"You always go calling with a Glock in your hand?"

"It's a dangerous world. Never know who you might run into."

"So that's how it's gonna be?"

He smiled at Jay again. "That's how it's gonna be."

"On your feet and assume the position."

He knew what she was talking about. He leaned against the wall, legs spread wide, hands up and also spread wide.

Jay nodded at Scales. "Cover him."

Scales pointed the Smith at Crewcut's spine.

She leaned in, patted the man down.

The search produced keys, a wallet, a money clip, a penknife and a spare magazine for the Glock.

"My cuffs are by the bed," she said to Scales.

"My, my," Crewcut said. "What a fun time you must have had."

"Shut up. Would you get them, Rick?"

Scales did so. Jay cuffed Crewcut's hands behind him, made him sit on the floor again. The bleeding from his scalp had stopped but he had a line of partially-dried blood running from his hairline to his eyebrow.

The new pigskin wallet held a California driver's license in the name of "John Johnson" and a matching American Express card. There were eight five-dollar-bills and ten ones and nothing else. The money clip had two thousand in hundreds in it. The keys were to the rented Taurus. The pocketknife was a little Swiss Army model, with a toothpick and tweezers built in. The spare Glock magazine held a bunch of 9mm cartridges, as did the magazine in the Glock.

"I don't suppose you have any truth serum in your medical bag?" Jay asked.

Scales shook his head.

"Mr. Johnson here is a pro—though not a very good one, hey?—and my guess is the license and credit card are fake and there's nothing in the car we can use, either. And he doesn't seem disposed to tell us what we want to know."

"I do have a scalpel in my bag."

Crewcut laughed, a nasty four-part noise: "Heh-heh-heh-heh."

"I don't think he thinks we'll do anything to him," Jay said.

"He's wrong," Scales said. "Guys who come after me with guns go right to the top of my shit list. I can give him something that'll make him sleep like a baby and while he's out, amputate an ear or a few fingers."

"Heh-heh-heh-heh."

"Or poke out his eyes, maybe."

"Heh-heh-heh-heh."

"You white men have no imagination," Jay said. "Put him to sleep and while he's napping, take off his dick. How'd you like to go through the rest of your life squatting to pee, pal? Have to change your name, since your johnson will no longer be around."

Johnson didn't think that one was funny. Scales thought he paled a little but that might have been his imagination.

"You know what they say, don't you?" Jay continued. She put her gun on the counter top and went into the bedroom. Came out with Scales' medical case. "If you're captured by the Indians, don't let them give you to the women . . ." She opened the case, came out with a paper-wrapped disposable syringe. Opened the paper, waved the hypodermic and its covered needle at Johnson.

He bolted. Came up, dived at the door, knocked it open and fell onto the concrete.

By the time Scales got to the door, Johnson was five yards away and going strong, despite having his hands cuffed behind him. He headed for the freeway.

"Go, go!" Jay yelled.

His already sore feet hurt worse as Scales chased after the fleeing man. Johnson gained ten yards, twelve, and was moving faster. Pretty good for a man his age who smokes unfiltered Camels, Scales thought.

Scales didn't know where Johnson thought he was going. Even if he crossed the interstate, there was nothing on the other side but a dead and dry empty field, looked as if it ran for a mile in any direction. Those cigarettes would kick in sooner or later.

Behind him, he heard Jay yell something he couldn't make out.

Traffic at this hour was sparse. Johnson got all the way across three lanes of I-5 before he tripped and fell. He hit hard, nothing to break his tumble. He was already stunned from the rap to the head and he was slow coming up.

The big truck's airhorn blasted, a spooked dinosaur running at eighty through the summer night. Scales slid to a stop, yelling.

"No—!"

At the last instant, Johnson tried to get up and leap out of the way.

The truck driver saw him and switched lanes.

If he'd stayed down the truck would have missed him completely.

Johnson leaped up and right into the truck's path as the

driver stood on his brakes.

It made a loud noise when the truck hit him, Scales heard it even over the air brakes and constant horn, a meaty thump that tore up the grill and chrome bimbo above the bumper before the impact knocked Johnson fifty feet through the air like a tossed doll. He hit the road and bounced—

—and then the swerving truck ran over him.

Scales saw Johnson's head flatten under the wheel. Popped and spewed like a water balloon.

"Jesus Christ!" Jay said.

Scales started forward but Jay grabbed his arm. "Come on. You aren't going to help him. We need to get the hell out of here."

They turned and ran back toward the RV.

TWENTY-FOUR

Scales drove, wired, Jay in the passenger seat more rattled than she let on. At least that's how he saw her. They didn't talk about it for a long time. The rest stop was outside Ashland, itself just north of the California border, and the RV labored in the darkness up the hills and down. They didn't have any fruit to declare at the checkpoint going into California. They passed through Yreka, by Mount Shasta and the little cinder cone closer to the road. They kept going steadily south at the speed limit, I-5 through Dunsmuir, across Lake Shasta. If anybody had connected them to the dead man at the rest stop, there was no sign of it from the state cops they passed or who zipped past them, Oregon and then CHP.

After the sun was up and they were both finally adrenaline-depleted, Scales found a big shopping center in Redding and pulled into the lot. They parked, turned on the radio. Scales went to the kitchen section and made coffee. It was pre-ground, but a gourmet blend, good until it got stale.

It was going to be another hot one in Northern California. Looking for temperatures around 110 in Redding today, maybe even hotter down the valley between there and Sacramento.

There was nothing about a death at a rest stop in Oregon.

"Doesn't mean anything," Jay said, sipping at her coffee. "State boys in Oregon might not have filed a report yet and that far out, maybe nobody was up listening to the scanner that early."

Scale drank deeply from his third cup of coffee. "Yeah, but they are going to wonder about those handcuffs. Can they trace them to you?"

"No. Those were an old travel pair I used, either from the service or LAPD, before anybody started worrying about keeping serial numbers. Pick up similar ones at any pawn or gun shop in the country. I left my good pair at home. Besides, it wasn't like we killed the guy. He got hit by a truck. It really was an accident."

He shook his head. "I feel like that woman on that old mystery series, Jessica Somebody? Once a week like clockwork, somebody dies."

"Her, too," Jay said. "I think they cancelled that series, didn't they?"

He saw she was trying to lighten things up but he was still having trouble with it. That joy of going on vacation he'd felt was gone. Watching a man's head burst like a dropped pumpkin killed that in a hurry. Whoever had caused all this shit had a lot to answer for.

Hughes drank the last of her coffee and looked at Scales. He was upset, had every right to be, but she didn't know how to comfort him. She was more than a little bothered herself. This can of worms was proving to be a lot bigger than she'd imagined. Unless the dead man who'd broken into the RV had just happened across them at the rest stop—something she pegged as less likely than winning the Publishers Clearing House Sweepstakes—then he'd been following them since they'd left the reservation. Since she hadn't been looking for a tail after they left Port Townsend in the RV, she'd never spotted him. Hadn't seen him leaving Sekiu, either, and she had been looking there. Could have been a bug on the car or maybe he'd been better at shadowing than at picking locks. Whatever. She'd fucked up, missed the tail, and maybe whoever was running this show now knew where they were and what they were driving.

Maybe not. Maybe the guy had been planning to handle it on his own and then report in afterward. No way to tell. They'd have to be prepared for the worst.

There was a small park next to the shopping center, mostly a flat spot with dry and dying short-cropped grass, a few trees, a couple of swing sets and slides. As Hughes finished her coffee and watched, a 4X4 pickup and a van arrived at the park and several people got out and began setting up posts sunk in buckets of concrete. They strung ropes around these into big squared-off areas.

A few minutes later, more vans and trucks got there, a dozen additional people joined the work. They erected one of those blue and white striped awning tents, rolled and pinned the flaps up so it looked like a giant carport. Began setting up card tables inside.

"What are they doing?" Scales asked, coming out of the shower and drying himself with a thick green beach towel.

She shrugged. "I dunno. Wedding, maybe?"

He looked out through the window. "Not unless the bride is a real bitch." He grinned. "It's a dog show."

Sure enough, more vehicles pulled up and some of these had those big plastic or wire kennels in them.

"How'd you know that?" she asked.

"One of my sisters used to have show dogs. Pomeranians. I went to a couple of these things with her, long time ago." He nodded at the park.

He finished drying himself, went back into the tiny bathroom, began using an electric razor. Hughes watched the dog show people. She'd never had a dog of her own, though a lot of her extended family had them. She'd never wanted the responsibility of having to feed and look after a pet. Although lately, sitting on the porch and petting the dog seemed like it as if it might be a lot more fun than once she'd thought. Looked as if the ones at this show were like those her uncle in Port Townsend had, German Shepherds, at least all the ones she could see were of that breed. Some of the owners had the dogs out now, on leashes, and they were jumping up and barking and generally having a good time.

"Want go over and take a look?" Scales said.

"What, the dog show?"

"Why not? We're not in a hurry, are we?"

"I guess not."

She went to the sink and rinsed out her cup while he finished dressing. Maybe a little walk around in the hot sunshine and then a shower and a nap would be a good idea. Some lunch or breakfast or whatever the hell the next meal should be and they could get back on the road. Like he said, it's not as if they had an appointment or anything.

Scales and Jay stepped out into the hot day. An oven-dry wind leached them as they strolled toward the dog show set up in the little park a couple hundred meters away. Shepherds, ranging from black and silver to black and red to almost pure black. No white ones. The dogs he saw looked young and frisky. An old man in a suit and tie with a name tag—he must be dying in those clothes—stood inside one of the roped-off areas with a clipboard making notes. Two women shuffled papers and took applications and money at a table under the awning. A few hucksters set up displays, using available shade or making their own with beach umbrellas or covered stalls. There were leashes, collars, big rawhide chews and doggy pillows for sale. One owner had a big battery-powered fan with a block of ice in front of it blowing cool air at her kenneled animals. People had spent a lot of time and effort on these critters.

Jay said, "What's it all for? The point of the shows?"

"Improving the breed—in theory. In practice, it's probably about ribbons and ego and money. Champion dogs are worth a lot, as are their offspring. Pick up a dog at the pound, it costs a few bucks for shots and a license. A pure-bred like one of these out of the classified adds in any big city, might run you eight, nine hundred bucks. But a dog that's won a major show? That will set you back a couple thousand or three on the low end, many times that much higher up the line."

"Really? If I spent that much on an animal, I'd be watching it full time, afraid it would catch cold or eat something bad and croak."

"It wouldn't be the kind of dog you'd let run around in the neighborhood eating other dogs' turds, no."

They approached a short, busty woman in hot pink shorts and a lime green tank top who had three dogs on roll-up leases. One of the dogs, a puppy, came toward Jay, tail wagging, front end low to the ground, wanting to be friends.

Jay grinned, bent. "Okay to pet her?"

"Sure," the woman said. "But soon as you do, the others'll be all over you. They're like two-year-old children, can't love on one without loving on 'em all."

Sure enough when Jay scratched the puppy behind the ears the older dogs were right there, nosing her hand, moaning and whining in voices that seemed ridiculously high for such big dogs. They sounded like Chewbacca the Wookiee.

Jay smiled and Scales squatted next to her and helped her pet the dogs. He got licked, groomed and pawed for his efforts.

"Hate to break it up," the owner said, "but I've got to get ready for the ring. See you."

She heeled the Shepherds and moved away.

Scales stood, as did Jay. She said, "You like dogs, right?"

"Yeah. Haven't had one since my ex and I split up but I've thought about getting another one. A dog is always happy to see you come through the door. You leave the dog inside and go check the mail and when you get back, it's, "Oh, wow! You're home! You were gone but now you're back! I'm so happy to see you!" A dog doesn't care if you've shaved, if you made a killing in the stock market or lost your shirt playing poker, he's just happy to be with you. There's an old saying, 'The more I learn about people, the better I like dogs.' "

"Great, coming from a medic."

"Sickness brings out the best and the worst in people. I once stitched up a guy who had a to-the-bone cut from his shoulder to his wrist and he kept apologizing for bleeding on me. Most of the time, it's the worst. I once had a woman with a cold threaten to kill me if I didn't do something to make her feel better. People are complex. Dogs are simple. No guile, no hidden agendas. Feed 'em, exercise 'em, let them be part of your pack, that's all they need."

Another owner went past, a short-haired red-and-black bitch walking in step with him. The dog smiled, its big tongue dangling as it watched its master for signals. Yeah, he liked dogs.

They walked over to the ring and watched as the judges,

led by the old man in the suit, checked numbers on their clipboards.

Jay smiled at the woman who'd let them pet her dogs as she moved past the outside of the square. They watched a young woman in a dress walking a female dog around inside the rope.

Scales said, "That's one of hers the handler has. Watch what she does when the girl runs the dog around the ring."

Jay watched. The owner moved down to the end of the rope square and when the girl with the dog trotted around toward her, the short woman began running along the outside of the rope, calling to the dog:

"Princess! Wooo, princess! Look at Mommie, baby, baby, baby! Princcceesss!"

The dog lifted its head but did not try to run to her mistress. The short woman ran past, breasts bobbing under the tank top.

"What was that all about?"

"They're allowed to do that. Get the dog to look alert for the judges. Wait until they run the whole group. We don't want to be standing here, we'll get trampled."

Sure enough when the judges had a dozen of the Shepherds looping around, eight or nine people thundered along the outside of the rope line, calling to their dogs:

"Peep-eye! Peep-eye, look at Daddy!"

"Sweetie, here, lookie, lookie, lookie!"

"Poopie! Poopie, poopie, poopie!"

Jay said, "If we get a dog, you have to promise you won't call it 'Poopie.' And no little hats or shoes or raincoats, either."

He felt the smile all over. If we get a dog.

We. Us. Together.

It was the first real sign she might be considering a future with him and he couldn't believe how good it made him feel. Them. Together. That it was happening here, at a dog show in the middle of a hot summer's day was just one more surreal brick on an already-unbelievable load. A future.

Assuming somebody didn't kill them before they got back.

TWENTY-FIVE

They were both exhausted and the idea of driving for hours held little appeal for either Scales or Hughes. They found an RV park south of Redmond with some shade. They pulled in, rented a slip and parked the RV under what looked like a cottonwood tree. It was still hot, but once Scales plugged in the power line and hooked up to the water and sewage drains, it had all the comforts of home. More, since Hughes didn't have an air conditioner at her house. The two overhead AC units were enough to keep the place cool, albeit they were somewhat noisy.

She took a shower, dried off, and got into bed next to Scales. They cuddled under the sheet but didn't make love.

Hughes dropped off without realizing it. When she awoke, Scales was in the kitchen cooking. She looked at her watch. It was late afternoon, she'd been asleep for almost six hours.

She padded naked into the bathroom, yawned, waved at Scales. From inside the bathroom she said, "Boy, I slept like I was dead. How long you been up?"

"About thirty minutes. I feel a lot better."

"Me, too."

She came out of the bathroom, saw that the back of his T-shirt and shorts were smudged with dirt. "Been cleaning the floor with your back?"

"No, I crawled around under the RV looking for bugs."

She nodded. "Find anything?"

"On the table."

She turned, looked. Sure enough, there was a black plastic box about the size of a non-filtered cigarette pack there. She picked it up. There were two thick magnets mounted on one side, a stubby, plastic-coated, thumb-long aerial sticking out of one end. The on-off switch was a recessed button.

"Well, shit," she said. She should have run the bug detector, like at the clinic. Or had she left it in his car, back in PT? Either way, she should have at least thought about it.

"No way to tell if it was still working when I pulled it from the frame."

"This was probably how Johnson tracked us. I'd guess he put it on while we were in the store in Port Townsend."

"He might have a friend," Scales said. "When we pull out, I think we should turn it back on, find a big truck going north and stick this on it."

She looked at him.

"Hey, I watch TV, too." He stirred sausage links around in the skillet. The smell of cooking was pleasant. Hughes realized how hungry she was.

He said, "You think they know where we're going?"

"Not unless they're psychic. Whoever they are. If it were me, I'd assume that we got scared and ran. Heading south is pretty much the only way we could go from where we were, unless we wanted to swim to Canada."

"Sausage is almost ready. How do you like your eggs?"

"Fried. Sunny side up or over easy. Three of them—what the hell—four."

"I'll use the sausage grease. The rate we're going, we won't have to worry about living long enough to have a heart attack."

"I'm going to go put some clothes on," she said.

"Why? You look so good naked."

She smiled. "Well, if for no other reason, I might drop a piece of hot sausage in my lap."

"I gotta a piece of hot sausage I could drop in your lap," he said, trying for Groucho Marx. He waggled his eyebrows.

She laughed.

After they finished eating breakfast—though it was closer to supper time—he washed the dishes. Jay stood next to him, dried plates with a dish towel. She said, "Are you scared?"

"Me? Nah. Hell, I'm from Texas. Shoot, a trip to the outhouse there is scarier than this. Snakes, wolves, bears, red Injuns. No offense to present company intended."

She wasn't smiling. He knew it wasn't the Injun joke.

He blew out a sigh. "Yeah. I'm scared. I don't know what the fuck is going on—I'm not sure I want to know, in one whole way—but if we don't find out, we're screwed. I don't think we get our lives back like they were before unless we unravel this. Maybe not even then."

She said, "I feel like I'm on some kind of psychedelic drug trip. None of it seems real. I keep thinking I'll wake up and it will have all been a strange dream."

"That include me?"

"No. I don't want to wake up from you."

He finished scrubbing out the skillet. She took it, dried it out, set it on the non-skid shelf liner under the counter.

"Thanks," he said. "So, are we ready to roll?"

"Might as well. Can't dance."

They stuck the little transmitter under the bumper of a tour bus heading for Seattle. They found the bus at a big truck stop just off the interstate. That was an experience in itself, Scales had never been inside a place quite like it. It was huge, there were dozens of big tractor-trailers parked in rows on a monster lot. Inside the main building, there was a restaurant, a small motel, a place to do wash and take showers, and a store that stocked everything from chrome bimbo mudflaps to big leather wallets with chains to tapes by stand-up comedians specializing in trucker jokes. They didn't really need anything but they walked around looking. Jay pointed out a display of Zippo lighters with truck emblems, skull and crossbones and American flags on them. "Bet most of the drivers are Republicans," she said. "I don't see a lot of liberal stuff for sale."

"What is 'liberal stuff'?"

"Peace symbols, 'Save the Whales' stickers, old Clinton or Gore or Kerry buttons."

He shook his head.

"Not into political humor?"

"It was a Democrat who sent me to Vietnam. He quit, but the Republican who replaced him kept me there. I don't have much use for either of them. Nor for the current idiot who thinks God has made him the World's Sheriff. Last time I voted, I wrote in Donald Duck. I figured I could understand what he said about as well as any other politician I've ever heard."

"Yeah, that was the thing with Nixon. What was so bad about Watergate was not that he was a crook—I figure they're all twisted by the time they get to that level—it was that he was an inept crook. You have to believe that Eisenhower and Kennedy and everybody back to Jefferson and Washington did illicit stuff, too, but they didn't get caught."

"Since they're all bandits, better an adept crook?"

"Sure," she said. "What else? Watergate was great theater and a lot of people got disillusioned, but I bet it didn't change anything about the way business gets done—except make the cat burglars be more careful."

"You could have a point. Hey, want to buy a suicide knob for the steering wheel?" He held up a rounded and blunt cone, bright orange plastic with a clear window on the fat end. There was a picture of a naked woman under the window.

"You are pushing your luck, white man."

They drove down I-5 for several hours. Made it past the turn off to Sacramento, bypassed San Francisco well off to the west. It was after dark and they thought about looking for a place to stay the night. There was a long and desolate stretch between there and Bakersfield, another six or eight hours. But they decided against it. It might be better to get to L.A. in the dark. Herding a big RV into town would be easier when the roads were less crowded. These days the city never slept and there was always traffic on the freeways, but it was still not as thick at three a.m. as it was during rush hour. So they drove all night, switching off, stopping a couple of times for gas or to stretch out. They watched for vehicles that might be following them, didn't spot any, though they couldn't be sure.

It was almost four in the morning when they crested the grapevine and started down into the basin.

"I have a couple of people who owe me big favors," Jay said. "We can park this beast in somebody's back yard and get some rest. Then I'll get them to rent a car for us."

"And then . . . ?"

"We pay a call on a certain pharmaceutical company."

The fear came back, twisting his belly and bowels. "Yeah."

TWENTY-SIX

Jay didn't want to use their cell phones except if there was a major emergency, just in case. They pulled into a Carl's Junior with a phone near the entrance and Jay made a call. She came back to the RV. It was just after five a.m.

"We've got a place to park," she said.

"Must be a good friend if you can call them this early."

"She is. Cop I used to work with, Bridget. She's black and a lesbian. I stood up for her when she had a departmental beef with a bigoted Sergeant. She lives with her girlfriend Sally, a criminal defense attorney who used to be a DA with the county prosecutor's office. Sally quit during the O.J. trial and went over to the other side of the aisle."

"You're not worried about us hiding out with a cop?"

"She doesn't wear the badge to bed. Besides, there isn't anybody after us for criminal activity."

"Not that we know of," he said.

"You worry too much. Bridget is cool."

Bridget was also tall—she looked into Scales' eyes from dead-level—and built like an Amazon. About thirty, she had a close-cropped Afro, wore black shorts and a white tank top, rubber sandals, was wide-shouldered and sculpted lean and tight. Here was a lady who was familiar with pumping iron. Next to her stood a petite blonde about the same age in a blue flannel bathrobe. That would be Sally.

The three women hugged each other like sisters at a family reunion and when they were done, Jay introduced Scales.

Bridget looked him up and down and grinned. "You lift?"

"A little."

"Shouldn't have told her that," Sally said. "She'll take you out into the gym and try to make you look bad." Sally dropped her voice half an octave and did what was probably a pretty good imitation of Bridget: " 'Yo, pendo, how much can you bench?' "

"Wouldn't take much to make me look bad," he said. "An empty bar will wear me out."

Bridget grinned, looked at Jay. "He's okay—for a pendo."

Scales looked at Jay, who translated: "Short for pendulum."

"Ah."

"Please come inside," Sally said. "Bridget's manners don't kick in until about noon."

The house was a two-bedroom tan stucco in a quiet residential neighborhood in West Hollywood, not far from the old Goldwyn studios and close to Television City. The inside was clean, recently painted, and the kitchen was Tweety Bird-colored—bright and cheery yellow. Somebody had made coffee and it smelled as if they knew what they were doing. Scales took the offered cup and tasted it. It was excellent. He said so.

"Fine coffee."

"That's Bridge's department," Sally said. "Where she's from, you had to be able to stand the spoon up in the sludge or it wasn't dark enough."

Bridget smiled, a flash of white against her chocolate

229

skin. "And if I hadn't already heard you talk, that 'Fahn kawffey,' by itself would give you away. Texas?"

Scales nodded. Guessed at her accent. "And you'd be . . . Louisiana? Mississippi?"

"Jackson. Give the man a cee-gar."

They passed a few minutes exchanging news. Then Bridget said, "What can we do you for, Jazz?"

Jay told her.

"No problem. You can leave the beast parked in the driveway alongside the house and we'll pass by the car rental place before my shift begins."

"Thanks, Bridge," Jay said.

"No problem."

"It's kind of weird, what we're doing, but there's no official heat shining our way," Jay said.

"I didn't ask if there was," Bridget said.

"I wanted you to know. We'll explain it all when we get through it."

"You don't have to explain anything, sister."

The two beamed at each other.

"Hey, that's enough of that," Sally said. She looked at Scales. "We better not leave these two alone. Bridget'll make another convert."

Scales grinned.

Bridget said, "C'mon, Sal, I'm just glad to see her. You know."

"Easy, big fella. I was just kidding." Sally put her hand on one of the taller woman's heavy shoulders and rubbed it. For the attention Bridget paid them, Scales and Jay could have just turned invisible; the love that shined from the black woman's face at Sally was so bright you could almost read by it.

It was nice to see.

★ ★ ★ ★ ★

The car from Rent-a-Heap was a gray Nissan about three years old and Hughes picked it because it looked like nine million other cars on the road. Bridge went off to work and left Hughes and Scales in the rental. Sally had a case in the valley somewhere and would be gone all day.

Hughes drove the Nissan back to the house and parked in on the street while she and Scales showered and changed clothes. She was tired and would have rather gone back to bed to sleep for a week but that wasn't why they were here.

"You ready?" she asked him.

Scales nodded. "I guess."

"This is just a scouting run. Get the layout, a feel for the place."

"Yeah."

He wore faded jeans and a sloganless black T-shirt, the belly pouch with the little Smith in it, black running shoes. He'd wet-combed his hair and it still lay flat and slick against his head. She also wore jeans and a T-shirt, a sleeveless photographer's vest over the shirt and low-top white tennis shoes. Under the vest, her .357 was tucked into a high-ride FBI-tilt pancake holster. The holster had a thumb-break snap to keep the gun from falling out—in case she needed to do a double back somersault or something.

It wasn't that long a trip from West Hollywood to Westwood, straight down Santa Monica a few miles. Hughes drove, noticed how things had changed but how the streets had also stayed the same.

Where they were going was in the Village, just north of Wilshire. Not a place where Hughes expected to find a drug manufacturing concern. Scales had told her it was a branch office.

When they passed by the Medical Frontiers Corporation

building, Hughes realized he was right. There was a commercial building there, all right, a small three-story structure.

"Probably the actual pharmaceutical manufacturing is in Mexico or Korea," Scales said. "Much cheaper labor that way."

"Is this going to do us any good?" she asked

"I don't know. Depends on what you want to find."

A pair of college students crossed in front of them, in the middle of the block, not looking to see if there were any cars coming.

"Fools and small children," Hughes said. She braked. The students, two young women lugging books in backpacks never looked in her direction, just kept talking to each other.

"We're looking for something to tie the killers to the company," she said. "Those two in Neah Bay and the one at the rest stop, long as we're at it."

"Place might have access to personnel records," he said.

Hughes turned, to circle the block and make another pass by the offices.

"A lot of companies allow their branch offices to log onto the corporate mainframe. If they did and if something is there and if I can find a password, I might be able to dig that out."

"Lot of 'ifs.' "

"Yeah, well, add, if we could get inside and if we could keep from getting our asses shot off by a guard or some of your old buddies in the LAPD. Plus five or six other ifs I can probably come up with."

"I'll take care of that part," Hughes said.

They went back to Bridge and Sal's and spent the afternoon sleeping. Or trying to, in his case. By the time Sally arrived, they were ready to leave. Jay didn't want to have to explain where they were going, so they found a restaurant, ate, then went to a movie. A Schwarzenegger flick, lots of explosions and shooting and a little sex. Funny, him being the Governor here now. Who'd have ever guessed that watching the Terminator?

"All that money," Jay said, shaking her head.

"Hey, Arnold, he's the wind in your hair and the hollow lurch in your belly when you hit the first drop on a roller coaster."

"Come on."

"You ever been to Disneyland?"

"Yes," she said.

"You expect to find Jesus during the Pirates of the Caribbean?"

"Well, it would have made it real interesting, but— no."

"The E-ticket rides are supposed to be exciting and fun, that's what you pay for."

"They don't do E-tickets any more," she said. "But I get your meaning."

"Good. You being a backwoods savage and all, I can see I have much to teach you about American culture."

By the time they got back to the area near the pharmaceutical offices, it was almost nine.

Jay explained that this was the perfect time. Late enough for the employees to have gone home but not so late a passing police unit would automatically assume they were up to mischief and check them out. They had, she said, about a two-hour widow to work in.

Jay parked the Nissan a block away. "I'll be back in half an hour," she said. "Stick close to the car, look at your watch now and then, pretend you're waiting for your married lover to ditch her husband for a little waterbed motel rendezvous."

"My, how you do go on." He paused, nervous. "Listen, you be careful."

"No problem. I'm in and out, just a quick run to make sure it's safe for you to go play computer nerd. Thirty minutes."

She kissed him, hard and with a flash of passion, smiled, then slid out of the car and walked across the street as if she owned it.

Scales got out of the car, moved to the sidewalk, stood there trying to look as if he had a good reason to be occupying the space. He lost sight of Jay as she neared the building.

Ten minutes dragged past, they felt like centuries. There wasn't much traffic on the street, a car now and then, and a few pedestrians. He was worried about her, a lot.

As he stood waiting, four kids ambled along the sidewalk toward him. They didn't look like college students, he decided. They looked more like predators cruising a grazing ground looking for fat prey. He saw them spot him, saw them decide he was maybe tender enough to eat. A white guy wearing a belly pouch? Had to be some yuppie scum. Sheeit, money on the hoof.

He watched them come, the four sterling examples of suburban trouble, hair cut short with designs etched in, or in one case, shaved so the kid looked like a tall and skinny two-tone dark-headed kitchen match. The quartet wore baggy shirts, baggy shorts, two of them had baseball caps turned backward—one cap, green, the other one orange— two were bareheaded. Diamond stud earrings. Business must be good. Bloods? Crips? Scales tried to remember which color which gang wore. Red, that would be Bloods.

No red he could see, no blue, either. Unaffiliated wanna-be types, maybe. He pegged them at fifteen, maybe sixteen and no less dangerous for their youth.

Definitely not UCLA's finest.

"Good evening, sir. May we help you?" Orange Cap said.

Scales smiled. "I don't believe so. I'm waiting to meet somebody."

"He waitin' to meet somebody," Match-head said. "Imagine that." He grinned, exchanged low-fives with the one in the green cap.

"Contrary to appearance, this is perhaps not the best neighborhood for a single man to be idling." Orange Cap said. His voice was even, his speech educated.

Idling. An erudite gangbanger.

"I'll be careful."

"Hey, Pro-fessor, man say he be care-ful," Match-head said to Orange Cap. His voice and tone were more along the lines of what Scales thought of as black urban patois. He wondered if it was a put-on.

Maybe he had been a parrot in a past incarnation.

"Perhaps you might care to take out some . . . insurance?" The one called Professor said. "Health, life, like that. We offer several policies. We live in violent and dangerous times. It would be a prudent investment."

"I don't think so. But thanks."

"C'mon, man, guy like you, gotta have money you don't need," Match-head said. "Right? Whachoo got in that little purse? We take cash, we take American Express, we take MasterCard. Fact, we will take them all, if you know what I'm sayin'."

"I'm really not interested in contributing to your delinquency," Scales said.

Match-head took umbrage at that. "You gotta attitude, dude. Unless you some kinda kong-foo expert, you axin' to get it straightened out. You need to learn to count, too. There's four of us and only one of you."

"Well," Scales said, feeling the sudden rush of adrenaline pop like hot grease in him, "that's not strictly true." He unzipped his belly pouch, slowly, offhand, no sudden moves. "There's actually three of us. Me and . . . Smith and Wesson—" he produced the .38 from the pouch and held it so the short shiny barrel pointed straight up.

Somebody said, "Fuck!" Scales didn't catch who.

"My, my. It appears as if you aren't in need of any insurance after all," Professor said. "Have a nice night. Gentlemen, let us depart."

"He ain't gone use that," Match-head said.

"James, James, haven't I taught you anything at all? White people are prone to violence, it's genetic. The man has a gun and if he wishes to use it, you have no means of preventing it. It is always less than wise to aggravate a man holding a firearm. You should moderate your tone." He smiled, gave Scales a military bow. "Another time, sir."

With that, the four moved off.

Surreal, that's what it was, surreal. A black gangster who talked like an English teacher. One more such fantastic event in the whole pageantry of the last couple of weeks. If he survived, he'd be able to dine out for weeks on this story alone.

He realized how rattled he was as he tucked the gun away. His hand shook. Then he saw Jay approaching.

"Making new friends in the big city, are we?"

"They needed direction," he said. "I told them where to go."

"I bet. Well, come along, Mr. Wizard. The place is

about as secure as Social Security. No guards, a simple alarm and crappy locks."

"Nice to know all your police experience is good for something," he said.

"Yeah, it is, isn't it?"

He took a deep breath, let it out. "Okay. Let's go."

They went.

TWENTY-SEVEN

There was a back entrance to the building that looked out on a parking lot, a lot empty save for a beat-up orange VW beetle missing both bumpers.

Hughes saw Scales look at the car. She said, "It's been parked there awhile. See the eucalyptus leaves piled up against the tires?"

Scales nodded.

The peppery, minty-smelling tree responsible for the leaves clumping against the VW hung low over the lot, stirred a little by a warm breeze.

She looked around, then pulled the heavy glass plate door open.

"What about the alarm?"

"See that big bar magnet?" She pointed at the top of the door frame. "Long as it stays there, the alarm bypasses this door."

"Wow. It's that easy?"

"Scary, ain't it?"

"And you picked the lock?"

"Just like in the movies. Well, almost. It took ten minutes, I bent my torsion tool, broke two picks and I won't even try to relock it. Let them think they forgot. The alarm will still be on."

Inside, she led him to the elevators. "They didn't even bother to shut them off. Pitiful."

Inside the elevator, she punched a button. "The personnel guy is on the second floor."

The elevator opened, the *ching!* it made loud in the quiet building. She went down the hall, Scales right behind her. The hall lights were on. The place was generic office—short, gray wall-to-wall carpet, drop ceiling panels and cheap repro sea- and landscapes on blue pastel walls. The recycled air had a stale smell to it.

"Shouldn't we be using flashlights?" he asked.

"No. A building with lights on doesn't make a street cop nervous, probably somebody forgot to turn 'em off. A flashlight beam waving around in the dark—that draws attention."

The office was a two-parter—a small outer office for the secretary and a slightly larger cube through an unlocked door. The larger office had a couple of file drawers, a big Eagle gray steel cabinet, a love seat and an oak veneer desk with a leather office chair behind it. No window. Upon the desk were two chromed wire baskets, out and in, a computer and monitor, a picture in a plastic cube of a woman and two small children. A crude, two-toned lopsided pottery jar half full of pencils and pens stood next to the picture. Bet one of the kids made it, Hughes thought.

Scales moved around the desk and looked at the computer.

"A Mac," he said.

"That good?"

"It is for me. I hate playing with Windows. I think Microsoft is a tool of the Anti-Christ."

He sat.

"I'm going to look through the paper files," she said.

Scales nodded, already tapping at the keyboard.

The screensaver, a colorful moire pattern, vanished when Scales tapped the first key. He used the mouse to se-

lect the hard drive, opened it, and saw that the computer
had local files and a network link to another system.

Local stuff first.

He clicked open various files. Christ, the guy didn't even
have his stuff password protected. He found the local employee list, opened it. He turned, looked for the printer.
Nothing. He got up, went out into the secretary's office.
Ah, there it was. A little HP inkjet, next to the secretary's
computer.

He flipped on the printer's switch, heard the power hum,
went back into the larger office.

Jay glanced at him.

"Printer," he said. "Might want hard copy if we find
anything."

She nodded, resumed going through the folders in the
drawer again.

He began lining up documents in the print monitor
queue. The employee file, the addresses and phone numbers of the other company offices: They had branches in
New York, Baltimore, Washington, D.C., Atlanta and even
Biloxi, Mississippi, as well as plants in Seoul, Korea and in
Hong Kong—the latter which was apparently being closed
soon.

He knew he could spend forever reading, so he just
downloaded anything that looked useful to the printer.

He looked for a Security or Investigation file but
couldn't find one.

Time to see if he could log onto the company mainframe. He was pretty sure he'd need a password for that.
Probably it was something the guy knew, a name or
birthday or somesuch, most people picked something they
wouldn't forget just so they didn't have to write it down. He
opened drawers, looked around, checked inside the phone

book and address book. Nope.

Scales got up again, went into the secretary's office. Pulled out the sliding shelf above the drawer on the left. Nothing. Did the same with the shelf on the right . . .

There was a little slip of paper taped to the shelf, hidden unless you pulled it almost all the way out. It said:

Ron's Passwords -
HQ - log on - ali / Personnel - liston
Biloxi - Contract Employees - tyson
D.C. - spinks
Hong Kong - lee

Scales smiled. Apparently old Ron was a fight fan. Except for the last name, the passwords were all former heavyweight champion boxers. Hong Kong, he figured, was Lee, as in Bruce Lee.

He copied the names onto a yellow Post-it note and went back into the inner office. Found the communications program, lit it, had the computer dial the HQ number he found in the directory, apparently they were on dedicated lines. No modem beeped dial signals at him. The computers connected. An icon appeared; a window grew from it and he got a log-on message.

Name?

He looked through the out basket, found a letter to be sent, looked at the signature.

Ron Gold, he typed.

Welcome, Ron Gold.

Password?

A-l-i

The screen flowered and the host computer gave him a list of folders. He clicked on the one marked *Master Per-*

sonnel. The host asked him for another password. He gave it *"liston."* It opened.

They might have a tracker set up to show who accessed protected files but as long as it would let Scales in, he didn't care; that was something old Ron could explain later.

Lord. There were ten subfolders, set-up for different locations, and altogether had to be more than a thousand employees divided up in those, including their home addresses, phone numbers, vital statistics and social security numbers.

He sent the main folder to the printer.

He connected to the other branches and scanned what files he could reach.

When he got into the Biloxi system, he came across a subfolder buried three down in the Contract Employees folder marked *Special Operations.* When he tried to open it, he found it was password protected and 'tyson' wouldn't get him in. He tried Ron's other passwords, then every heavyweight boxer he could think of, including John L. Sullivan and Joe Louis, but it wouldn't open. Nor could he download it to the printer. He was finally able to copy it to a disk, though he couldn't open it from there without the password and the security program that created the file in the first place, which apparently wasn't even on this machine. Worse off than before.

"You got something?" Jay asked.

"Maybe. I don't know."

"Wrap it up. Time for us to leave, grasshopper."

"Leave? I just got started."

"You've been sitting there for almost two and a half hours."

He blinked, looked at his watch. Son-of-a-bitch.

Scales exited the system, shut folders, put the desktop

back in the same shape he'd found it. Ejected a newly-burned CD with the copied security file. He got up, realized how stiff he was, and walked to the printer in the next room. There were a couple hundred sheets in the tray. He'd lost all track of time. He gathered the printout together and shut the printer off. "I've got everything I can think of," he said. "Let's go."

They headed for the elevators.

"So, what do we have?" Hughes asked him, as they drove away from Westwood.

Scales said "I dunno for sure. We'll have to go through it."

"Anything promising you noticed?"

"I've got all the regular employees and their addresses. And there's a locked file that might be interesting."

"Can you get it open?"

"Not me. I know a guy who might be able to."

A cop in a black and white pulled up next to them on Wilshire. Hughes nodded and smiled at him. He smiled back and pulled away when the light changed.

They headed for the RV in West Hollywood.

TWENTY-EIGHT

Scales sat on the edge of the bed in the RV, staring at the bottom of his bare right foot. He frowned.

"I thought it was palms the gypsies read, not arches. Any answers there?" Hughes asked.

He looked up at her. "Nope. Just more questions. When I ran across that parking lot after Johnson I was churning along pretty good, no shoes on. I noticed it hurt at the time, even with the adrenaline blowing through me like water through a firehose. My feet ought to be all abraded and raw. They're not."

She gave a little shrug. "You got a lot to worry about, don't you?"

He gave her a wry smile in trade for her shrug. "Yeah, I suppose."

"So, what do you think?" She waved at the papers spread all over the inside of the RV. They'd spent hours going through the hard copy they'd printed out at the pharmaceutical offices. It was almost three a.m. and they were exhausted, at least she was, and from what she could see, he didn't look much better.

"What I think is, we have a lot of information and none of it seems to be particularly useful. The company apparently started in Biloxi, Mississippi, just after the second World War—I got that out of a PR flack's form letter. The founder was one Winward "Win" White, an Army Major who'd spent some time in China between battles and came across some of the health roots and herbs the Chinese used, ginseng, ma huang, like that. He thought he might be able to peddle them here and apparently was right. Went from a one-man operation in a shack behind a local drugstore to a multinational corporation, making himself a millionaire a dozen times over in the process. Took twenty years. He retired in 1980, lives in Miami and Winward White, Junior, is now CEO and Chairman of the Board. Junior lives with his wife at the family estate, Six Oaks, not far from Jefferson Davis's final home of Beauvoir, in Biloxi. Junior and his wife have three grown children, a son and two daughters. The White family owns seventy percent of the company's stock."

"Fascinating. Anything in there about them hiring thugs to kill off the Indians up in Puget Sound?"

"I haven't come across that part yet, no."

"So now what?"

"The CD with the locked file," he said. "I have a friend in Houston who is a computer expert. I'll call him in the morning, we can FedEx or UPS it or maybe upload it over the wire to him. If anybody can open it, he can."

"Might be like Al Capone's vault," she said.

"Might be. Only one way to find out."

"How about we go to bed?" she said.

"I thought you'd never ask."

He should have slept until noon but after five hours, Scales was awake. He left Jay snoring gently, showered, dressed, and went to find a phone booth and, he hoped, something that might pass for coffee.

His luck was good. Within a few blocks, he came across a Starbucks wanna-be store called Caffeine City. There was a phone across the street on the wall of a gift shop. There was a drugstore nearby and he went in and bought a ten-buck phone charge card. Then he went back to the coffee store, got a large cup of plain coffee and crossed to the phone. He called information and got Bear's number. Did the little dance with the buttons that let him put the call on the untraceable-to-him card.

The coffee was passable.

Travis "Bear" Meyers was a shaggy mountain of a man, six-four, two-seventy, who had been a patient at the hospital where Scales did an allergy rotation during his training. Every so often Bear would blister, blow up like a horned toad and start wheezing so bad he sounded like a stadium full of asthmatics. Somebody would haul him to the nearest ER where he'd be pumped full of epinephrine, steroids and Benadryl. This had happened six times, and three of those he'd come close to dying. He'd been poked, prodded and injected with hundreds of substances without finding out what caused the reaction. Scales had been assigned to retake Bear's history, on the off chance the other sixteen physicians, med students and PAs who'd gone before him had missed something. He didn't expect to find anything.

Sometimes when you expect to lose and don't care, you win. The gods must have been feeling bored and benevolent.

Scales went through the questions that had been covered before, diet, environmental exposure, work habits. Bear was a programmer who did troubleshooting for several software companies and to look at, the antithesis of a computer nerd. He ran his office out of his house, a typical small business operation, computers, desk, chairs, office stuff.

Scales took him through the litany of what he handled each day.

"Mail, yes, I use regular mail when I can't modem stuff."

Back then, Scales didn't know what a modem was. He asked.

"Modulate, demodulate. Mo—" he waved one hand in a big arc, "—dem. It's an electronic converter that sends information signals over a phone line. Shoot, I can squirt stuff almost as fast as I can type it, three hundred baud!"

Scales assumed he was supposed to be impressed. "Uh huh. Well, when you aren't mo-dem-ing, do you lick the stamps you use on your letters?"

"No. I thought about that. I sponge 'em. Besides, they tested for glue allergy. Nada."

Bear reached up and scratched at what was one of the thickest beards Scales had ever seen. He had a pretty good razor burn and rash under his chin where the pelt had been scraped away.

It came to him in a flash what the problem was.

Later, Scales wondered how he'd come up with the leap, it was intuitive, but way beyond any reason he would have thought up to link the two things together. Something akin to the *Augenblick* he was just discovering he had, maybe.

"You ever scratch your chin after you sponge your stamps?"

"Huh?"

"Like you're doing now."

Bear jerked his hand down. "I don't know. I suppose I might."

"Bring in that sponge and some of the stamps you use."

Bear, it turned out, was allergic not to stamp glue, for which he had indeed been tested, but to mold spores. The sponge he used sat in a dish of water and both sponge and dish had collected a thick solution of glue over the uncleaned years. A culture of the solution grew out a weird mold that had died but left spores behind. When he wet the stamps by pressing them against the wet sponge, he managed to transfer some of the spores to his fingertips, then autoinoculated himself by scratching at his barber's rash. His immune system went bananas when the spores came to visit and Bear went into a reaction as bad as a werewolf touching silver.

It was luck that Scales figured it out but Bear had been more than grateful. They'd stayed in Christmas-card touch over the years and he was always offering to help Scales upgrade his computer system or to send him pirated software.

"Tumescent Systems," came the voice over the phone.

"Bear. It's Rick Scales."

"Doc! How the hell are you? You still living up there in the woods with Bigfoot and the polar bears?"

"More or less. I'm, uh, on the road at the moment."

"Vacation, hey? Still divorced?"

"Still divorced. Listen, Bear, I need a couple of favors."

"Call it."

"I've got a CD with a locked security file on it. Mac format. I don't have the program that coded it, nor do I know the password. Could you take a look at it and see if you could open it?"

He could almost hear the man grin. "Sheeit, Doc, is that all? Can you upload it to me?"

"I guess I could."

"Lemme give you my secure email. Squirt it to me and I'll have a look."

"It might have a virus."

"Teach your Grammy to suck eggs."

"Thanks, Bear."

"No sweat. You want me to call you when I get it open?"

"No, let me get back to you, I don't know the number where I'm staying, I'm calling from a booth."

"Fine. Call back around—what time is it now, ten-thirty?—gimme an hour and a half, that's noon my time. If it's commercial security, I'll have it by then. Military-grade takes longer. Hell, better gimme two hours, just in case."

"You can do it that fast?"

Bear laughed. "Well, since you ain't a paying customer, I guess I can tell you. It'll probably take me thirty minutes. The rest of the time is for a beer and burgers. Man's gotta eat."

Scales laughed.

"You said a couple of favors—what's the other one?"

Scales thought about it for a second. What the hell.

"I need something done to my credit cards. Can you access that kind of stuff?"

"Does the Pope shit in the woods? Gimme a break here, Doc, how long have I been doing this?"

"Sorry, didn't mean to insult you."

"You want me to wipe your balance clean? That's a snap."

"No, here's what I need. I think somebody might be looking for me. I haven't done anything illegal but whoever it is has got big resources. I need to use my MasterCard or Visa without anybody being able to track it to me. Is there a way to do that?"

"You mean you want to get the bills like normal?"

"Yes."

"Jeez, Doc, you probably pay for long distance, too, don't you?"

"Guilty."

"Well, I can fiddle around with some code. Make it so somebody scanning for transactions won't see them but that the cards'll still be good and the billing will go out in thirty days."

"That would be perfect."

"Consider it done."

"You need my name or numbers?"

"Why do you hurt me like this, Doc?"

Scales grinned, hung up and opened the phone book. He found a 24-hour print shop within walking distance, somebody trying to take business from Kinko's. It was a mile or so away. He walked there.

They had Macs, yessir, and high speed broadband, scanners, printers and as long as he wasn't sending any pornography, for twelve dollars an hour, he could use the computer all day.

It didn't take long to ship the file. It blew the material along the broadband lines or cable at gigabyte speeds—a hell of a lot faster than the 300 baud of the device Bear had thought so incredibly quick when first they'd met.

Scales was able to rent the computer, log on, open the disk and send the file two thousand miles away—all before he finished his coffee.

Amazing to be living here in the future.

He headed back to the RV.

Jay was up, showered, dressed and cooking breakfast. Thin steaks, eggs, English muffins and chopped apples and bananas. She had a pot of coffee on, too.

"Hi, Ward? Hard day at the office, dear?"

He did Ricky Ricardo to her June Cleaver: "Luuccy? Why'ju make jokes like that? You bin up to sonthing?"

"Only advantage to having an old fart like you around is that you know the classic TV shows. And that you don't come before your zipper gets all the way down."

"One does what one can," he said.

"Sit. Eat. Talk."

He slid into the bench by the table, felt good that she was cooking for him. He'd been doing that for himself for so long he'd almost forgotten what it was like.

She heaped food onto a plate and set it down in front of him. Poured him a cup of coffee, then filled her own plate and cup, sat. They ate for a time in silence.

"So? Enjoy your walk out in the smog?"

"Yep. I called my friend Bear and found a print shop that let me ship him the file. I'm supposed to call him back around ten-thirty our time."

"Bear?"

"Doesn't sound like a computer whiz, does it? But he can make those pixels dance."

He took another bite of the breakfast steak and told her the story of how he'd met Bear.

By the time he was done, most of the food was gone from both their plates.

She smiled at him.

"What?"

"Oh, just that there's a lot about you I don't know. It's going to be interesting to find it out. People our ages, we come with pasts."

"Well, that's what wisdom is, isn't it? Experience?"

"Oh, so you're wise?"

He grinned. "Not me. Wiser than I used to be, but that's a relative term. When you start out fairly stupid, it doesn't take much to improve."

"You know, Scales, I don't think you were ever really stupid."

"Shows what you have yet to learn. I could tell you some stories."

"That's what I said. Tales to keep us warm on those cold winter nights."

"I've got a better idea of how to do that."

"Well, sure, but a man your age, you can't keep things up all night. Once the newness wears off."

"I might surprise you."

"Oh, that would definitely surprise me."

They grinned at each other. He was really getting used to having her around. It felt altogether too good.

"You cooked, I'll get the dishes," he said.

"Deal. But how about we let them soak for a few minutes first?"

She raised an eyebrow.

"You want to get married?" he said. "Seriously?"

"Maybe. We can talk the talk later. What say we walk the walk?"

"If that's what you want to call it, fine by me."

At ten-thirty and after another giggly shower, they walked to the phone across from the coffee store. He punched in the card number and called Bear. Smiled at Jay in her T-shirt and tight jeans. A car rolled past and somebody wolf-whistled at her. It pissed her off, but it also pleased her. He could tell.

"Tumescent Systems."

"Bear, Rick."

"Ah, Doc."

"So, what's on the disk?"

"Now that's what I like to hear, complete confidence that I did the job. What it looks like is some kind of employment records from some chemical company in Mississippi. Names, dates, places, airline schedules, pay vouchers, like that. I don't see why somebody went to the trouble to encrypt it, even a cheapjack commercial program like they used. Took me fifteen minutes to pop it. Eighteen, tops.

You want me to fax or squirt this to you?"

"Fax'll be okay, I don't have my laptop here. I'll have to get back to the print shop and get a number for you. You said there were some names—give me a couple of them, would you?"

"Sure. John Smith, John Jones, John Johnson, John Jackson, John Jefferson—lotta guys named 'John.' "

Bingo!

"I'll call you back in about ten minutes," Scales said.

He turned to Jay.

"What are you grinning for?"

"We got 'em," he said. "Smith, Jones, Johnson—they're in the file."

"Damn!" she said.

Oh, yeah.

TWENTY-NINE

"Bear?"

"The one and only, Doc," came the voice over the phone.

"Here's the fax number." Scales rattled off the digits on the print shop's machine.

"Got it. Be on the way in a minute. Oh, and that other thing you wanted? I fixed that, too. All your cards are invisible for the next billing cycle. And while I was at, I increased your limits. You're good for fifteen grand straight across the board, Doc. Have fun."

"Thanks, Bear. I appreciate it."

"Por nada. Every time I remember one of those nasty hospital visits, I think about how much I owe you. This is nothing."

"No, it's a big help. I'll talk to you later."

"Adios, amigo."

Scale cradled the phone and turned to Jay.

"Bear says it's on the way."

It was. It came out to five pages and Jay collected them while Scales paid the girl behind the counter. By the time they got outside into the hot and gritty L.A. afternoon, Jay had already done a quick scan.

"So?"

"Project L.F."

"L.F.?"

"Mean anything to you?"

"Look Fool?" Scales shook his head. "Lady Finger? Let's Fuck?"

"I see the names," she said. "This is where our hit men came from. I also see who is in charge of it, at the bottom of each page are the initials 'W.W.' "

"Winward White?" Scales said, a little more seriously.

"Probably not too far a stretch. This is run out of Biloxi, White supposedly lives there. He owns the show."

"Why would a good old Mississippi millionaire want to get involved in something like this?"

"Why did Nixon get involved in Watergate when the election was a lock? If I gave you a million bucks would it change you?"

"I'd get a new car," he said. "Maybe take a few days off and go to Hawaii. I've had my eyes on some neat new Nikes, but they cost."

"You know what I mean."

"My basic personality, I don't think so. I'd hope not, at my age."

"I knew a couple of people with money when I worked here," she said. "A rock music producer, a movie director. The music guy loved mystery-meat hot dogs with American cheese and canned chili and the director never ate a lunch that cost less than forty bucks but they both took their pants off one leg at a time just like everybody else."

Scales found himself suddenly awash in a foamy breaker of jealousy.

She saw it. "Something wrong?"

He was quick to answer. "No, nothing."

She grinned.

Damn. She knew. Way too perceptive for somebody he'd only been with such a short time. He tried to smooth it out. "Your past is your business."

Her grin got bigger.

"It's a negative emotion," he tried.

"And anybody who says he never gets one of those is a liar," she said.

"I don't own you. Not then, not now."

"I know that. I like it that it bothers you. I'd rather have you jealous than not caring. Long as you don't do anything stupid about it."

He gave her a half grin. "Thanks."

"No problem. You look at another woman lustfully when we're together and I'll take you off at the knees, white man. Um. Anyway, what I'm saying is, because a guy has money doesn't mean he's a saint. The one thing big wealth does is give its owner a sense of power, of maybe being a better than ordinary folk. Of being above the rules. Throw enough money at it, you can bury almost anything."

"So, what do you think?"

She said, "I think maybe we should take a trip to the land of magnolias and Spanish moss. Perhaps even speak to Mr. White. Poke around at the very least. You got any time left on that phone card?"

"Few bucks."

"I want to call my uncle in Port Townsend."

"Is that a good idea?"

"We're leaving here soon. Even if they've bugged everybody we know, time they get here, we'll be gone. And I don't think they have the manpower to tap dozens of phones, not if these names are the only players. Half of them are gone."

"You're the ossifer, ossifer."

Jay picked up the phone and called.

She told her uncle they'd be hanging on to the RV for a while, would let him know how long later. From her expression, he couldn't care less. Then he said something that got her attention.

"What? When? Lord, lord. Yeah, I'll tell him. Thanks. Send my love to my mother, tell her I'm fine and I'll explain it all when I get back."

She hung up.

"What?"

"Your clinic burned down. The fire marshal they sent out thinks somebody firebombed it. They are still going through the wreckage."

"Fuck," he said. Aside from what he packed for this trip, everything he owned was in the clinic. His clothes, business and personal records, his computer. "Fuck."

"Could have been worse—you could have been in it," she said.

Scales blew out a sigh. Yeah. He could buy a new computer. He was insured.

They left her uncle's RV with Bridge and Sal, along with a promise to let them know what was what as soon as they could. She and Scales packed, unloaded and put the handguns into a bag they planned to check, locked inside a plastic case Hughes had. They took a shuttle to LAX, bought two one-way tickets to New Orleans on Delta. Showed all kinds of ID. Hughes declared the firearms at the ticket counter, made sure the agent put the identifying tags inside the bag.

Scales paid for the tickets with a credit card. He'd told her that his friend Bear had fixed it so it couldn't be traced. That worried her but even if somebody could run it down, they'd have to be real damned fast to get the info and beat a five-hour flight.

As they walked to their gate, Scales asked about checking the guns.

"It's a federal rap not to tell them. No law against transporting weapons, long you let them know. And they aren't loaded."

They had seats over the wing, by the emergency exit of the big jet, she thought it was an L-10/11 or maybe a DC-10, something like that. Wasn't a 747 because it didn't have the hump on its head.

They got settled in, had the row to themselves. The flight attendant came by with earphones for the movie and music. Another attendant went through the safety lecture with the seatbelt and oxygen buttercup.

The plan was to rent a car in New Orleans and drive to Biloxi.

"It's only an hour, hour and a half," Scales said. "Just off I-10 on the way to Florida."

He'd made the trip a few times, he'd told her.

The takeoff was uneventful. The giant metal beast lumbered down the runway, bellowed louder and jumped. It always amazed her something the size of a small bowling alley got up and stayed up. The craft circled out over the water and away from the valley. From the air, L.A.'s basin was a ragged bowl filled with civilized guck: Smog lapped at the mountains, sloshed over the buildings, a translucent yellow-brown fluid that seemed to thicken below as they gained altitude.

A few years back, living in L.A. was supposed to be equivalent to smoking two packs a day. It was better now, but it didn't look good from a distance.

She was tired. The drone of the engines lulled her into a doze.

When she awoke, she was leaning against Scales' shoulder, the armrest between them pulled up and the seats leaned back. She didn't remember him doing that. Her mouth was gummy and tasted bad.

She sat up. "Unnh. Where are we?"

"I think we might be in Kansas, Toto. Or thereabouts."

"How long have I been asleep?"

"A while."

"Bathroom," she said. "Have we eaten yet?"

"They've started serving." He nodded toward the aisle and she saw the attendants pushing their metal carts and pouring drinks.

"Back in a minute," she said.

"I'll go with you."

"No offense, Scales, but the last thing I feel like doing right at this minute is joining the mile-high-club."

"I just need to pee, Jay. I've been sitting here for a couple of hours, too."

"Sorry."

"Don't be. After we clean up, maybe I'll knock on your door."

She glared at him.

"Or not."

In the bathroom, which bounced up and down as she sat on the tiny toilet, she discovered part of the reason for her irritation. Her period had started.

Great. Just what she needed.

She found a beat-up tampon in her purse and used it.

Scales was waiting for her in the corridor.

"Escort you to your seat, ma'am?"

"Why not?"

"You okay?"

"Yeah, fine. The red snows have started."

"Ah." He'd been married. He got it. Said, "Better you than me. You want me to get you some aspirin or something?"

"I'll have a glass of wine with lunch. I won't start

cramping for another day or two. I can live with it."

They got back to their seats in time for the overly-cheery attendant to deliver their meals. Scales took the chicken, she had the steak. The steak was about as big around as a Coke can, overcooked and the consistency of an inner tube. She sawed at it with the dull plastic knife and managed to tear off gristly chunks she could chew on. The white wine tasted as if it had been stored inside an oil drum. The butter was ice cold and so was the stale bread it was supposed to be spread upon.

"Elegant," she said to Scales, around a bite of neoprene.

"Makes you wish for the old China Clipper days," he said. "I saw a PBS special on it once. Flights going across the Pacific used big four-engine prop planes, some of 'em had sleeping compartments. They would put down on little islands in middle of nowhere, everybody would get off the plane, go sit down to a chef-cooked meal, wander around, then get back on the plane and take off again. When you did eat on the plane, you had real silverware, china, and the food was cooked onboard. Much more civilized than this."

"Not as efficient as fast food and tight seats," she said.

He held up his fork, looked at the piece of overcooked chicken drooping from the tines, popped it into his mouth.

"And Delta's food is better than most. A shame," he said. "There is something to be said for elegance."

From the air, you could smell the swamps outside New Orleans, a unique odor that Scales hadn't sniffed in a while but could hardly forget. The cypress jutted up from the gray water in sticky wet clumps and Scales told Jay that seeing alligators wandering around below wouldn't be any surprise. The sky was overcast, and when the big bird put down on the runway, the concrete was wet and another thunderstorm flashed in the distance.

When the door opened, the humidity oozed into the jet, a heavier stench of swamp accompanying it.

"There's no place like home," Scales said. Texas was not that far away.

"Maybe for you," Jay said. "I'm not buying any real estate here."

They made their way to the luggage carousel, found their two small bags, then went looking for a rental car. They found a bank of phones with nice little pictures and numbers.

"Hertz?"

"Why not Avis?" she said. "They try harder."

But neither Hertz nor Avis had any vehicles available. There was a trio of big conventions filling up the hotels in Nola and apparently all the attendees, their spouses and children, liked to drive.

Alamo, Enterprise and Dollar were likewise tapped out and though they were all expecting returns any minute, most of those were going to be turned around in a hurry to customers waiting for them, sorry.

The guy from Budget was also sorry.

But the woman who answered the phone for Thrifty did have something. Scales said, "We'll take it." He gave her his American Express card number to hold it. She said she'd send the pick up van for them.

When they got there, Scales filled out the paperwork while Jay went to the bathroom. When she came out, she said, "We need to find a drugstore. I need some supplies."

"Supplies?"

"Female supplies."

"Oh. Oh, yeah."

They went out to get the car. When the guy pulled up,

Jay turned and stared at Scales. "A Miata? A two-seat arrest-me-red convertible?"

"It's what they had," he said.

"Come on."

"I swear."

"And here I thought you were secure in your masculinity."

He didn't bother to speak to that.

The trunk was not much bigger than a backpack, though they managed to jam their suitcases into it, after Jay sneaked two of the three guns out. A few fat drops of rain began to fall as they got into the little car. It was a tight fit with the roof up, Scales had about an inch of clearance over his head and it was sort of like getting into a big glove. Enough leg length, but not much room on either side of his knees. He was going to get familiar with the emergency brake lever and the left side panel in a hurry.

The rain increased, thumped on the vinyl roof and quickly blurred the glass all around.

"Doesn't look as if we get to put the top down," Jay said.

"Maybe later."

He started the car. The exhaust had a throaty, deep rumble when he gunned the engine. The controls were simple, the dials analog—a speedometer, gas, oil, temp gauges, a tachometer. Air bags on both sides.

"Red lines at seven thousand," he said, nodding at the tach.

"Vroom, vroom," she said. "Yeehaw, cowboy."

"Better than walking, ain't it?"

"Listen, white man, if my feet and ankles swell up, you are going to spend hours rubbing them."

"Of course," he said.

He pulled the little car out onto the street.

They found a market, a Piggly Wiggly or some such non-sense. Jay ran in, came out with a plastic bag and a couple of Cokes. "Okay. Now I'm prepared to travel."

Hughes hadn't been in rain this hard in a long time. It came down pretty good at times back home but this was tropical stuff, falling in buckets. Even with the wipers going full, it was still almost impossible to see. They drove north on the state road until they got to I-10, then headed east.

Scales nearly missed the turn, it was coming down so hard.

At least the Miata cornered well.

They drove across the narrow part of Lake Pontchartrain and by the time they reached Slidell, the rain had stopped and the sun peeked out from behind patchy clouds. It couldn't get any more humid but the heat went up fast.

"This thing have an air conditioner in it?"

"Are you kidding? Doesn't have power windows, power steering or a hot tub, either. This is a roadster!"

"Pull over and let's put the roadster's fucking top down, then."

Scales nodded. "Yes, ma'am."

"And don't be condescending, Scales. It's not just hor-monal."

"No, of course not," he said. He tried to keep a straight face, almost managed it.

She laughed.

Long as he could make her laugh, he was safe. He knew it, too.

They pulled onto the shoulder and stopped. Dropping the top took about ten seconds and they did it sitting down. Scales unzipped the plastic rear window, unsnapped the two latches over the sun visors with a springy tang, folded the roof frame back one-handed.

A lot like the old MG Midget he'd once owned for about fifteen minutes, he told her. Neat little car, the few times it actually ran.

"You want to drive?" he asked.

She thought about it. "Sure. Why not?"

They got out, swapped seats. She adjusted the mirrors, slid the seat up an inch or two. Started the car. The throw on the shift was very tight and short. She fed the engine gas and the back wheels spun on the wet pavement as they pulled onto the interstate. It was kind of fun to drive. They'd be there soon, it looked to be about fifty or sixty miles from the little rental car map they had.

"Vroom, vroom," he said. "Ride 'em, squaw woman."

She smiled and shook her head. So it was a lot smaller than the RV. Driving a little droptop roadster in the warm sunshine with a man who could make her laugh and who thought she was something special?

There were worse places to be.

THIRTY

They were passing a truck and in the wrong lane, so they missed the Gulfport exit from I-10. They drove a little farther and took I-110 south. When they got to Highway 90, Beach Boulevard, they turned and headed west, the slightly-ruffled Gulf of Mexico sparkling off to the left. It was warm and humid but all that water was worth a little cool breeze. Some dark-bottomed clouds piled up offshore, but they didn't appear to be heading their direction.

It had been more than a few years since Scales had been to this area and it had changed considerably. Jay idled the little red car along a hair faster than walking speed in the line of traffic and Scales looked at what time had wrought. The stretch along the broad sandy beach had built up, despite the hurricanes that whirled in every so often and stomped flat half of everything in their way. When he'd been a kid, the storms had names like Audrey, Betsy and Camille. Now they might be named Raoul or Sam or Jerry—no doubt that had done a whole lot to advance equal rights for women. And maybe there was something to global warming, too—there had been a dozen tropical storms named so far this year and the season wasn't half over. Living on an island in the Gulf of California or the Caribbean this year was a more dangerous business than usual.

Gambling had been legalized in Mississippi, at least the riverboat kind, and there were dozens of casinos now floating in the shallow Gulf. Some of these were real paddlewheelers that would have looked at home plying the

Big Muddy; others were huge moored barges made to look like castles or pirate ships or famous buildings. Big white-washed antebellum homes still sat across the highway, drowsy dowagers taking the sun, cloaked in old-fashioned bathing suits of live oak and Spanish moss, all but asleep on this warm summer afternoon. But what he remembered as quiet and stately was now interspersed with adult video stores, pawnshops, garish souvenir places and a lot more motels.

Civilization of a kind had come to Mississippi. It was a mixed blessing.

Jay read his memories. "Must have been pretty nice here twenty or thirty years ago," she said.

"Yes and no. It looked a lot better. There's an Air Force base here, so the coastal strip was relatively liberal, but you didn't want to go into the heartland unless you were a White-Anglo-Saxon-Protestant. Or you knew your place, which was downhill, downwind and three steps back."

"How lovely," she said.

"Statues of the southern generals all face north, you know. There are places down here where we are still fighting the War—and still losing. You know Mississippi didn't get around to making slavery technically illegal until 1995? 'Save yore Dixie cups boys, the south'll rise agin.' "

"Jesus. Where does that name come from, anyhow? Dixie?"

"South of the Mason–Dixon line. You didn't take any history classes as a kid?"

"At my school, we were more interested in trying to put a new spin on the great white heroes who slaughtered our women and children. Way we learned it, Custer's Last Stand was actually *Custer's Last Run*—most of his men were shot in the back or the ass—and that wasn't because anybody snuck up on them."

"Well. They were outnumbered in a big way."

"What they were were arrogant and stupid. Custer thought he was invincible, that with a few men he could defeat a nation of savages, every day of the week and twice on Sunday—after church, of course."

"Okay, okay, you can have Manhattan Island back—we shouldn't have cheated you out of it. I'm sure I speak for all white men."

They saw a few red neon vacancy signs lit along the main drag and they passed Jefferson Davis's old estate of Beauvoir.

"Six Oaks must be around here somewhere," she said.

But they couldn't spot it and they didn't want to ask somebody who might remember that they had. Jay passed a convention center and a Holiday Inn, pulled into a convenience store's parking lot. Scales went into the store, paid four bucks for a city map.

Back in the car, they found the White family estate. The PR flack's "not far" from Beauvoir translated to a little over a mile. That wasn't so bad. In the south, "Up the road a piece," could be anywhere from fifty yards to fifty miles.

Jay pulled back out onto the highway headed east, had to punch it a little to keep from being run over by a van full of teenagers in bathing suits.

"There it is," Scales said, nodding at the place, "on the corner."

Six Oaks was currently misnamed. There were four thick and tall live or pin oaks to the west and north of the house and probably twenty much smaller ones in front of it. The building itself was a huge, two-story white structure with a high gray roof. Four man-thick fluted columns were linked at the top by three arches that looped over the upper porch.

The lower porch went all the way around the front and sides of the house. Both verandas had waist-high balustrades, the lower one gapped in three places by sets of steps. Probably could put up the local football team and give each of the players their own bedroom. It was a big house.

The yard was lush green St. Augustine grass, neatly mowed. A fountain centered in a circular, raised-brick pond pumped an arm-thick column of water ten feet up from what looked like a giant, corroded and ornate copper bird bath. A sheet of water undulated and spilled over the edges of the copper fountain's bowl into the pond. A whitewashed wrought-iron fence, seven feet tall and spiked on top, surrounded the estate. Scales saw a security company "Armed Response" sign near a wide front gate. An intercom speaker and a TV camera were mounted on a pole next to the gate, inside the fence.

"Probably don't get a lot of door-to-door salesmen," Jay said.

"Probably means if we go calling and demanding explanations for murder and mayhem in the great Northwest we won't get very far."

"Looks like a public beach across the street here. Maybe we can work on our tans," she said.

"Like you need one."

"I'll keep you company, you're pale even for a white man. You could use a little color."

"Let's go around the block."

"I've been around the block a few times, Cowboy."

They made a U-turn farther down the strip, passed back in front of the estate and hung a right on a street that ran along the western side of the white iron fence.

There wasn't a street directly behind the place, so they went up a few blocks and turned around.

"Fence goes all the way around, looks like," Jay said. "There's a big garage and a gate and driveway on the side, see?"

Scales nodded. "Got it."

"Want to park and sit on the beach?"

"Probably ought to get a room first," he said. "And maybe pick up a bathing suit and some Coppertone. I burn easily."

"The Holiday Inn had a vacancy," she said.

"Or maybe we ought to take a run past the company before it gets dark, too."

"Okay. We'll get a room and then go find Medical Frontiers."

The Holiday Inn room was standard issue: a queen-sized bed, night stands, a table, short couch, TV and clock radio in the main room, a closet and a bathroom. They took turns in the bathroom and once they were feeling a little more human and little less like walking bladders, they headed back out to the car. Scales put the top up and this time, he drove.

Medical Frontiers Corporation was a few miles inland, in the middle of what looked like it had probably once been a cow pasture. There were four buildings, all single-story, the largest of which was the size of a big department store. All painted an ugly lime green. There was also an eight-foot-high chainlink fence topped with razor wire and a guard kiosk at an electric gate in the front.

"Doesn't look like they want people wandering in for a chat, either," Hughes said.

"I'd guess that would be standard procedure for a place that makes drugs," Scales said. "Dopers thought it was an easy mark, they'd be breaking in pretty frequently, wouldn't they?"

"Give the man a prize," she said. "Okay, we've seen it. Now what?"

"Why don't we go get something to eat and then back to the room? Get an early start in the morning?" he said. He wasn't really that tired, the flight and the drive in the warm sun hadn't taken the toll he would have figured, but Jay looked pretty worn out. "How you holding up?" he said, meaning her period.

"Fine. It's not like this hasn't happened to me every month since I hit puberty. Except for three months when I was sixteen."

They found a seafood restaurant in among fishing and pleasure boats in town, a blue wooden structure with a big parking lot. The place was crowded, the waitresses wore white dresses with black aprons, and the smells were wonderful. They got a table after ten minutes and looked at the menus.

"Any suggestions for this southern cuisine?" she asked.

Scales grinned. "Anything fried. Nobody does fried the way they do down here. You can sit and listen to your arteries get hard and plug up but it tastes so good you don't care. Catfish, shrimp, oysters, soft shell crab, crawfish tails when they're in season, whatever. Get some hush puppies and French fries to go with it, a green salad to make you feel virtuous. Stay here more than a week and we'll gain twenty pounds."

"You sure know how to say the right thing, Scales."

The waitress came. "Whutkin ah gitchawl?"

Scales looked at Jay. She shrugged. He said, "Seafood platter for two."

270

"Chuownto drank?"

"Iced tea," he said. "For the lady, too."

The waitress left.

"I'm glad you're here to translate, white eyes. I'd starve before I ever figured out what she said."

"Talk to me sometime after I get off the phone with my mother," he said. "I sound like a character from *Gone with the Wind*. Or maybe a bareback rider at the Texas State Fair."

"Yeeedoggie," she said.

Eventually the food came. The platter was piled high, enough to feed a little league team.

"This is good," she said around a mouthful of fried shrimp.

"Told you."

Between the two of them, they went through a pitcher of iced tea and the entire platter. It took them thirty minutes.

"Definitely we go back to the motel," she said. "I think I might sleep for a week or two."

On the way to the car—which Scales thought he might have trouble shoehorning himself into it after that meal—Jay reached over and took his hand in hers. He felt a sudden rush.

Weird as all this was, he was still having a good time. More or less.

THIRTY-ONE

The two time-zone change didn't seem to bother Scales any. He woke up at seven—that would have been five, west coast time—and headed into the bathroom. Hughes heard the shower crank up, then Scales as he got under the spray and began to sing softly to himself. She listened to "Hey, Jude" as it drifted out of shower into bed with her. He wasn't bad—on key, at least—though she doubted the last two Beatles would come looking for him to replace John or George.

With any luck, they'd make this sad song better, too. Somehow.

The water stopped. She heard the plastic shower curtain rings *clack-clack-clack* as the curtain slid back. She imagined she could hear him toweling himself. When he finished, he came back into the bedroom and looked to see if she was awake. He had the towel around his waist. His hair was wet-combed.

"Hi," she said.

"Hi."

She got up, brushed past him and into the bathroom. When she returned, he was cross-legged on the bed naked, looking at her.

"I had a thought," he said.

"Yeah?"

"We don't know that the head honcho down here is involved with this whole mess. Could be somebody else with his initials or maybe he just signs off on stuff without reading it."

"Okay. So?"

"So maybe before we corner him at the 7-Eleven and start hammering him with questions, we might ought to see if we can come up with more information."

"That sounds reasonable," she said. "How?"

He grinned. "Well, that's the part I haven't figured out yet. I wanted to leave you something to do. You know, so you'd feel useful."

"Thanks ever so much. Any other clever thoughts to go with this one?"

"I kinda figured maybe I should call my niece. I can get another one of those prepaid phone cards and see if she's got anything new on the medical end. Or use the cell phone."

"All right. While you do that, I'll come up with the other part."

When he came back from using the pay phone in the lobby, Scales looked agitated. He wore a pale blue T-shirt and darker blue shorts, white socks and running shoes. And the belly pouch.

"You look like you spent ten years in a cave in Alaska," she said. "You really are pale."

"Yeah, it takes me two weeks in the sun just to go from bright to white. Five minutes and I start to turn lobster-red and peel. If they made a sunblock SPF two thousand it'd be barely enough."

"So, how is your niece?"

"She's fine. I'm fine. We're all fine here."

"Are we?"

He shook his head. "I dunno."

"If you could explain that, in terms I can understand, that would be good."

He said, "According to Dana, all this stuff about DHEA

and apoptosis and dismutase and immune system shit is the hot new thing in medical research circles. Thing is, the top five or six scientists playing with such things have lately been out of pocket."

"Out of pocket?"

"They've stopped publishing their research. They are keeping low profiles. When she tried to get hold of one of them she knows, she says the guy's secretary told her he was on a leave of absence. She reached out through a friend of a friend and found that another one of these whiz kids is on vacation and has been for three months. And yet another professor quit her position with the university where she has tenure and supposedly got another job—only nobody knows where. Something of a mystery in certain circles."

Hughes said, "Yeah, and more of these nasty coincidences littering the ground like autumn leaves after a wind-storm."

"Dana says this kind of thing sometimes happens when people are on the trail of a major breakthrough. They shut up and lay low so nobody swipes their work."

"I don't like it. Do we know who these Nobel candidates are?"

"Yeah. I got three of their names." He held up a torn-out piece of phone book yellow page with scribbles on it.

Hughes, now dressed in a tank top and cut-off jeans, slid off the bed and went to the table where the stack of print outs they'd swiped in L.A. sat. "Rattle one off," she said.

"Joseph Michaels," he said.

Hughes found the list of employees. It took a few minutes. "Well, well. Looky here."

He moved to peer over her shoulder. It was in section marked "Subcontractors - Biloxi." There it was: Joseph A. Michaels.

"Hanah Smith-Welch?"

She rattled papers. "Two for two."

"Lawrence Mendleson?"

"We have a conspiracy, folks."

Scales blew out a sigh.

"This circumstantial evidence is getting pretty thick," she said.

"Still doesn't mean that White is the man to see," he said. "He could be a hands-off manager."

"What would it take to convince you?"

"Something linking him to them directly. Or to somebody."

"And how do we get this wonderful information?"

Scales nibbled at his lower lip. "I dunno. Maybe we watch him, see where he goes, what he does?"

"That's a possibility. Or we could maybe do a little more research. I assume this place has a newspaper and a library. We could look up back issues, stories about the company and White."

"Sounds good," he said. "I'll drop you at the library—"

"Wrong, white man. You do the library, I'll sit on the beach."

"Why is that?"

"Well, first because I'm a trained police officer and I know how to do surveillance. Second, because I can sit on the beach and not look like I just crawled out from six years hibernating under a rock. Third, because you're the computer nerd and a lot better suited to perching on a stool in a microfilm room staring at a screen."

"Okay, I get your point."

The Sun-Herald, the local paper, had offices a couple of miles from the motel, in Gulfport. Yes, they had a library and yes, one could do research in the stacks or microfilm section. The entire run of the paper had not been indexed and computerized—they were working on it—but Scales was certainly welcome to come by and check the last few years by title or subject and then dig that roll of microfilm out for viewing. The office was on Debuys Road, not far from the railroad tracks.

Jay drove the Miata to the office. "I'll hang around on the beach and work on my tan for a couple of hours," she said. "See if anybody comes and goes from Six Oaks. Pick you up around noon. I need to go find a camera place first. I want to rent a videocam with a zoom or at least a tele-photo 35mm."

Scales could see the need for that.

She dropped him off and drove away.

Scales signed in, told the helpful librarian he was doing research for a book, and was given access to a computer. He ran the name Winward White, came up with two dozen references and pictures, and started going through the micro-film, rolling it through the viewer and making himself dizzy.

He printed out several articles, including an architectural piece on the main house at Six Oaks, complete with diagrams and pictures. There were also photographs of White with other company officials; with the governor of the state; with a vice-presidential candidate from a couple of years back; with his wife, his grown children and here was one of him wearing a yellow hardhat, using a shovel to turn the first spade of earth at the construction site for a new plant to be built outside of Natchez.

There were no pictures of White passing thick envelopes of money to hit men, nor of him kicking dogs, nor of him spitting on the sidewalk.

Scales looked up and realized it was almost noon and he

was hungry, having had nothing more to eat or drink than a cup of nasty coffee in the motel room several hours earlier. He shut down the microfilm viewer, returned the film to the librarian and thanked her kindly. He took his sheaf of photocopies and left.

Outside, it was about five minutes before Jay showed. She had the top down and looked gorgeous in the little car. The sun glared and it was hot and humid. Rain clouds built to the southeast and it looked as if this storm might be rolling toward them.

"Hi, sailor. New in town?"

"How much you charge?" he said.

"Better put those in the trunk," she said. "So they don't blow away."

She popped the trunk lid and Scales put the photocopies into the tiny trunk. He saw a video camera and two spare batteries already there.

He climbed into the car and Jay pulled away. "How about some lunch?" she said.

"Good idea. So, how'd it go?"

She drove south, toward the coast highway a couple blocks away. "Well. Three men tried to pick me up even though I'm sure two of them thought I was black. The lifeguard stared at my ass so hard I thought it might burst into flame. Two kids kept running past and kicking up clouds of sand. A dog chased a Frisbee and once, he peed not too far away."

"That interesting, huh?"

"A limo did come out about ten o'clock. The windows were all blacked out but I followed it to a high-class restaurant where the passenger, a thin and rather athletic woman of about fifty dressed in a couple thousand bucks of tailored silks and Italian leather alighted and met another woman for breakfast. Mrs. White, I suppose, unless they pay the maids a lot better than I suspect. I managed to get a few feet of tape as she went in to the restaurant. Other than that, no activity from lovely Six Oaks, except for a gardener who spent the morning trimming trees. A white man, like yourself. I thought that was unusual down here. I got some video of him snipping branches with a long handled clipper. Never a dull moment. How about you?"

"I got a bunch of articles and some pictures. He's very popular around here, is Mr. White."

They drove to the same restaurant where they'd had dinner the night before, reasoning that it if was good then it might still be good now. They took a booth, ordered fish and chips and beer, and Scales spread out the photocopies.

"He looks familiar," she said, when she saw the first pictures. "And yes, that's Mrs. White—holy shit."

"What?"

"The gardener. Guy clipping branches—that's him. White."

"Come on."

"You can check the tape when we get back to the room, but it's him. Took me a second to make the connection."

"You'd think he could afford a yard man."

"Everybody needs a hobby, I guess," she said.

They were about to get out of the Miata at the beach, Scales slathering sunblock on his neck and face, when another limo pulled out of the side gate at Six Oaks.

"Whoops. Show time," she said. "Different car, too."

"How do you know? Limos all look alike to me."

"I'm a trained investigator. I notice the little details, microscopic differences in paint tone, tiny chips on the glass, like that. And the license plate numbers. That one is different than the one I wrote down when the missus went out." She pulled a notebook from the sunvisor over her head and tossed it to him.

Sure enough, the number was a digit different.

The limo pulled out onto the highway and headed east. Jay followed, three or four cars back, and they all moved down the road at jogging speed.

"One good thing about heavy traffic," she said. "They can't get too far ahead of us—unless they catch a light and we don't."

Which happened as soon as they reached the thick part of town. Fortunately, the limo was easy enough to spot. They saw it pull into the parking lot of a casino shaped something like the Lincoln Memorial. Jay did a fast U-turn and zipped into the lot.

The limo stopped in front of the casino's entrance.

"Go!" she said. "I'll park the car and catch up to you!"

Scales piled out of the car.

"Wait. Leave the gun. They won't let you in if you look like you're carrying."

He unsnapped the belly pouch and dropped it on the seat. He started up the walk.

He saw White get out of the limo. The man wore an ice cream-colored linen suit and tan shoes. Didn't look much like a gardener in it. The man was about five-eight, maybe one-sixty, and seemed fit enough from his walk. He didn't exactly bounce but there was a certain athletic grace to his steps. Gray hair, neatly trimmed, a deep, dark tan. At first glance, Scales would have pegged him at forty, forty-five, when he was, according to his bio, in his mid-fifties. Maybe all that tree-trimming kept him in shape. White walked to the sliding glass doors and inside. Scales didn't know how far away he should stay, but he didn't want to lose him, so he bustled in twenty feet back. At least White didn't have a bodyguard.

White ambled into the place as if he owned it. Maybe he did, for all Scales knew.

The sights and sounds washed over Scales in a noxious wave. The smells of air-conditioned cigarette smoke and nervous sweat blended with some kind of deodorizer as ranks of zombie-ized players mechanically fed coins into video poker, video blackjack and video slots. Machines burbled in musical chords that brought to mind a demented circus calliope. Now and then sirens wailed and colored strobe lights blinked brightly, prowl cars and fire engines and ambulances unmoving, to remind the zombies that the machines actually paid off. Waitresses moved back and forth, dispensing drinks and change. Scales glanced down and saw a big freestanding ash tray full of what looked like black volcanic sand. Farther on, bored dealers stood gazing at craps or blackjack tables. Security men in blue blazers with radio earplugs roamed around, hard eyed and watchful.

Reno, Vegas, the reservations, here—these places all had a sameness to them. Loud, obnoxious, desperate . . .

White strolled into a bar. The bartender waved at him, received a raised hand in return.

There was a door in the back of the bar and White went there. A uniformed security guard who stood there admitted White, shut the door behind him, went back to staring off into space.

Probably Scales ought not to try to follow him, he figured.

He bought a beer, sat at a table where he could see if anybody came or went from the guarded door. Tried to look like a gambler taking a break before going back to lose more money.

Ten minutes passed. Scales nursed the beer. That was easy, since it was a bottled Bud and he had given up that brand a long time ago.

Where was Jay?

Another couple of minutes went by. Jay walked in, spotted Scales, moved to sit across from him.

"Stupid son-of-a-bitch wanted me to check my camera at the door," she said. "I didn't want to leave it, in case we have to split in a hurry, so I had to go back to the car and lock it in the trunk. Next to our guns. I hope nobody steals the fucking car."

"I guess there are people in here who might not want to show up on the evening news back home," he said. "Or get shot down by a crazed loser."

"Yeah, I should have known better. Where is he?"

"Past that guard over there. Must be an office or a private gambling room or something."

As he finished speaking, the door opened. A short, dumpy woman of about sixty emerged. She wore a khaki shirt, a black skirt to mid-calf and sensible walking shoes. Also black-rimmed glasses. Her hair was mostly gray, might have been red once from the streaks in it, and she wore no makeup that Scales could tell. She carried a plastic tray piled high with gambling chips, and a brown leather purse slung over one shoulder.

Win White was right behind her. They two of them talked as they walked toward the bar's exit. The conversation was friendly. The lady had just won a lot of money. Thousands, Scales gathered from what White said as they passed.

Scales and Jay watched them peripherally until they moved from sight.

"Girlfriend?" he said.

"I doubt it. Let's go."

White accompanied the woman to the cashier's booth where she traded her chips in for cash. A security guard was summoned and he accompanied the woman and White to the front door. White got into the back of the limo. The woman and the guard started down the ramp.

"Stay with her," Jay said. "I'll tail White."

"How am I supposed to stay with her? Flap my arms and fly?"

"Get a make and model on her car, license number, which way she goes, like that. I'll come back for you once White lights somewhere."

Jay headed off into the lot at a brisk walk.

The woman and guard walked to the street. They waited for the light to change, then crossed into the lot of a five-story hotel. They went into the building.

What the hell, Scales thought. He followed them in.

Sensible Shoes and the guard went to the elevators. Scales walked up as if he belonged there, smiled at them. Got onto the elevator with them.

"Floor?" the guard said to Scales.

"Three, thanks."

The guard nodded. Pushed three and then five.

Scales got off on three.

Well, so much for that.

He went down the corridor toward the front of the hotel, found a stairwell, and hurried down it. Outside, he moved to one side of the hotel's lot and found a palm tree thick enough to shield him from the hotel's front entrance.

Three minutes later, the security guard from the casino came out and crossed the street.

Scales guessed that Sensible was staying at the hotel, and likely on the fifth floor. If this were the movies, he would go to the front desk, make up some story about Sensible being his aunt or something and get the clerk to tell him what room she was in. But he didn't have a lot of confidence in his ability to pull that off.

Instead, he went back across the street and waited for Jay to come back.

THIRTY-TWO

Apparently sports cars were common here on the Gulf coast. In the space of ten minutes, Scales saw two Miatas, an MGB and a Honda Del Sol, and those were just the red two-seaters.

A third Miata pulled into the lot and to a stop where Scales stood in the shadow of the casino's palm-tree flanked sign.

He got into the car and Jay pulled out of the lot.

"White went home," she said. "How about the woman?"

"She's staying in the motel across the street," he said. "Fifth floor." He paused and pretended to shoot his non-existent cuffs. "The name is Bond. James Bond."

"Room number? Her name?"

"Uh, well . . ."

"Uh huh. I don't think Her Majesty's Secret Service will be pounding down your door to get you to replace 007 any time soon. Bond would have charmed that information out of somebody. Rockford would have scammed the desk clerk. Mike Hammer would have pistol-whipped a manager and got her room and name."

"I didn't want her to see me."

"Even so."

"Okay, Modesty, how would you have done it?"

A car full of teenaged girls zipped past on their left in a top-down Jeep. The four girls were young, tanned, slim, and wearing about as much among them as half of Scales' T-shirt would cover if he cut it up into little triangles.

Maybe less. They yelled and moved their hands palms-down over their heads at Jay.

"What does that mean?" she asked.

"I think they think we should have the top down."

"Oh. I thought maybe they were trying to tell us how anything requiring more than a bust-size IQ goes right over their heads."

"Ooh. We're in a good mood, aren't we?"

The Jeep gained ahead of them, the girls laughing and enjoying the sun. They were young, free, going to live forever. Even if it was possible, Scales wouldn't go back to that age for a fortune—but there was much bliss to be found in teenage ignorance.

He said, "As you were saying about how you would have found out more about Sensible?"

"Sensible?"

"From her shoes."

"Ah. Attend, grasshopper, and learn."

Jay pulled into a liquor store's parking lot, got out of the car and went into the place. Scales waited in the car. While she was gone, he put the top down.

Jay came out with a paper bag. She handed it to Scales, climbed back in behind the wheel.

He slid the bottle out of the covering. "My. Moet & Chandon Brut. Good stuff. What are we celebrating?"

"You know, this thing really is fun to drive," she said, as she caught rubber leaving the lot.

In the lobby of the motel across from the casino, Hughes asked for and was directed to the bell captain. Scales watched her from a nearby couch overhung with potted palms and ficus trees.

"Help you, ma'am?" The bell captain was on the slow

side of forty, what hair he had combed straight back and held down with something greasy. He was short, dark and broad. He'd probably been pretty muscular once upon a time in his glory days of hauling bags, but now his gut stretched the button threat on his blue blazer to near the breaking point. He had brown, bloodshot eyes and a lot of burst vessels along the sides of his nose. A drinker. No smell, so she guessed he had a half pint of vodka tucked away in a pocket somewhere.

"Yes, please. My husband's aunt is staying here. She just won a jackpot across the street and my husband wanted me to give her this to congratulate her." She raised the bottle of Moet & Chandon. "Thing is, it's embarrassing, I went blank and can't remember the old lady's name."

The bell captain grinned. "I see. And what does she look like, your husband's aunt?"

Hughes described the woman. Ended by saying, "I believe she told him she was staying up on the fifth floor."

The bell captain smiled again. "I think I know who you mean. I'll be happy to deliver it for you."

"Well, I'd really rather surprise her myself."

"I'm sure you would," he said. The smile faded and his face went flat. "Two hundred."

"One-fifty," Hughes said, an automatic reflex.

"Do I look like the K-Mart here? Two gets you the name and room number. No discounts."

"You got it," she said.

"Be right back," he said. He headed for the front desk.

Hughes smiled at Scales. Raised the bottle in a mock toast toward him.

In a minute the bell captain returned. "You have something for me?"

Hughes reached out and shook his hand. The transfer of

cash, two four-folded hundred dollar bills, was invisibly made. The bell captain dropped his hand toward his pants pocket, glanced at his palm, saw the denomination on the tightly folded bill. Even if she'd stiffed him—and she hadn't—he saw he'd get at least a hundred out of it.

He smiled. "Five-thirty-one," he said. "Miz Hanah Smith-Welch."

Hughes nodded, kept her face neutral. Damn!

"Want me to deliver that?" the bell captain said, nodding at the champagne.

"No, I don't think so," Hughes said. "I must have gotten the wrong hotel. Doesn't sound like my husband's aunt at all."

"What a shame." They smiled at each other.

We're all professionals here—nice doing business with you.

As they headed for the car, Scales said, "Motherfucker. Hanah Smith-Welch. One of the hotshot scientists."

"So it would seem. Want to bet that the other missing white coats are also working for him? And that Hanah didn't win those chips she cashed in?"

"White," he said. "He buys chips, gives 'em to her, chalks 'em up as a gambling loss. Nothing shows on his books. She declares them as a win, pays taxes, everything is apparently legit. Man. How did you get the guy to tell you about her?"

"Bell captain in a place like this is usually too savvy to go for a simple con. It's always worth a shot, you never know, but I wouldn't think anybody mentally older than twelve would actually fall for the champagne trick. And if I'd flat out asked him for the name and room number, he might have told me to fuck off. But a crappy story and a couple hundred bucks will get you much further than a great story and no money. And this way, we get to keep the champagne."

"I bow to your expertise. You are the master. A question?"

"Sure."

"Can I drive this time?"

Jay put the champagne bottle into one of the room's little gray plastic trash baskets, took it to the ice machine and packed it full of ice. She wrapped a damp towel around the bottle's neck and set the makeshift ice bucket on the bathroom counter.

"Give it an hour and we can go for it," she said.

Scales was stretched out on the bed. She joined him. They lay side by side.

"So, do we have enough to convince you that White is involved in whatever this whole mess is?"

Scales said, "Yeah, afraid so."

"All right, Mistah Bond. What do you think we should do next?"

"Probably we should speak to Mr. White in person. He doesn't seem to have a bodyguard."

"Not to walk into a fairly security-conscious casino that he probably owns a big piece of—if not all of," she said. "And I'd guess the chauffeur has a degree in defensive driving and is also armed. We'll have to watch White for a while and see if he ever goes anywhere on his own. But I doubt we can count on it. That kind of money is always a target and a smart man would cover his ass."

"We could hop the fence while he's clipping the bushes, maybe," Scales said. "Tell him how much we admired his botanical work and by the way, what the fuck was he doing hiring murderers?"

"I doubt we'd get much of a conversation going before his security service and the local cops swarmed us," she said. "Millionaires get fast service when they ring the bell."

Scales leaned back on the two pillows propped against the bed's headboard. "Ideally, we need to get him somewhere alone long enough to have a friendly chat."

"Not that I want to rain on your parade," she said, "but even if we could manage that—suppose he likes to wade out into the Gulf all by himself or something—what exactly are we going to say to him?"

Scales raised his eyebrows. "How about, 'Listen, White, we know all about your evil insidious plan! Confess or we call the law and have you put away for a thousand years. Hee, hee, heee.'"

She laughed, picked up one of the pillows and thumped him with it. He didn't move to block, just let it lay on his face. She pulled the pillow away.

"And he says, 'Fine, go right ahead and do that,' knowing that if we had shit for evidence, we wouldn't be here talking to him, we'd be at his arraignment watching from the spectator's seats. What we have is shaky, circumstantial, and in point of fact, we don't know what his evil insidious plan is."

"We know there are a lot of dead people," Scales said. "We know that through Reuben, White's company was testing some kind of experimental cancer cure, sure as fuck not FDA approved. Even if we can't get him convicted of a crime, we can throw a big monkey wrench into whatever he's up to."

"Maybe he won't care," she said.

"And maybe he might care a lot. If you're willing to kill people to cover something up, it seems to me you really don't want anybody to know what's going on. Let's say, hypothetically speaking, that White does have this cancer cure almost ready. But if the FDA finds out he's been using it without proper protocols, at the least, the project starts in a deep hole. He's looking at fifteen years, several million bucks to get the thing approved and to market—assuming the studies show it doesn't have any nasty side effects. And if the G-men don't decide to try and put him away in a federal pen somewhere for messing with them. The FDA is like the IRS, it has a lot of power it can exercise just by decree. It could cost him a lot of time and money if he really pissed them off."

"Granted," she said. "But that still doesn't do us any good. There's no reason for him to take us seriously. And even if he did take us seriously, so what? Are we going to tape record him confessing that he is responsible for murder? Gun him down in a fit of street justice?"

Scales chewed on that for a few seconds. "I have a reason for him to take us seriously. Couple million reasons, actually."

She raised herself up onto one elbow and looked at him. He rolled over to face her, mirroring her pose.

"We'll blackmail him," he said.

"Wow. Hold on a second. I'll get the champagne," she said.

"It can't be cold yet."

"It'll be cold enough."

THIRTY-THREE

After two more days, Jay's tan was probably coming along pretty well. It was hard to tell, she was so dark. Scales, on the other hand, was a scorched red, despite the high-numbered sunblock, and if he planned to spend much more time on the beach, he was going to have to spring for a big umbrella or risk cooking. He could tan but it took a couple of weeks of carefully protected exposure to do it without looking like as if he'd been dropped into a vat of acidic dye.

"You want something to drink?" he asked Jay. They had a picnic basket full of sandwiches and fruit and a cooler with a dozen cans of Cokes and club soda all iced down.

"No, I'm good," she said.

"That's true."

So far, it had been a dull morning, insofar as activity from Six Oaks. Mrs. White—Maureen—had gone to breakfast with yet another of her many sharply-dressed and chauffeured lady friends. White himself had not left the estate—they theorized that he was on vacation or did his business from home, since he had yet to go to the local plant. He seldom went out, at least as long as they had been watching him.

"Maybe we could go back and have a little talk with our scientist friend?" Scales ventured. He popped the top on a can of bubble water.

"I doubt she knows more than just her piece," Jay said. "I imagine she'd be horrified to know what White did. Or what we think he did."

"Maybe not. If she collected her money in chips, she has to know something is not on the up and up."

"That's a reach," she said. "All he had to do was tell her he's having tax troubles or he's overspent his research budget or something. He didn't have to bring up the body count."

"Maybe we could get her to give him a call. Get him to come to her room and then we could have our conversation with him."

"Right. I'm sure she'd be thrilled to hear us demanding a shitload of unmarked cash from him or we go to the feds. If she's still there. My guess is that she's collected her money and checked out."

"We could see."

"Yeah, we could. We'll do that. Meanwhile, I have to go pee."

Jay stood, wiped her face and neck with a towel. There was a public bathroom not too far away. "Don't eat everything in the hamper while I'm gone," she said.

"I'll save you some bread crusts," he said.

He watched her trudge away, heard her bare feet making the little cheek-cheek noises sand sometimes made when you walked on it.

He ate a sandwich, finished his can of club soda. Ate an apple.

Six Oaks sat quiet in the afternoon sun, a little breeze ruffled the tree leaves and waved her Spanish moss back and forth.

When Jay hadn't come back in twenty minutes, Scales got a little antsy. Give her another few minutes, he thought. Probably just had to do more than pee.

Thirty minutes. Thirty-five.

Now he was worried. Jay had left her gun, holstered and wrapped in a towel. He put on his T-shirt, strapped his belly pouch on, picked up her towel-wrapped revolver and headed for the bathroom. He had that pit-of-the-stomach feeling, as if something were alive and working its way down into his bowel.

He didn't see her at the bathroom. He stopped a teenage girl going inside. "Excuse me, but my wife is not feeling well and I think she might be throwing up or something in there. Would you tell her I'm out here?"

"Sure."

"She's tall, dark, black hair. Name is Jasmine."

"Okay."

But when the girl came back out, she said, "There's nobody in there."

The thing in his bowel twisted, kinked, took his breath away and started his heart racing. Oh, Jesus! Where could she be? She ought to know better than to wander off without telling him!

His rational brain fought with the thing that lived in the cave inside his mind. She's okay, she just needed to walk to the market and pick up something, that's all.

No, the thing in the cave said, *No, something happened to her. Something bad—*

When nobody was looking, Scales went into the women's bathroom. The girl was right, there was nobody else in there.

He hurried frantically across the street, looking for her. Jay wasn't in the little market, they hadn't seen her.

She hadn't gone to the gift shop next door, nor to the motel.

He re-crossed the highway, headed back for where they had been set up on the beach. He could see their rental car parked where they'd left it, top up to help keep the seats cool.

Where are you?

Once, when his older daughter was five, she'd disappeared. She'd had an argument with her mother and when Janet had gone to let Shannon out of her room, she was gone. After looking everywhere inside the house and in their yard, a panicked Janet called Scales at work.

Scales had rushed home. They turned out the neighbors, called the police, went house to house, searched the yards, dug through every trashcan. All the while Scales had kept an outward calm. She's okay, he told himself. She's just run away, fallen asleep somewhere, we'll find her, she'll be fine.

But another voice had also been in him, a voice fueled by fear and imagination. She's dead. Some child molester got her, did unspeakable things to her, strangled her—

No matter what he had done, he couldn't shut that voice up.

Eventually they found Shannon. And the voice of reason had been right. She had gotten upset with her mother, had run off, managed to get a mile or so away before finding a doghouse in somebody's back yard. The dog that had lived there was on vacation with his mistress and Shannon had dozed off, tired from her walk. One of the Boy Scouts who'd joined the search found her there, still asleep. The relief Scales had felt had overwhelmed the anger, but the anger was still there. He wanted to hug her and shake her at the same time. "We were so worried about you," he told his daughter. "We missed you so much!"

Now, he felt that same sense of anger and worry. How could Jay do this, how could she worry him so?

Maybe because she didn't have a choice. Maybe somebody got her.

He couldn't make that thought go away, either.

★ ★ ★ ★ ★

An hour later, Scales was convinced. Jay wasn't at their room, she hadn't gone back to their spot on the beach. He had driven up and down the highway looking, but there was no sign of her.

Now, he drove back to the motel, thinking hard.

Either she had just up and walked away, something Scales could not believe, or somebody had taken her. If the latter was true and it wasn't some wandering psychotic who just happened to be passing by, then the obvious suspect was White. Somehow he had spotted them. He knew who they were and he had sent somebody to get Jay.

That made sense and as scary as that was, it was something Scales could deal with. Back at the room he had all that paperwork and in it somewhere was Winward White's private phone numbers, at work and at home. It was time to make direct contact with that bastard, fuck all this sneaking around. Scales was enraged, truly pissed off, and he had guns. If anything had happened to Jay, if she had been hurt—

Or killed—

Then Winward White was a dead man. No power on Earth could save him.

THIRTY-FOUR

As he walked toward their room, it suddenly occurred to Scales that if White had sent somebody to get Jay, it was very possible that the man had also sent somebody to collect him, too.

That they were waiting for a less-than-public place to grab him. Like inside his room.

The thought stopped him before he got to the door. Between the time he'd come back here looking for Jay and now, a small army could have moved into the place, could be waiting there for him to step inside. If somebody is out to get you, it isn't paranoia, it's healthy realism. Given the way things were going, it was a good idea for him to start paying better attention to such things.

Scales did a quick scan of the parking lot. There was a woman with two small children, all three in bathing suits, heading toward the pool just around the corner. A white Chevrolet pulled out of the lot, he couldn't see the driver. Other than that, he was alone.

There was only one way into the room. The door had a large window next to it but the heavy double curtains were mostly drawn, leaving but a three-inch gap in the middle.

Scales walked to the door, kept looking around for anybody who might be watching him. He didn't see any observers.

He unzipped his belly pouch and eased toward the gap in the curtains. He did a quick glance and moved away, didn't see anybody inside, then moved back for a longer look.

If anybody was in there, they had to be under the bed, on the floor on the other side of it, or in the bathroom. Under the bed would definitely be a problem if you were planning to jump out and surprise somebody in a hurry. Ditto lying on the floor—you might fall asleep or get too stiff to come up quickly, like when your quarry opened the door and waltzed in. If somebody was hiding in the room, then they'd probably be in the bathroom. If somebody was.

Scales swallowed, his mouth dry. Probably nobody was in there and he was going to feel real stupid if he went barreling in waving a gun around like he was Brad Fucking Pitt.

Then again, if nobody was home, then nobody would see how stupid he felt. And if somebody was in there . . .

The door's lock was magnetic, you used one of those little plastic cards. Slip the card in, the little red diode turned green and then you could turn the handle. Quieter than a key.

He took a deep breath, let it out, took another and held it. Slid the keycard into the slot with his left hand. Grabbed the butt of the revolver in the unzipped belly pouch with his right hand. Put his finger on the trigger.

The light on the lock turned green.

Should he push the door open slowly? Or shove it wide as fast as he could?

Fast, he decided. If somebody was inside, they might have put a can or something behind the door to make noise. Moving slow would only warn them. Besides, he needed to move fast.

He let his in-drawn breath out, took another one—

—shoved the door open, leaped into the room, pulled the Smith, all at once—

Somebody stepped out of the bathroom. A man. He had a gun, was raising it—

Scales snapped the little revolver up—

Hughes wasn't handcuffed or bound in any way. She sat in a comfortable, overstuffed leather chair in a tastefully-appointed study, lots of hand-waxed and rubbed wood paneling—pecan, she guessed—shelves of books, like that. There was a large painting on the wall of a man in hunting clothes holding a shotgun and a brace of pheasant, a black dog standing next to him. Definitely a man's room.

She was free to move, but White's chauffeur stood behind her and to one side, ten feet back with a .40 caliber SIG pistol in a shoulder holster under his unbuttoned jacket. She was pretty sure he could get that gun out and working before she could move far in any direction. And from his angle, he could shoot her without endangering his boss. For now, they were being relatively civilized. When she'd come out of the bathroom on the beach, the chauffeur's gun had been hidden under a folded newspaper. Just like in the movies. He'd opened the paper enough to show it to her, then covered it. Even if she'd had her piece with her, she'd never have gotten to it before the chauffeur cooked her. He was a pro.

Behind an oak desk across from Hughes sat Winward White. He wore a white silk suit, a pale pink shirt, a blue tie. She had seen his feet and instead of some handcrafted European loafers, he wore a pair of Nike running shoes. They were black leather, but she could make out the black swoosh. He had lots of smile wrinkles at the corners of his eyes and the easy look of old money.

Hughes had an urge to blurt out something like, "You can't get away with this!" but she kept quiet. Probably he could get away with it, unless Scales could figure out what had happened to her and what to do about it. She loved Scales, she had realized that, and there was much about him to admire, but this wasn't his thing. He wasn't James Bond.

"If you're worried about your friend Mr. Scales," White said, "don't. He's going to be along shortly." He had a deep, soft voice with a syrupy, southern overlay. Very genteel. It was easy to picture him sitting on a veranda sipping at a mint julep watching the slaves pick cotton in the fields.

What the hell, she might as well give it a try. "Kidnapping is a fairly serious crime, Mr. White."

"Call me 'Win,' please. Because that's who I am and that's what I do—win."

That had the sound of something he had said a few hundred times, polished smooth like an old banister.

"Yes, ma'am, Miz Hughes, kidnapping is a serious crime. Pretty much a drop in the bucket though, all things considered, don't you think?" He smiled. Nice white teeth, probably bonded.

Hughes didn't speak to that. But she didn't need to. He knew who she was and that meant something.

He went on. "I don't know exactly how much you and your friend Mr. Scales have found out, but I do know somebody broke into my computer system and had a look at some records I thought were supposed to be private. Those records, by the way, no longer exist. In case you were wondering."

Hughes stared at him.

"And I know that several of my people are . . . no longer with us, at least two of them dispatched by you or your friend's hand."

Two?

Again, he seemed to read her mind. "There was one unfortunate fellow wounded by a shotgun up there in Warshing-ton, another one who was apparently pushed in front of a truck in Ory-gone."

"We didn't push him. It was an accident. He fell."

White waved one hand in dismissal. "It doesn't really matter, darlin', they were paid soldiers, they knew there were risks involved. The problem is, you and Mr. Scales have managed to dig up all kinds of things that were better left buried. Things I'd just as soon not have dragged out into the light and put up for public view. So we have to set down, you, me and Mr. Scales and decide how best to resolve this whole unfortunate situation."

This was where she was supposed to denounce White and his evil scheme—whatever the hell it was—and tell him they weren't making any deals with the Devil. But the dry mouth and thumping fear in her kept Jay quiet and seated. With a wave of his hand, he could have her killed. She wasn't ready to die. So she just nodded and said, "Okay."

Chances were good that he might have them killed anyhow, but maybe not. Maybe Scales was right, maybe he was the kind of man who thought that if he threw money at a problem, he could make it go away.

She sure hoped so.

The phone rang.

"That would be my trusted soldier, Jules," White said. "Calling in regard to your Mr. Scales." He must have seen something in her face, because he let the phone ring again as he said, "Don't concern yourself, darlin'. Long as Mr. Scales didn't do anything foolish, he'll be just fine."

Jest fahn. She was really beginning to hate that term.

White reached for the phone.

★ ★ ★ ★ ★

When the man came out of the bathroom, Scales was stretched as tight as the e-string on a violin. All he needed to see was that the person in front of him was not Jay. Then he saw the gun. His vision tunneled, his hearing went away and all he could perceive was that black pistol, moving up in slow motion . . .

Scales shoved his own weapon out as if punching with a silver fist.

Time stalled . . .

The gun facing him drooped, fell to the floor, the man holding it crumpled . . .

His vision expanded, his ears began working again. Scales hadn't heard his shots or if the man from the bathroom had gotten off a shot. What he heard now was a mechanical, repetitive clicking, very fast, snap, snap, snap, snap—

His gun. It was the sound of the hammer hitting the empty shells in the cylinder.

He lowered the gun, stopped working the trigger. He had shot it empty, five rounds, without being aware he had done so—and kept going. Had the gun held thirty, he would have shot them all. Lord—

The man on the floor was wheezing, drawing great bubbling breaths, struggling to get air.

Punctured a lung, Scales thought. He moved toward the injured man.

The wheezing stopped.

Scales dropped to his knees, checked the carotid pulse. Nope. He was gone. The man wore a green tank top and shorts. There were at least three blood-oozing holes grouped over the man's sternum, Scales could have covered them with a playing card. A fourth wound was lower and to

301

one side. Three in the heart and lungs, one right in the liver. CPR would just pump him dry, assuming he had much of a heart left.

He wondered where the other bullet went—?

Scales suddenly realized the man might not be alone. And his gun was empty—

He grabbed the black pistol and hoped it was ready to shoot. Spun and looked around wildly.

Aside from the dead man, he was alone.

He ran to the door, jerked it open, looked into the parking lot.

If anybody heard the shots, they hadn't come out to investigate. A short fat man in Bermuda shorts and a Hawaiian shirt and flip flops ambled across the parking lot toward the beach. A maid pushed a cleaning cart across the lot toward another section of the motel. Neither of them looked in his direction.

How could you shoot a gun five times in a crowded resort town and not have people come running? What kind of a world was that? Weren't they worried about terrorism?

Scales shut the door. Realized that he still held the dead man's weapon. Good thing nobody had glanced his way.

The gun felt oddly off-balance in his hand. He looked down at it.

The slide was bent, and half the muzzle was covered by a silver and copper-colored smear. It took him a second to realize what had happened: the missing bullet. He had hit the gun that he was most focused on. If he had tried to shoot this thing, it probably would have blown apart in his hand. Great.

He went back to the body. Stood there staring at it, feeling nauseated, hot, jittery. He took a couple steps back, sat heavily on the bed. He'd just killed a man, blam, just like that.

Jay.

He went to the stack of printouts, dug through them, came up with the phone listings. He found the number he wanted, got an outside line, punched in his call.

The phone rang. Rang again. He glanced at the body on the floor. Wasn't a lot of blood, considering, but what was there soaked into the carpet. Going to be a real mess to clean up.

"Hello?" came the voice from the phone.

"Mr. White? It's Rick Scales."

There was a long pause. "I see. I don't suppose it would be possible for me to speak to my, ah, associate, Jules?"

"Jules is . . . indisposed."

"I see. Well. I suppose we'd better talk."

"You suppose that right, too. Is Jay Hughes there? Is she all right?"

"Yes to both."

"Good. Let's cut to the chase, Mr. White."

"You on a public phone, Mr. Scales? It would be prudent for you to speak with care."

"Care? All right. Here's the deal. I am in possession of certain . . . technical information that I believe you will find quite valuable. I believe it is absolutely essential for the continued well-being of your corporate interests."

"Yes?"

"I'd like to sell you this information, after which I and my associate, Ms. Hughes, will no longer have any use for it."

"I see. And how much do you figure this information is worth, Mr. Scales?"

Scales thought about it for a second. It had to be enough

to convince him they were serious but not too much to spook him. He said, "Two million. That's firm."

Another long pause. "And if I decide to enter into this agreement, I can be assured that none of my . . . competitors will ever come across this information?"

"I guarantee it."

"I believe we can do business, sir. Tell me where you are, I'll send a car."

"I have my own transportation. I'll call you back in an hour to arrange a meeting place."

"You're welcome to come on by the house," White said.

"I don't believe so. You'll need time to arrange for payment, won't you?"

"For two million, I can walk to the wall safe, Mr. Scales. Why don't you just drop on over? Miz Hughes and I have been having a nice talk. I'm sure she would be glad to see you."

He had to ignore the implied threat. If he walked into the lion's den with them waiting for him, they'd eat him and Jay both. It was hard, but he said, "I'll call you back in an hour with the meeting place."

He hung up the phone. Looked around the room. There was nothing here worth dying for. His target pistol and Jay's revolver were locked in the Miata's trunk. He didn't think White wanted the cops to find the shot-up body of a man connected to him in a motel room a mile away from Six Oaks but that was his problem.

Scales wiped the black pistol off with a towel and stuck it in the dead man's hand. If the local police did find the body, he could always argue self defense, if it came to that. He came back to the room, somebody he didn't know jumped out with gun, he could sure as hell pass a lie detector test on that part of it.

Scales went outside. Paused long enough to hang the "Do Not Disturb" sign on the door. He didn't want the maid dropping by. He hurried to the car, got in, pulled out of the parking lot.

He had an hour to get into Six Oaks and rescue Jay.

THIRTY-FIVE

White cradled the phone and smiled at Hughes. "Well, well. It would appear that your Mr. Scales is more resourceful than I had thought. It has been a while since I underestimated an opponent, it's a good lesson to have brought home now and again. Keeps one humble."

Hughes wondered exactly what Scales had done. From the sound of White's end of the conversation, the guy who had gone to grab Scales wasn't coming back under his own power.

"Lawrence, where was it that Jules intended to collect Mr. Scales?"

The bodyguard/chauffeur said, "At his motel room."

"Best if you send Leroy and Joey there. I expect Mr. Scales will have departed but his room will probably be in some disarray. Have them clean it up and dispose of the remains."

"Yessir. What about her?"

"Miz Hughes and I will be fine. It seems that we have come to terms and I'm sure she wouldn't want to jeopardize her chance to become a millionaire."

Lawrence nodded. Turned and left the room.

"You really have that much money here? Two million dollars?"

"Why, Miz Hughes, I do believe you were eavesdropping on my conversation. Yes. I keep small amounts on hand for this and that. Nice, clean, untraceable hundreds. That much will fill up a small suitcase, that's twenty thousand bills, you know."

"And you're just going to give it to us?"

"Why not? It's only money. Look at it from my point of view. It is much better to have you as rich and happy accomplices than as enemies, don't you think?"

Scales must have something in mind. Whatever it was, she figured it was wise to play along with it. "Yeah, I can understand that."

"Good. Would you like to see your money?"

"Sure."

He stood, moving with easy grace, and sauntered to the oil painting. It was hinged down one side, covering a good-sized wall safe. He dialed in the combination, swung the door open. "Have a look."

Hughes stood and stepped over next to White. Looked into the safe. There was a little light on inside, must be like a refrigerator bulb or something. The safe had two compartments, with a half-high divider separating them. On the left was a stack of money that filled the space, on the right, several small leather cases and what looked like gold-edged bonds.

Lawrence returned. "Leroy and Joey are on their way to the Holiday Inn."

"Good. Would you get a case and put two million dollars in it for me?" White nodded at the safe.

"Yessir." Lawrence left the room again.

"Please forgive me, Miz Hughes, I'm being a terrible host. Would you care for some refreshment? A drink to seal our bargain? Some bourbon and branch water? A mint julep? Although I have to tell you, mint juleps are one of the nastiest-tasting concoctions on God's green Earth."

Hughes' mouth was dry. "Maybe a glass of water?"

"Certainly." White moved to his desk, pressed a button inset into the top. A black woman in a maid's outfit arrived within seconds. "Lorrie, would you bring Miz Hughes a glass of ice water? And a Southern Comfort on the rocks for me?"

"Yassuh, Mistah White."

Lawrence returned yet again with one of those airline travel bags that had a handle and wheels so it could be pulled behind you like a wagon. He unzipped it and began filling it with crisp bundles of hundred dollar bills. His lips moved as he counted the stacks.

The maid returned with a silver tray, upon which was a tall frosted glass filled with water and ice and a whiskey sour glass with about three fingers of pale brown liquor over ice in it.

Hughes took the water, White the blended whiskey. Lorrie turned and left. White raised his glass in a toast. "Here's to our new partnership," he said.

Hughes trusted this man as far as she could pitch him one-handed. She didn't believe for a second that he was just going to hand over two million dollars and wave bye-bye. What she believed was that she and Scales would become another clean-up chore for Leroy and Joey, but she raised her own glass. Let him think she believed it.

They drank.

White said, "Please, have a seat. Mr. Scales—who is understandably cautious, though it is not really necessary here—will be calling back within the hour to arrange a meeting place where we will finish our negotiations. If you would speak to him and assure him of my good intentions, that will probably go a long way to relieving his mind of worry." He smiled, took another sip of his drink.

Hughes sipped at her water and worried on her own. This whole little show with the suitcase full of money was for her benefit. She was supposed to convince Scales that all was sweetness and light. And this man was altogether too smooth and too sharp to mess around with. He held all the aces.

She sure hoped Scales had something going. Whatever it was, it would have to be good.

THIRTY-SIX

A storm cell blew in from the Gulf, complete with strobe lights and sound effects, and the first fat drops started to fall. Scales risked the drive past along the side of Six Oaks. He reasoned that nobody would be standing at a window looking for him and even if they were, the thickening rain should offer some cover. As he drove, he looked at the estate. Nothing had changed outwardly. He knew he could leave the car, move along the back fence and find a place where he could climb it. That would be the easy part. But the fence itself might be wired into the alarm system, there could be motion sensors in the yard, and for sure the doors and windows would be rigged. He didn't know enough about this kind of stuff. He'd seen movies, read books and knew that some alarm systems went off if the power was interrupted and some had battery back-ups that kept them online even if the juice was cut off. Some of them sent a call for help out on the phone lines.

He didn't know enough and time was running out fast.

What came to mind was something he remembered as a twelve-year-old boy visiting an uncle in the city. It was a terribly hot summer evening and almost dark and everybody's air conditioners were running full blast. Scales had been in the back yard, playing with his cousins in a treehouse they'd built when there came an explosion. It was a hollow *boom!* that echoed over the treehouse. It sounded like a cherry bomb going off inside a big steel garbage can.

"Jesus, what was that?"

310

One of his cousins, Kyle, said, "Aw, just a transformer blowing up. Lookit th' house."

Scales looked. The house was dark. The whole street was dark and the ever-present rumble of air conditioners was stilled. It was spooky how quiet it was.

"What happens is, the oil inside the transformer gets too hot and it explodes. The power company has to come out and put up a new one. Takes 'em a couple of hours."

More than thirty five years ago, that memory, but now it might be just what he needed. Most of the power here was underground, you didn't see electrical lines on poles as much as you used to, but there was a power substation not far from here—he remembered seeing it when they'd been driving around and scoping things out. He could be fairly certain that a lot of the area's power went through that sub-station, a collection of steel boxes and giant transformers and heavy cables draped from tall towers.

He drove to where he remembered the substation was.

THIRTY-SEVEN

White looked at his watch. "Won't be long now," he said to Hughes. "Another half hour or so. I hope the rain lets up. With all those young people speeding, the roads are real dangerous when they get wet." He smiled at her.

Hughes' water glass was almost empty and as a result she needed to pee but she didn't want to bring that up.

As if making idle conversation, White said, "So, where are you and Mr. Scales going to live, once you become people of independent means?"

"I don't know. Probably we'll go home, for a while, at least."

"You ever read anything by Mr. Thomas Wolfe, Miz Hughes?"

"I don't recall that I have."

"When I was at Yale, the English professors were quite high on his writing—Mr. Wolfe's. You should try reading him. Especially those novels published posthumously."

Now what did that mean?

White said, "You know, I do have to congratulate you all on getting this far. It appears that Dr. Reuben made an error in judgement of Mr. Scales."

She didn't say anything, waited for him to continue.

"See, Mr. Scales was supposed to be a burned-out case, out there in the woods, marking time. No ambition, indecisive, not sharp enough to pick up on what was going on, or even if he did, he wouldn't care. Dr. Reuben told me your friend was a loser, no offense, Miz Hughes. You must have helped him along considerably."

"The other way around," she said. "I was looking for a reason somebody killed one of my people. Without Scales, I never would have gotten off the reservation."

White nodded, sipped at his drink. "Interesting. I would have a few words with the good Doctor Reuben—but I guess he paid for his mistake, didn't he?"

Again the toothy smile.

Hughes repressed a shudder. This man found death all too amusing. It did not bode well for her future.

THIRTY-EIGHT

Under a pouring rain from inside a tiny fogged-up convertible, the power substation looked pretty formidable. There were big, painted metal boxes, man-high transformers with cooling fins, steel frames that looked as if they had been fabricated from a giant erector set to support a bunch of incoming wires and glass or ceramic insulators as big as Scales' arm. A couple of tall power towers bracketed the whole affair. A ten-foot-tall chain link fence with warning signs in English and Spanish surrounded the place, and the coil of razor wire looped atop the fence was a good indication somebody didn't want stray visitors. Being inside a place like this in the middle of a thunderstorm didn't seem particularly wise; Reddy Kilowatt's big electrical brother might come to call. And even if he could scale the fence and get inside, what good was that going to do him? Wet as it was, if he touched anything, he'd turn into something that looked like a strip of overcooked bacon. Once, onboard a ship with the Marines off the coast of Vietnam, Scales had seen an electrician who had grabbed the wrong power cables. The swabbie's skin was burned black and oozing serum from cracks in it by the time somebody killed the juice and got him off the wires. He looked liked a piece of barbecued chicken left on the grill too long. And there was that hunter hit by lightning in Idaho last year, the bolt had blown his shoes off and driven his feet into the ground like tent pegs. He'd been lucky to survive. Big power was nothing to fool around with.

He could maybe rig the car's gas pedal with a stick or something to crash into the place. If it got through the fence and if it hit the right thing, that might do it. Of course, he was a mile away from Six Oaks in a driving storm, and he had twenty minutes left before he was supposed to call back. He'd play hell getting there on foot, over the fence and inside in that time. If the car would do the job anyway.

It was all iffy as shit any way you looked at it.

But he remembered something else he and his buddies used to do when he was a teenager, when they were out rabbit hunting with their .22s or .410s.

Scales popped the trunk, got out, and grabbed his target pistol. He also collected the light windbreaker he'd packed. It wouldn't do much to keep a rain like this off, but it would give him something to hide guns under. He was soaked by the time he got back into the car.

It was awkward, but he slid Jay's service revolver's holster onto his belt. Along with the belly pouch and the reloaded snubbie in it, he felt pregnant but now he had two weapons on and another on the seat next to him. Three-gun Rick.

Jesus.

The substation was just off the road in a field. A gravel path led to the gate. Scales pulled off the road and onto the gravel, drove to within a few yards of the gate, then jockeyed the car back and forth until he was parked crossways on the gravel, the driver's window facing the transformers. He rolled the window down.

The power hum from the substation was a heavy drone, thrumming with energy, a giant wasp in a bottle, and well able to fatally sting anybody stupid enough to mess with it.

He loaded ten rounds into the pistol's magazine, slid it into the butt and worked the slide. Automatically he snicked the safety on. He pulled a set of foam earplugs from his case and put them into his ears. He twisted the dot scope's on/brightness control to full, propped the barrel of the .22 against the window frame and held it there with his left hand. He looked through the scope, both eyes open, and saw the tiny glowing dot appear in midair. He moved the gun until the dot was on one of the big ceramic insulators, just under the wire it supported. It was about fifty feet away, he guessed. The dot bobbed up and down in tune with his heartbeat. He clicked the safety off. The rain kept falling.

Steady . . .

He fired. Saw the dark ceramic insulator chip an inch or two away from the wire. He heard the whine as the tiny bullet bounced off.

He re-sighted, fired again. Another chip, but the tough material held.

He pulled the trigger. Again. Again. The sound was muted by the plugs but still loud under the vinyl roof and falling rain. He hoped nobody lived behind the station anywhere close, he was sending ricochets all over.

On the eighth shot, the insulator had enough. It shattered and the heavily insulated wire snapped away, draped itself across the top of the fence.

Scales removed the magazine and reloaded it. With the one in the chamber, he now had eleven shots. He lined the sight up on the wire where it touched the metal fence.

It took three shots. The third round tore enough of the insulation away for the wire under it to make contact with the metal bar at the top of the fence.

There was a giant blue-white flash, a *boom!* and the power hum died. The smell of ozone and burned metal and grass rolled over the Miata. The metal bar atop the fence glowed orange, smoke rising from it.

That sure as hell threw a breaker.

Gulf States or whoever owned this place was going to hate him.

He put the gun down and started the car. He had fifteen minutes.

He drove fast, got to a spot near the western corner of the whitewashed wrought iron fence surrounding Six Oaks and pulled the car to a stop. The rain slapped at him as he left the car. He ran along the north side of the fence, didn't worry if anybody saw him. There was a field to his left, a few trees growing in it, but none close enough to the fence so that he could climb one and drop inside. It didn't matter.

He heard sirens in the distance and guessed that enough of the city had been blacked out that the cops were going to be busy at intersections where the traffic lights were out, as well as checking for burglar alarms that went off during power failures.

He ran. Or rather, he slogged. There was an inch of standing water where the ground was level and more than that collected in hollows, muddy brown puddles as deep as his calves, some of them.

He came to a place where the bushes and trees inside mostly blocked the fence from the house.

He hadn't had to climb a fence in years but it came back in a hurry. The points on the top were more ornamental than useful, rounded little balls on them like the tip of a fencer's foil. He levered himself over and dropped, hit the wet ground hard but stayed on his feet. It must be the adrenaline, that seven-foot fall was like nothing.

No time to be patting yourself on the back, Scales. Move!

He ran toward the house.

There was a back door that probably went into the kitchen, a set of French doors halfway down the house that were probably an entrance into a bedroom or a living room, and a covered walkway to the garage. Scales ignored these and headed for a large window nearest the east corner of the house. If the window was unlocked, that would be a better way in, assuming the room behind it was empty.

He reached the window. There were gauzy curtains draped over it but they were mostly transparent. It was a bedroom with a big four-poster bed and some antique chests and dressers in it. Empty.

He didn't hear any alarms from inside, so maybe the system was off. Or maybe the fence and yard weren't set up to detect movement. Maybe, maybe, maybe! Stop thinking and move!

He peeped around the corner of the house. Saw one of those metal boxes marked with a bell mounted on the wall.

Telephones.

He moved to the box, saw that it wouldn't open without a screwdriver.

Fuck this. He stood to one side, kicked the box until it fell off the wall. Saw the bundle of wires going through a hole in the wall. Pulled out his pocket knife and hoped they didn't have much juice in them. Cut the wires. Didn't even feel a buzz.

He headed back around the corner.

The window was a wooden-framed weighted-sash job but it was locked. One of those pivoting hooks at the top where the frame and window met. Damn.

Lightning flashed. Scales looked around. He pulled Jay's .357 from the holster. Waited.

When the thunder crackled and rumbled four seconds

later—close, less than a mile—he used the butt of the gun to break the glass. He reached in, unlocked the window, shoved it up.

Inside the house, an alarm began hooting over and over. Fuck!

Well, at least it wasn't going to call out for help now.

He didn't have time to worry about it now. Speed was going to have to serve in place of finesse. He climbed through the window. He wished he could remember the layout of the house's interior from the article, but it was all a blank.

Hughes really needed to pee and the sudden screaming of an alarm didn't help. The lights had gone out a few minutes ago, but a back-up lighting system mounted in the room's corners had clicked on. White did not seemed concerned. It happened all the time when it stormed, he told her.

Lawrence ran into the room, his SIG out and at port arms. "Mr. White? You okay?"

"Yes, yes. It wasn't the panic button. Might have been a branch fell on the house, I haven't gotten all the widow makers out of the big pecan out back." White looked at Jay. "Sometimes a strong gust of wind will set the system off." To Lawrence, he said, "Go and make sure that's all it was."

Lawrence nodded and was gone. After a minute, the alarm went off.

White said, "You don't think your Mr. Scales would be so foolish as to try to break in here, do you?"

"He's not that kind of guy," Hughes said.

"I'm sure my man Jules would be happy to know that. Still, chance favors the prepared, you know. And given as how we have underestimated Mr. Scales before, it wouldn't be wise to assume that he's what we once thought." He opened a drawer in the desk and pulled out a small chromed or stainless steel pistol and slipped it into his jacket pocket.

She didn't get a good look at it. One of the little .380s, PPK, maybe a P5. Looked like a mother-of-pearl handle. Not much weapon but big enough to kill you with.

Scales ran through a doorway and into a hall—

And smack into a large obstacle—White's chauffeur.

The chauffeur was bigger but Scales had the momentum. They slammed into a wall behind the chauffeur. Scales lost his wet-handed grip on Jay's gun. It clattered to the floor as he and the chauffeur bounced off each other.

The chauffeur had a gun, too, and his grip was better than Scales'. He shook off the impact, started to bring the gun up—

Scales' panic was hot and immediate. He couldn't get the belly pouch open in time, no way, Jay's gun was on the floor, might as well be a million miles away he'd never get to it fast enough, he had no weapon and the guy was going to shoot him—!

Scales heard himself growl like some demented animal. He leaped at the chauffeur, snapped his hands up and shoved as hard as he could—

In a quarter-second, all those years of bench pressing, of straining under the iron on the bar, it all paid off. The effect was astounding.

The chauffeur slammed back into the wall behind him so hard the plaster and lathe shattered. His head snapped back, hit—and the wall gave way. He went into the wall, wedged between two wooden uprights so tightly he couldn't fall, even though he was unconscious. The gun dropped onto the top of his left foot, bounced onto the Oriental rug runner. Looked as if it was gong to take a crowbar to get him out of the wall.

A woman said, "Sweet Jesus Almighty!" down the hall to Scales' right.

He spun. A black woman in a maid's outfit stood there.

Scales bent, picked up Jay's gun. "Where is Mr. White and the woman with him?"

She pointed down the hall. "In the s-s-study! D-D-Down and right, then left! Don't s-s-shoot me, mister!"

"I'm not going to shoot you. You go find somewhere to sit down for a while. No point in trying to call the police, the phones don't work."

"Yes, sir!"

Scales turned and went to find the study.

The house shook, Hughes felt a vibration through the wall, but she didn't see a flash of light or hear thunder. She looked at White, who frowned.

White stood and moved from behind the desk toward the room's entrance. He pulled the little pistol from his pocket and stood facing the closed oak door. To Hughes, he said, "You stay right where you are, darlin'."

From the tone of his voice, he expected her to do just that. Hughes realized that this rich Southern white man was used to having everybody obey him, especially a woman who was as dark as his black maid was. It would never occur to him to think otherwise. Injuns, niggers, spics, wops, they were all inferior to Winward White, he couldn't believe otherwise. She could feel it in him. He was one of the Chosen and everything around him proved it to him.

The door handle turned, slowly.

Scales.

It had to be him. Somehow he had done it. He had gotten in, gotten past Lawrence and whoever else White had out there. And if he came in with a gun, White would shoot him, all the crap about paying them off no longer necessary.

The door began to slowly swing open.

White raised the pistol and smiled.

THIRTY-NINE

Scales didn't want to rush through the study doorway, in case somebody had a gun pointed at Jay and they panicked. So he eased the door open . . .

Scales saw White extend one hand with a sure enough fucking gun in it—

—saw Jay leap up from a chair and yell "Scales, down!" as she lunged at White—

—time went rubbery yet again and Jay's flight slowed—

—White turned toward her—

Jay slammed into White. His gun went off but Jay kept going, pushed, knocked White off balance—and Scales finally found his voice:

"Freeze! Move and you die!" He held Jay's gun with both hands, sights locked and aimed right at White's left eye.

White froze.

"Jay, get his gun."

She took the pistol from White's hand.

Scales felt a great wave of tiredness flow through him but he kept White covered.

The man turned and smiled at him. "Ah, the redoubtable Mr. Scales. I am pleased to finally meet you in person—though I do feel as if I already know you. You are much more adept than I expected. I stand corrected."

Scales was not in the mood. "Sit down, White. Right fucking there."

White sat in an overstuffed leather chair.

"Jay, you okay?"

"I am now." She turned to White. "Where is the nearest bathroom?"

When Jay returned, Scales sat on the edge of the desk with the gun resting on his knee, looking at White, who seemed as unconcerned as if all this had been no more than a spirited bridge game.

"All right, sir. Miz Hughes is fine and that suitcase over there is full of your money. Why don't you all just take it and leave? We'll all just go on about our business."

"Just going to give us two million dollars? Right. I want some answers first."

"And what if I'm not disposed to give you any?"

Scales grinned. "I will shoot you somewhere that will hurt you. I'll keep on doing that until you are disposed to give me anything I damn well ask for."

Jay said, "You learn pretty quick for a white man."

"Thank you."

White said, "Well. Let's keep things friendly here. How much of it do you have? To save going over that you already know."

"We know that your company has developed a new drug," Scales said. "That you were testing it illegally on patients—on my patients—with the help of my late employer, Dr. Reuben. Where did you know him from?"

"He worked briefly on the project for my father when he first left medical school. The tools were not up to the job, the project was put on hiatus. Reuben went on with his life. When I restarted the project, I thought to look him up—he was a brilliant man when he was younger. Unfortunately, he no longer had the skills we needed. But they also serve who provide a field test."

"This anti-cancer project has been in progress since the fifties?"

White laughed, a high, cackle. "That's quite funny. You think you know what is going on but you don't."

Scales wanted to smash the man's face. He held onto his temper. "I know that two of your men killed Jimmy Lewis to keep him quiet, and that several of my other patients with sudden remissions are not to be found and they are probably dead, too. I know you tried to have us killed in Oregon and I know that by the time the FBI, the FDA and a shitload of state police get through bouncing you up and down, a lot of things are going to fall out of your pocket. You're gonna have law all over you like white on rice."

"Do you know what this project is called?" White asked.

"Project L.F.," Jay put in.

"Do you know what that means?"

Jay and Scales exchanged glances. "No," Scales said.

" 'Live Forever,' " White said. "I don't have the science to explain it to you and you wouldn't be able to understand it if I did. It's a drug, it's hormones, it's tailored-viruses. It's recombinant DNA, it's the biggest thing to ever happen in the history of man. We've developed a true adaptogenic, a substance that makes fire and the wheel look like monkey toys."

He smiled, a genuinely happy expression.

"We've developed a cure for almost everything known that affects human cells adversely, including cosmic rays, free radicals, the Hayflick Limit and bad Mexican food. It isn't just cancer, Mr. Scales, it's AIDS, plague, the common cold. We've created the elixir vitae, the fountain of youth. Once this stuff is in your system, it fixes what ails you, almost everything that can possibly ail you. It makes your immune system bulletproof. Viruses, bacteria, they bounce right off. And if our projections are right, unless they get hit by a truck or fall off a building, anybody who takes this substance will live a *very* long time. Maybe forever."

Scales felt the force of that hit him. No. No way. Oddly enough, he thought about his feet. How fast they had healed. Maybe that part of it was right, but living *forever* . . . ?

White continued. "Of course, there is one theory that your brain will still use up all its bits or bytes or neurons or whatever in a few hundred years and you'll go senile. Although there is another theory that says that won't happen, you'll make new ones and the older memories will just . . . fade away if you live long enough. In five hundred or a thousand years, you'll be a new person."

"I don't believe it," Jay said, echoing Scales' own thought.

White favored her with a smile. "Oh, you can believe it. We have a set of special short-lived mice who normally survive only six months who are four years old and the most careful examination shows them to be in their physical and mental prime. That's eight times their normal spans and they're still going strong. We have a dog that we have infected with forty diseases, most of them fatal, including Bubonic plague and rabies who is, according to our scientists, the healthiest dog on the planet. We've got a monkey we've started a dozen fatal cancers in who shakes them off like water off a duck's back. And we have Mr. Scales' patients and others in several locations around the country who have come back from the brink of death from cancer, AIDS, hepatic failure, heart damage, lung damage, you name it. What part of it don't you believe?

"You take a pill. One pill. The stuff in it gets into your system, replicates itself, insinuates itself into every crack and cranny, becomes part of you. Alters your cells, every system, your very DNA right on down to the core.

"You see why two million dollars means nothing? The man who controls this treatment—and it only takes one dose!—will be able to control the world. How many billionaires on their deathbed would give it all for a reprieve? How many kings or presidents or dictators would rob the national treasury for a guarantee against the Reaper, Miz Hughes? Think about it."

"My God," Scales said. "My God."

The size of it was overwhelming. If this was true—if half of it was true—it would change the world. The haves and have-nots would never have been so far apart. It could rip civilization to shreds if the knowledge became common. And given what he had learned . . .

"God? No, I wouldn't say that," White said. "But I will be the man who can give long life. Even if it peters out in a hundred or two hundred years, think about that. To be disease-free, as fit at a hundred and fifty as you were at twenty-five. Think of it!"

He still didn't accept it but Scales wanted to keep him talking. "What about side-effects?"

"There's the center jewel in the crown. We have eliminated nearly all of them. A few people are allergic to some of the components. Even though we are messing with major hormones and body chemistry, the treatment seems to be less dangerous than aspirin. We were willing to live with a mortality rate of thirty, forty percent. If we had to, more for major problems and guess what? There aren't any. Isn't that something? God loves a winner."

"Man," Scales said. "It can't be." But that was a reflex more than reason. He believed it was possible.

"No? What about your patients? The cancers, the AIDS,

the liver? We did that, we cured them. You know it's true. You were there. You can't deny it."

No. He couldn't deny that.

"How long were you planning to sit on this?" Jay asked.

"How long? Well, for a few years. The rabble would go mad if they knew it existed and they couldn't get it. We plan to be very, ah, selective in our patients."

"Billionaires, kings, despots?" Jay said.

"Maybe a senator or two. Republicans."

"You bastard," she said.

"Miz Hughes, such language. What is the problem?"

"This ought to be available to everybody, if what you say about it is right. There are thousand of people dying every day and you could save them all!"

"I'm not my brother's keeper, Miz Hughes. I'm a businessman. And in a few years, I'm going to be the richest businessman in the world. Besides, there wouldn't be room for them all. Nobody dies? Too many fleas destroy the dog."

Jay flared again. "What is to stop us from walking out of here and spilling all this to the nearest honest cop?"

"There are plenty of those in Mississippi," White said. "Most of them would probably think you'd slipped a cog, but even if you could find one who would listen to you about one of the state's most well-respected citizens, you'd first have to overcome a few problems of your own."

Scales said, "What do you mean?"

"Miz Hughes and I spoke of the writer Thomas Wolfe, earlier. Do you know his work?"

"I read some of it."

"And what is Mr. Wolfe perhaps most noted for?"

"Listen, White—" Jay began.

" 'You can't go home again,' " Scales said.

White beamed like a teacher at a bright student.

"What does that mean?" Jay asked.

White said, "There was a fire at Mr. Scales' clinic recently, did you know that?"

"We heard about it," Jay said.

"Did you also hear that body was found in the rubble?"

Jay and Scales exchanged looks. "A body?" Scales said.

"Yes. A drug dealer from Seattle. He was shotgunned to death. I believe the state police will surely have found by now the weapon that did it in a garbage can behind the clinic. I am given to understand that while shotgun ballistics are hard to determine, if they have the weapon it is easier. And the shells of a certain lot can be matched. Your gun, your shells. Your place."

"You're trying to frame Scales for murder?"

"His clinic burned down shortly after he left town in a hurry. A dead dope dealer—shot in the back, by the way— was found in the ashes. A big old lump of melted cocaine will eventually show up there, too. Certainly suspicious, wouldn't you say?"

"I can vouch for Scales," Jay said. "I was with him when he left the clinic. It didn't burn until later and there weren't any dead dealers in it."

"Ah, but you have problems of your own, officer. You're involved sexually with the suspect. And it gets better. Did you know that an anonymous tip to the state police resulted in a search of your office on the reservation? And that a half-kilogram of high-grade cocaine and eighteen thousand dollars in cash were found taped under your desk? And that your personal bank accounts, yours and Mr. Scales, have both been fattened by large deposits in the last few days? About eighty thousand dollars each?"

"Motherfucker," Scales said.

"And that's even without the late Dr. Reuben. Who did the police find with him when they arrived? And who had just recently written him a nasty, threatening letter and faxed it to him from your computer?"

"I never threatened him!"

"Well, then, somebody must have broken into your house and used your computer while you were out. Though that might be hard to prove, your computer being a melted puddle at the exact center of where the fire started. The fax was folded up and in Dr. Reuben's wallet. Didn't think to look there, did you? No reason you should have, since you didn't know it existed."

"Shit," Jay said.

"You two are sharp, I'll give you that, but my daddy didn't raise no fools. I made his company a lot bigger and stronger than it was when he gave it to me. You all take the money and run," White said. "Buy a condo in Hawaii, a grass shack in Tahiti, a villa in Spain. You live low key, it'll last for thirty or forty years. Enjoy yourself. It's not like you have a choice. I'm holding all the trump cards here. You been playing out of your league and the game is over, you lost."

"I've got a gun pointed at you. That puts me in your league."

"No, sir. If you shoot me, I'll be dead. But Project L.F. doesn't just go away. You're already wanted for questioning in a murder case, maybe two by now. The police will certainly investigate my death vigorously and you checked into the local Holiday Inn under your own name. That can't look too good."

"You had your men clean that room out," Jay said.

"I'm not talking about Jules. If I'm dead, they'll tie you to it, I guarantee it."

He gave them another smile. "And pretty soon now, the armed guards my alarm system has summoned should be arriving."

"I cut the phone lines before the alarm went off."

"And when you did that, you automatically called them." He looked at his watch. "They're just rent-a-cops, probably not very good against desperate and armed people such as yourself, but—do you want to kill a couple of innocent men? Once the shooting starts, the police will surely arrive soon after—the guards have radios.

"I don't want to see the police. Do you?"

Fuck!

"He's right," Jay said, the realization bitter in her voice. "He's set us up. By the time we get through trying to clear ourselves back home, he'll have wiped all his records."

"No, ma'am. Those records are already gone. As are those in your motel room. You don't have anything. You can't get anything. You did good to get this far, but this is the end of the road."

Jay stared at him as if he had just turned into a giant snake. She looked at Scales.

White said, "It's what you call a no-win sit-u-ation. Suppose even you had the evidence? Rich men don't go to the gas chamber in this state, we aren't California. I had lunch with the Governor last week and even if I did get the death penalty, I can guarantee you the Governor would give up re-election and his political career to pardon me. Then when he left office, he'd retire a very rich man. I might do a couple of years waiting. I could do it standing on my head—see, I have taken the drug!"

"You couldn't buy the feds," Scales said.

Jay shook her head. "Yeah, he could. Put yourself in the shoes of the federal prosecutor. 'Want to live forever, counselor? Make a mistake in your case that gets it reversed on appeal and we'll give you a very special pill and enough money to enjoy it for a long time.' How tempting would that be?"

"Miz Hughes is a very smart woman. You're lucky to have her. But like I said, you're not playing with some hayseed just off the farm. Y'all better take off. The guards never take more than fifteen or twenty minutes to get here, even in bad weather with the power out."

Damn! He had them. He had been a step ahead of them the whole way.

"Don't you move a fucking muscle," Scales said. He started for the door. He paused by the suitcase. Picked it up. It was heavy.

"What are you doing?" Jay asked.

"He's right. We'll need the money. We can't go home."

They glanced at each other. Scales turned to look at the smiling White. Scales said, "You haven't seen the last of us. This is not over."

"Bye-bye," White said. He waved, using just his fingers. He smiled. "Y'all don't come back now, you hear?"

Scales' rage flared and he was tempted to blast the smug expression off White's face. The man was a killer, even if his hand hadn't held the weapon. Cock the hammer, point the gun, pull the trigger, he fucking deserved it . . .

No. He wasn't that far gone. He could shoot to protect himself or Jay, but he couldn't just murder a man, even a man like White. He was a healer, not a killer.

Jay moved. She took three steps, doubled her fist and smashed White's face. He went over backward, took the chair down with him. He hit the bookcase, knocked several books off. The falling books clattered and thumped to the floor. He raised to a crouch, put his hands to his face, came away with blood on them. He wasn't smiling now.

"You broke my nose!"

Jay nodded. "Yeah, I did. Don't worry. It'll heal, right?"

It was absurd, but Scales felt a lot better seeing White squatting on the floor with blood streaming from his nostrils. At least the bastard wasn't invulnerable.

"Come on, Scales," Jay said. "Now we're done. Let's go."

FORTY

The rain had slackened but it was still steady. Scales and Jay ran to the side driveway gate. There was a mechanical crank in case of power failures and Scales cranked it just enough for them to slip through. They hurried to the Miata.

There was barely room in the trunk for the suitcase full of money.

They drove toward the highway.

An alarm company vehicle made to look as much like a police car as possible went past in the opposite direction, lights flashing but no siren.

Jay turned and rubbed condensation off the plastic back window as the car reached the driveway and stopped. Scales saw in his mirror two uniformed men with drawn guns leap from the car and head for the still-open gate.

"He wasn't lying about that," Jay said. "The son-of-a-bitch."

Scales pulled out onto the highway, turned right, put one hand on her leg. "You're alive and in one piece, that's the important thing."

"I guess."

"Listen, this isn't over, Jay."

"No? You heard him. He's got all the high cards. We're fucked."

"I heard what he said, but he's afraid of us. If he wasn't, he wouldn't have tried to kill us, or bothered to frame us. He won't sic the cops on us. I think he will try to run us down with his own people, but we can still get him."

"How?"

"We're free, we've got two million dollars in the trunk." He dug in his watch pocket, found the capsule he'd wrapped in plastic back in Sekiu, what seemed like years ago. He fished it out. The rain hadn't soaked through the Saran Wrap. He held the capsule up for her to see, handed it to her. She stared at it.

"We've got each other," he said.

She looked away from the capsule and at him.

"We can work this out. It might take time, but we have plenty of that. I already took mine. That one is yours."

She nodded, the realization dawning on her. "Yeah. I guess you're right."

He up shifted and accelerated along the highway. Maybe a condo in Hawaii wasn't such a bad idea. A place to sit and rest and come up with a plan. Because like he'd told her, they had plenty of time.

Maybe forever.

About the Author

Steve Perry has been a swimming instructor and lifeguard; toy assembler; hotel gift shop and car rental clerk; aluminum salesman; martial arts instructor; private detective; Licensed Practical Nurse and Certified Physician's Assistant. Perry has written short stories, novels, animated teleplays, non-fiction articles, reviews, and essays, along with a couple of unproduced movie scripts. He wrote for *Batman: The Animated Series* during its first Emmy-award winning season, and during the second season, one of his scripts was nominated for an Emmy for Outstanding Writing. His original novelization of *Star Wars: Shadows of the Empire* spent ten weeks on *The New York Times* Bestseller List. He did the novelization for the summer blockbuster movie *Men in Black*, and his collaborative novels for *Tom Clancy's Net Force* series have also been bestsellers. For the past several years, he has concentrated on books, and is currently working on his 55th novel. He lives in Oregon, with his wife of thirty-nine years. They have two children and four grandsons.